LOVE STRUCK

NIKKI ASHTON

For the incredible NHS Staff and Key Workers who kept us all alive and well during such an awful time. 2020 is a year that will never be forgotten, and neither will all of you.

PROLOGUE

The young boy with the big blue eyes held his breath as his stepdad watched the boy's mum button up her coat. She was going to the doctor's surgery to get his new baby brother or sister checked out because there wasn't long to go now before the baby would be there. The boy was glad because maybe with a new baby in the house his stepdad would be too busy to bother with him. It wasn't his stepdad's baby, not *this* stepdad anyway, it was the one before; but the boy didn't think this stepdad cared.

"How long will you be?" his stepdad asked.

His mum shrugged. "Depends if the doctor is running late. I'll call at the supermarket on the way home and grab something for dinner." She turned to her son who was chewing on his lip. "Be good and make sure you tidy your room like I asked."

The boy bobbed his blond head and screwed his fingers together. He'd heard his stepdad complain about the mess in his room to his mum, he knew who thought it was messy.

His mum kissed his stepdad on the cheek. "See you later, love."

"Yeah, later."

When they heard the front door click shut the boy tried to run, but a big hand caught him around the arm and fat fingers pinched his skin through the SpongeBob t-shirt he was wearing.

"What did I tell you about keeping your room tidy?"

His stepdad always spat when he talked to the boy and there was always dried, white stuff at the corners of his mouth. He had bad breath too and the boy had no idea how his Mum could kiss him. It smelled like the pieces of old meat his first stepdad, Dean, used to catch fish with.

"I was going to do it, but Mum asked me to put the bins out," the boy said.

"Oh, and that takes all day, does it?"

The boy shook his head, his hair falling into his eyes. "I had homework too."

His stepdad let go of his arm and hit him around the back of the head, making the boy stumble forward.

"What have I told you about back-chatting me?"

The boy tried not to wince; it was better to stay still. He also knew that the slap around the head was just the start of what was to come. It never stopped with one slap and angry words.

"Not to," the boy said. "But you asked me a question."

If he was going to get hit, he might as well make it worth the while. No point getting a beating just for not tidying his room.

"You little fucker."

Spittle hit the boy's cheeks and as he lifted a hand to wipe the wetness away, a punch landed on his stomach.

It was hard and fast, and it made all the air rush from his lungs. He tried hard not to make a noise, but when he fell back onto his bum, he couldn't help the groan that barked into the air.

He didn't have time to try and drag a breath in before he felt a boot in his back. It wasn't a kick, but more of a push that sent him sprawling onto the thin brown carpet. His chin hit the floor and his head bounced like his football did when he was practicing his dribbling skills in the yard. As it came back down the boy felt his teeth bite into the inside of his bottom lip instantly filling his mouth with blood.

A hand then grabbed the front of the boy's hair and pulled his head back until his neck was straining and he was almost choking. The boot came again, this time in his side before he was flipped onto his back and a heel was plunged into his stomach, in the same place the punch had been landed.

All the time the boy tried hard not to cry. The pain was horrific, but the shame of crying would be worse.

Pride had become his shield. Pain had become his motivation.

As more blows were rained upon his small body the boy closed his eyes and imagined his stepdad dying a horrible death. Maybe falling off a ladder and landing onto a spiked fence; a long thin spike pushing through his stomach and coming out through his back.

One day the boy would make sure he did die, maybe not with a spike, but maybe when he was bigger, he would punch him to death. Until that day the boy knew he would never trust anyone ever again. It would be better to hurt them before they could hurt him.

When his Mum came home later that night with minced beef to make burgers for dinner, the boy was tidying his room. When she put dinner on the table, she asked the boy if he was okay because he looked pale.

"I'm fine thanks," he replied. "Dinner is nice."

His mum gave his stepdad a strange look and then took a huge drink of her water, speaking to the boy without looking at him. "When you've finished your dinner go straight to bed."

The boy chewed the burger, which tasted like crap, the best he could with a swollen lip, and nodded.

He finished his dinner and went to bed, deciding that the next day he would tell someone other than his mum what his stepdad did to him. He'd tell his friend Ellis' mum; she was kind and gentle and had the most beautiful smile; she would believe him.

The next day his little sister was born, and the boy knew he couldn't tell anyone because even though he was mean and cruel, they needed his stepdad more now than ever.

1

ADAM

According to the dictionary, shock is the state of insufficient blood flow to the tissues of the body as a result of problems with the circulatory system. Initial symptoms of shock may include weakness, fast heart rate, fast breathing, sweating, anxiety and increased thirst. This may be followed by confusion, unconsciousness or cardiac arrest.

Add to that being struck dumb, and I had every reaction covered.

My dad strode towards me as though it was perfectly normal, as though he did it every day, yet I hadn't seen him since I was five years old.

Despite the years, I recognised him instantly from the old photograph that I'd looked at so many times. His hair was shorter, and he was wearing clothes of a much different style. He was dressed like... like a teacher. He *looked* like a teacher, any teacher, but still looked like the man from the picture who I'd been desperate to see. It was him. It was my dad.

With Sarah shaking and whimpering in my arms, I looked at him and my heart pounded like it was too big for my chest. It was about to burst with the pressure of the blood pumping through it. He'd come back, after thirteen years, and the sight of him made me want to puke. I'd always thought I'd run into his arms and tell him how much I'd missed him, but all I could taste was bitterness and fury.

"Adam, please make him go away." Sarah's pained cries brought me back to my senses and my gaze fell to her.

"I've got you," I whispered and pulled her tighter against my chest. "It's okay, you're safe with me."

"Adam," my dad said, his low growl startling me. Sarah shuddered with a fresh round of screaming. "We need to talk, son."

With my lips against Sarah's hair, I shook my head and croaked out, "No. You need to go."

I couldn't look at him, because I was scared that if I did, I might throw myself into his arms. Despite how much I wanted him away from Sarah, I needed him here with me. I needed my dad to hold me and tell me that no one would ever hurt me again and that he would protect me.

I'd always needed him, for thirteen long years.

A loud scream caught my attention and I glanced across the carpark. Sarah's mum ran towards us, cutting off anything else I might say to him.

"Get away from my daughter, you bastard, get away from her now."

"Mum, please," Sarah begged, as her fingertips dug into my arms, while the rest of her body shook. "Make him go. Adam, help make him go away." Wide, scared eyes pleaded with me.

Sarah's mum slammed fisted hands into my dad's chest, so much force behind each powerful thump that he staggered backwards.

"You're a dirty rapist bastard. You should be in prison."

Tears ran down her face, and her chest heaved as she threw blow after blow at him. He didn't respond, except to hold his arms out to the side.

"Just go," I shouted at him. "Get out of here."

Mrs Danes continued to hit him, but still he stood there, taking every hit, while Sarah's cries echoed through my soul.

"What the hell is going on here?"

I looked up to see Miss Daniels and Mr Brewster, our Deputy Head, had come outside. They must have seen the commotion from the window. My stomach turned at the thought, of who else might have seen. Too many people would now know Sarah's secret, which in turn was now my secret too.

"Get this man away from here," Mrs Danes cried, trying to take in gulping breaths. "He shouldn't be here. He should be in jail."

"I think you know that's not true," Dad said, and he took a step away from Sarah's mum. "I was found innocent. I *am* innocent."

"No, you fucking lied, you bastard." Mrs Danes pulled Sarah from me and enveloped her in a safety blanket of the purple wool of her coat.

Reluctantly I let her go but she reached out her hand, so I took it back gladly. I needed to touch her, but I also needed it to stop me from doing something that I might regret, like punching my dad or even hugging him.

"I think you need to go," Mr Brewster said, moving towards my dad.

He held up his hands and then glanced at me. "Okay, but can I at least speak to my son first?"

"You're his son," Mrs Danes gasped and pulled Sarah closer until our fingertips barely touched. "Oh my God."

I blew out a breath as I tried to hold my crumbling emotions together.

"I-I-I didn't know." I shook my head and just about managed to brush my fingertips across Sarah's. "I swear I didn't know."

Tears built against my lashes. Sarah stayed silent but stared at me with wary eyes. The moment stretched as I waited for the trust and bond we'd created between us to crumble into ash on the floor.

2

SARAH

I opened my eyes and winced at the pain thudding in my temples. Hazy thoughts of something happening caused fear to pump around my chest. Then I remembered.

He was here.

I sat up, gasping, and tried to catch my breath as I looked around me.

I was in my room at home.

I was safe.

I was in my room at home and I was safe.

My gut ached with tension as the vision of him walking towards me played on a loop in my brain. I wouldn't forget it; something chilling and terrifying to add to the memory bank of the other nightmares I'd gone through over the last year.

I needed to deal with it, couldn't ignore it, because if I did, I would surely go under. He'd been here—at my new school. My stomach rolled and I leaned over to drag in a gasping breath.

You are my sunshine, my only sunshine...

Breathing heavily, I pulled my feet from under the duvet and dropped them to the floor. With my head in my hands I tried to remember everything else that happened. I had no recollection of getting home. The last memory flitting through my head was being in Mum's arms, wrapped in purple wool, desperate for Adam's hand to be in mine, like both our lives depended on it.

Adam?

There was something about Adam that I needed to recall, something important. The more I tried to think about it, the more my head hurt. I pushed two fingers to each of my temples and massaged them in slow circles, following the breathing routine I'd been taught. Only at number seven I heard the raised voices; Mum and Adam shouting, at each other?

I pushed off from the bed and went to my door, cracking it open slowly to avoid the creak. They'd seemed to get on, why were they rowing?

I padded down the hallway but their voices weren't quite so loud as I'd first thought, although I could hear Mum crying.

"What's going on?" I asked. My eyes stung and I blinked fast, rubbing at them. "Why are you shouting?"

Mum rushed to my side and pulled me tight into her arms, cradling my head against her chest.

"Oh sweetheart," she whispered. "You should have stayed in bed."

"How you feeling?" Adam's voice was tentative, nothing like the confident, swaggering footballer that I'd grown used to. I struggled against Mum's hold to turn my head to look at him and I was shocked by what I saw. He looked drained, there was no colour to his cheeks and his eyes were heavy, devoid of any light. His hair was a mess like a thousand people had run their fingers through it, and his hands were shoved deep into the pockets of the hoodie that he was wearing over the top of his training shorts.

"Did you win your match?" I asked.

Adam shrugged. "I don't know. I skipped it to be here with you."

I pulled away from Mum and stepped towards him, but she pulled me back with her hand on my shoulder.

"Sarah, sweetheart. I think Adam should go home."

Her voice was hard, and it surprised me. She had no idea how he'd treated me those first few weeks I'd started Maddison High. As far as she was concerned, we were going out, and she liked him. I thought she was happy for me.

"No." I turned to her and narrowed my gaze. "I want him to stay. Why are you being like this?"

They exchanged a glance and Adam let out a pained groan.

"What's going on? Why are you staring at Adam like *he's* the devil?"

"Sarah—"

"No," Mum butted in. "She's had enough for one day. Adam, I think you should go."

"It's obvious she doesn't remember, and I don't want any secrets from her." Adam ran a hand through his hair. "I want to tell her."

"I don't think—"

"What don't I remember? What is it Adam wants to tell me?" I looked at Adam and gave him a smile. "Tell me, Adam because we don't keep secrets from each other, remember."

Adam blew out a breath and the knot in my stomach tightened. This was something big, something that had the ability to grind what we'd just started to a shuddering halt. I could feel it. I could see it in the tension of his shoulders and the caution in his blue eyes.

"I don't see how telling you will help anything," Mum protested.

"Maybe Adam can come back tomorrow, when you're feeling a little stronger. You might have remembered by then."

"I won't feel any stronger," I replied and rounded on her. "Joshua Mills is here, Mum. In this town. He's come for me, I know it. I don't see how I'll ever feel safe whilst he's here. And what the hell am I supposed to remember?"

My hand shook as I pushed it up the arm of my jumper in order to feel the comfort of the jagged scar on my wrist; it helped me to remember I'd survived this nightmare once and I that could survive it again. I rubbed at the raised skin while an image of Mr Mills walking towards me across the car park flitted in front of my eyes. I squeezed them shut to try and push it away. Another fractured image of him staring at Adam filtered into my brain. Mum whimpered and I looked at her; her palm anchored against her chest, covering her heart, as she looked at Adam with pain etched into the fine lines at the edges of her eyes.

Her fear told me that whatever Adam wanted to tell me, it would rock me to my core.

"Can I talk to Sarah alone please, Mrs Danes," Adam croaked. I switched my wide gaze to him.

"I-I-I don't know." My mum looked between us, evidently torn with what to do. Since the trial her need to protect me had been overbearing at times, but she hadn't been afraid to leave me alone with Adam before.

"Mum," I cried. "It's Adam. I trust him."

Adam let out a breath. Confused, I held out my hand for him and he rushed to take a step closer, not quite touching me.

I hated the space that remained.

"Please, Mum."

She gave a single nod and Adam was instantly at my side,

pulling me against his chest. He kissed my forehead, and then placed his hands on my shoulders and looked down at me.

"I swear to you, I won't let anyone hurt you." He looked at my mum, his eyes pleading. "I have to tell her."

My heart twisted and tumbled as Mum stood aside and Adam took my hand to lead me out of the kitchen and down the hallway to my room.

Once inside he ignored Mum's usual rule and closed the door, before scrubbing a hand over his face.

"I think you should sit down."

Frowning I sat down on the edge of my bed, the covers still rumpled from when I'd only got out of it a few minutes before.

"What's going on? Why didn't you go to your match?"

"Did you really think I would?" His neck stiffened as he drew his head back. "After what happened this afternoon? There was no way I could have played and kept my mind on the game. I can't believe you're even asking me."

He shook his head, blinking rapidly, and reached for my desk chair, wheeling it over to me and sinking down on it.

I reached up the sleeve of my jumper. "I'm sorry. I-I, well I guess I'm not used to people caring about me. I'm sorry if it gets you into trouble."

Adam's eyes went wide. "Sarah, I don't give a fuck about the match. I care about you and what happened. You were upset. Fuck you were hysterical with shock. How the hell could I even think about leaving you?"

I dropped my gaze to my lap as I enjoyed the feeling of my cool fingertips on my scar.

"Don't," Adam said softly, and he pulled my hand from up my

sleeve. "I need to tell you something. I don't think it registered with you earlier."

"About Joshua Mills," I stated and narrowed my eyes. My memory jangled, hinting at a jigsaw piece that I couldn't quite recall.

"Yeah," he said, letting out a long and exhausted sigh. "About him."

I didn't reply but watched as Adam battled with something going on inside of his head. He sat forward, resting his arms on his bare knees, and then flopped backward, the whole time looking tortured.

"Adam tell me."

He leaned forward again and looked up at me through his long lashes and I swallowed at the glittering pool of tears I saw there.

"I swear to you," he said. "I knew nothing about it. When he walked across the car park, I was as shocked as you."

He reached towards me and pulled my hands between both of his, encasing them in warmth. He wheeled the chair forward until his knees were almost touching mine, then he opened his to cage mine in. All his actions could have been seen to be time wasting, but I knew from the way his Atlantic blues gazed at me with sincerity and apology that he simply wanted me to feel safe.

"I didn't know he was coming here," he finally said. "I swear."

I was confused yet had a vague recollection that there was a reason why we were having this conversation, I just couldn't remember what it was.

"Why would you?" I asked.

"Because..." He let out a long exhale and then leaned his forehead against mine. "Because he's my dad, Sarah. He's my real dad. He's Glen Hudson."

I tried to pull away from him but as soon as I did, his arms went around me, and he dragged me onto his lap.

"Let me go, Adam, let me go."

I struggled but he held me tight with his lips at my temple, whispering, "I didn't know, I swear, I didn't know," over and over again.

"No," I cried, sick rushing up my throat, I swallowed it down. "No, tell me you're lying."

"I can't, Sarah. I'm so sorry."

"Mum," I shouted out.

"Please don't," Adam begged, bright pools brimming at his lashes. "Please let me talk to you about this. Please."

I looked into his eyes which begged for me to listen. His Adam's apple bobbed on a swallow and I clearly saw the distress destroying him.

I opened my mouth to speak, but my door flew open and Mum rushed in. "Are you okay?" she asked, her hands gripped into tiny fists.

Adam dropped his forehead to my shoulder and whispered softly, "Please, Sarah."

I inhaled and nodded. "I'm fine, Mum. I just wanted to tell you that Adam will be here for a while. He's told me the truth and I think we need to talk."

I chewed on my lip. Emotion and worry clouded her face.

"Honestly, Mum, I'm okay," I soothed.

Adam's arms squeezed me, and a soft sigh of relief left his lungs as Mum moved back to the door and cleared her throat. "I'll make us some dinner," she said pausing to look between Adam and me.

I nodded, but I knew I wouldn't eat. My stomach bounced like a trampoline and nausea rose with every minute.

"Adam are you staying for dinner?" Mum's tone was hard and accusatory.

Adam looked up at me and blinked slowly. "Yeah, Mum, he's staying." She went to leave but hesitated at the door, looking back over her shoulder at us. "Honestly, Mum, I'm good, I swear."

With a hand on her stomach she left, leaving the door slightly ajar.

Once I heard Mum rattling pans in the kitchen, I turned to Adam. "Was this all part of your plan?" I asked quietly

Adam reared back. "God no, I fucking swear, Sarah. I had no idea. I didn't know that my d-da... Glen was an art teacher."

Memories of that room, full of paint and brushes and the smell of turpentine and fear, invaded my senses. I felt like I was back there, it was all so clear in my head.

"Are you okay?" Adam asked, glancing down and taking hold of my shaking hands between his own.

I nodded. "Just tell me the truth, Adam."

"I am, I swear. When he was married to my mum, he worked for a garage that dealt in custom built cars. He did all the spray painting. Mum told me once that he'd been to uni and had a degree, but that was all she said, she didn't elaborate, so I had no idea what in. I guess it was teaching or art maybe. I have no fucking idea." He turned and looked out of the window where the sun was slowly going down. "I can't believe he's the same man that did that you, Sarah. I can't believe he's here."

"Really?"

His gaze swung back to me. "Yes, really. I told you. He left when I was five and I haven't heard from him, or seen him since; not until today."

I pushed back a little, wanting to look right into his eyes, but his arms wrapped around my waist, leaving only centimetres between us.

"Don't you think I would have called him before now if I'd known where he was?" Adam nostrils flared. "Do you think I'd have stayed with my mum, with that bastard Eric who beat me, if I'd known where he was. I'd have called him and asked if I could go and live with him."

That thought sent ice through my veins and I shifted to move off Adam's lap.

"*Would* have, Sarah," he said, his voice cracking. "Past tense. Not now. Now I have you and..."

"And your precious Dad raped me." I clutched my head and squeezed it tight, as if I could squash the pictures of his guilt into nothing. "How can I believe you?"

I heaved in a breath, dragging air into my lungs.

"I told you the truth," Adam cried. "I didn't know. Do you think if I'd known it was him, I'd have...?" He paused and dropped his head back. "Fuck, I don't know, Sarah. I don't know anything anymore. I'm just shell shocked by it all. My dad, who I've prayed to return every fucking day, is here, and I find out he might have raped my girlfriend and then there's—"

"*Might* have raped me," I cried, forcefully pushing my flat palms into Adam's chest.

His arms came back around me before I could properly get free. "I didn't mean it like that. It was just a figure of speech. I believe you, Sarah. I saw what seeing him did to you. Of course, I believe you." His eyes were fearful as his arms tightened around me. He pressed his lips to my temple, his whole body encompassing mine, swaddling me, as if he was never going to let go.

We lapsed into silence and exhaustion suddenly swamped me. I couldn't help but sag against him. His hoodie smelled of fabric conditioner and him and I breathed it in, calmed and comforted. I really wanted to believe he had nothing to do with his dad turning up at our school. Try as I might though, it all seemed too much of a coincidence; something that you only ever read about in a book.

When I yawned, Adam shifted in the seat and before I knew it, I was being carried to my bed and laid down.

"Lift your legs."

I did as I was told, and Adam pulled my violet coloured duvet over me. He went to sit back on the chair, but I pulled at his top.

"Lie with me," I said when he looked back at me.

He glanced at the door which my Mum had left slightly ajar and then his eyes were back on me. "Are you sure?"

"Yes. We need to talk some more, but I think we could both do with some sleep first."

"But your mum is making dinner."

"It's fine, she'll keep it warm."

Adam still looked cautious, nothing like the boy who ruled Maddison High School.

"Please Adam, I need to sleep, and I don't want to be alone."

He closed his eyes and let out a breath before quickly toeing off his trainers and pulling his hoodie over his head, placing it on my desk chair. He was still in his training gear which meant he probably hadn't even gone back into school once his... once Joshua Mills had turned up.

I scooted over to give him room and turned on my side to face him. Once Adam was in the bed with the duvet over him, I allowed myself to move a little closer. As I looked at him, I bit on my lip having no idea what I was doing. Should I have told him to leave and never speak to me again? Or was I right to keep him by my side for strength and comfort? I knew my Mum would have liked me to make him go, but in just a couple of weeks he'd become my person, the one who I wanted by my side at times like this. The fact that his own father was the product of my nightmares was strange, admittedly, but I couldn't imagine anyone else being with me. I knew Adam would guide me through what was bound to be one of the worst times of my life – hell, a continuation of the worst time of my life.

I chose Adam Hudson; I just hoped he'd be able to support me.

I yawned behind my hand and smiled when Adam immediately fought against one too.

"Sleep," I said.

Adam reached out with his index finger and slowly traced the outline of my nose. "I want to be awake in case you need me," he replied, edging closer to me.

"Just having you here will help."

His face softened and he moved his hand to just above the waistband of my skirt while he tucked his other under the pillow. His lips were pouty and kissable, and I couldn't help but lean closer and take his mouth in mine. As I took control and swept my tongue against his, he groaned and squeezed my waist, pushing his hips forward so that I could feel his erection in his training shorts. I raked my fingers through his hair, allowing my nails to graze his scalp and when his hand snaked down into the back of my skirt, I felt myself get wet. That was what he did to me, what his touch did to me; it made me forget.

As I moved a hand towards Adam's hard on, he pulled back and ended the kiss.

"What?" I whispered, feeling the loss of his lips on mine.

"For one your mum is only down the hall, and tonight she's not engrossed in TV. Tonight she's worried about her daughter and is likely to come and check on you at any point. And," he sighed, as he brushed my hair from my face, "for two, you've had a huge shock. You're emotionally fucked and need to sleep."

"Maybe it will relax me," I replied rubbing at the frown lines between his brows.

"Maybe, but it's not happening." Adam smiled and pulled me closer, tucking me under his chin. "Sleep, babe."

He kissed the top of my head and I sighed with contentment.

"How the hell are you still holding yourself together?" he asked, surprising me.

I answered honestly, without worrying that it might be the worst possible answer I could give.

"You," I replied. "You are how I'm holding it together."

Adam's body visibly relaxed against mine and then he too let out a sigh. Within minutes his breathing was steady and heavy in time with mine.

3

ADAM

I woke up wrapped around Sarah and for a second all the shit that had happened that afternoon didn't exist. I was just a horny seventeen-year-old lad with a hard on poking into my girlfriend's arse. But, when she stirred and whimpered, it all came flooding back.

My dad was back and had been responsible for raping my girlfriend.

I pulled her closer to my chest and smoothed her hair away from her face; she seemed to settle down. It looked like early evening from the twilight I could see through her open curtains. I could hear Mrs Danes in the kitchen and remembered that she was going to make us some dinner and thought we should probably get up. I didn't really want to wake Sarah though.

My gaze skimmed around the room I'd spent a lot of time in over the last couple of weeks, and I couldn't help grinning when they landed on her desk chair which I'd wheeled next to the bed earlier. We'd had sex on it only two days before when Sarah's mum said she was taking a bath. Sarah was sitting on my knee as we looked on the internet for part-time jobs for the summer, but as soon as we'd heard the bathroom door's lock click, it was all systems go. I'd had Sarah's knickers off and her straddling me in record time. Mrs Danes hadn't even finished her bath by the time we were both gasping for breath after coming hard.

Wishing we could go back two days, I blew out my cheeks and tightened my grip on Sarah's hip. I must have done it too hard because her eyes fluttered open.

"Hey." I leaned forward and kissed just below her ear. "How are you feeling?"

She turned over so we were almost nose to nose and gave me sleepy smile.

"I have a bit of a headache, but it's okay. How about you?"

I shrugged. "Don't know really. All feels a bit weird."

Sarah swallowed and her eyelids flickered. "I don't know how we should be dealing with this, Adam. I have no idea whether we…"

Her words trailed off and my heart thumped high in my throat.

"What?" I barely got out the question. I wasn't sure I wanted the answer to it.

Sarah's hand cupped my face, her fingertips warm against my skin. "I have no idea whether we should stay together, or whether this is just too big for us to deal with."

"I suppose that's up to you." I let my head fall back and sighed out a quiet groan. "I get it if him being my dad is too much for you, but I don't want us to finish. I want to be with you."

"Y-you do?"

I frowned and stole a quick kiss. "Of course, I do, but I have to be honest it isn't going to be easy. He's my dad and at some point, I'm going to have to talk to him."

Sarah stiffened and her breathing faltered.

"I *have* to. I haven't seen him in for almost thirteen years. My mum will definitely want to know."

"I know, but it's just the thought of him being here." She closed her eyes and shivered.

I'd never wanted to take away someone's pain and torment so much as I did with her. Usually I created it, but with her I'd do anything to make her feel better. Could I ignore my dad though?

While we lay in silence, Sarah still tucked under my chin, and I stroked down her hair, it would have been quite easy to forget the trauma waiting for us in the world outside. We were so content that we were almost asleep again when Mrs Danes tapped on the door and walked in.

"Dinner is ready." She cleared her throat and looked around the room, probably for evidence that we were naked under the covers.

Sarah answered her mum's questioning eyes by throwing the duvet off us. "Okay, thanks, Mum."

We both stretched while Mrs Danes busied herself by picking a pair of Sarah's jeans from the floor and throwing them into the wash basket by the door.

"Come on," she said as she paused before leaving. "You don't want it to go cold."

When she finally left the room, Sarah groaned and pushed the heels of her hands into her eyes.

"This is going to be awkward. She's either going to question you non-stop or give you the silent treatment."

"That's only natural. I can go," I offered. "If that's what you think is best?"

Sarah's eyes went wide. "No, I want you to stay. *Please.*"

I took a deep breath and gave her a single nod, because in that moment I'd do anything for her.

Sarah and I were sat in the back of her mum's car. Since I'd left my car at school, she'd offered to drive me home. Just as Sarah had thought, dinner had been a little uncomfortable. Mrs Danes had been silent throughout, alternating between picking at her food and watching my every move. Finally, after helping to wash the dishes I'd suggested I should go. I still had to tell my mum that my dad was back, and I wasn't looking forward to that conversation. I knew she'd turn it all around to be about her, that was just what my mum was like. Everything was about her - always. She'd have no concept of how it made me, or more importantly Sarah feel. Sarah and I had discussed it and agreed that we should tell Mum what Glen, Joshua or whatever the fuck he called himself, had done to Sarah. It wouldn't make a bit of difference though; Elouise Crawford would only think of herself.

As we pulled up at the end of the driveway, Sarah cuddled closer into me, which considering she'd had her arm wrapped around my bicep and been plastered to my side for the whole journey, was pretty difficult.

"I'd like to come in if that's okay." Mrs Danes glanced over her seat towards us.

"No, Mum." Sarah unclipped her seatbelt and pulled away from me to lean forward to get closer to her mum. "You can't just do that."

"They're expecting me."

Sarah and I both inhaled sharply.

"I called them when you were both sleeping. I told your mother everything."

"That wasn't your place, Mum. That was up to Adam."

Mrs Danes took a deep breath and turned to look out of the

windscreen. "You are my daughter. You're the only person I care about in this situation, so it *was* my place."

I placed a hand on Sarah's back and rubbed it gently.

"It's okay. Someone had to tell her, and I wasn't looking forward to it."

Sarah glared at me over her shoulder. "No, Adam. She had no right."

"*She* is your mother." Mrs Danes shot back around to look at us. "Which gives me the right. Now you either stay here, or you come inside with me. It's entirely up to you, Sarah."

Sarah's shoulder's sagged and she reached for the door, pushing it open. Mrs Danes and I followed her out and then I took her hand to lead her up the driveway. I didn't have time to pull my key out before the door was pulled open and we were faced with Roger, looking less than happy.

"You'd better come in," he said directing his words to Mrs Danes.

I moved to push past him, but he placed a hand on my shoulder.

"You okay?"

I dropped my head and exhaled slowly. "Been better." I didn't have the energy to fight against him. I just wanted to get seeing my mum over with. Once I'd done that I could then decide how the hell Sarah and I were going to deal with things.

Roger gave me a reassuring pat and for once it was welcomed. I gave him a nod and then walked into the lounge where, just as I expected, I found my mum sitting in an armchair sobbing her eyes out and rocking while she clutched one of Roger's hankies.

Fuck my life and fuck whoever decided the parents I'd got landed with.

"Mum?"

She looked up at me with red eyes and started a fresh bout of sobbing. "Adam, I can't believe it."

"Which part?" I asked as I took Sarah's hand and led her to the sofa.

As we sat down my mum watched Mrs Danes, her eyes flicking between her and Roger who was hovering in the doorway.

"Can I get anyone a drink?" he asked.

Everyone declined and so he sat on the other end of the new huge sofa that had replaced the one which had been perfectly fine. I personally liked the idea of keeping the other as it was where Sarah and I first had sex, but someone else in Maddison Edge was now enjoying it after buying it for practically nothing.

"I suppose I should just get down to it," Mrs Danes said. "Were you aware your ex-husband was now living as Joshua Mills and he was responsible for raping my daughter? In fact, did you know he was coming to live here?"

Mum drew in a breath and let it out with a ragged, "No."

Seriously, she could have won best actress award. I knew this would be a shock to her, but the weeping and fucking wailing was too much.

"Is there any need." I rolled my eyes and flopped back into the sofa, Sarah's hand still tightly in mine.

"You have no idea what this had done to me," Mum cried. "It's devastated me."

"Boo-fucking-hoo," I muttered under my breath and earned a nudge in the ribs from Sarah's elbow. "What?" I grumbled. "Everything is about her, all the time."

"Adam." Roger warned, his tone low.

"The point is," Mrs Danes continued, ignoring our little family spat. "I need to know if you have anything that can help us to get rid of him."

My body tensed and my stomach rolled. He'd only just got here. I hadn't seen him in almost thirteen years. They couldn't just make him go, could they?

"Are you okay?" Sarah asked quietly.

I nodded and gave her a quick smile. How the fuck could I tell her that I wanted the man who had ruined her life to hang around so that I could get to know him? More to the point, why the bloody hell did I want to?

"No," Mum replied and buried her face into Roger's hankie. "I haven't seen him since he left us. I didn't even know where he was."

Roger cleared his throat leaned back into the sofa and crossed his legs at the ankle, attempting to look casual but looking anything but. Something was off, I could just sense it.

I turned my head towards Mum. "You knew where he was, didn't you? All this time I wanted to find him; you knew."

She shook her head vigorously, her long brunette waves swinging as if she had the lead in in one of those stupid shampoo adverts. "I had no idea, sweetheart, I swear."

I could've asked her to swear on my little sister's life; but I wouldn't risk it. I bloody loved the little munchkin.

"You better not be lying to me, Mum."

"I'm not, Adam. I'm not."

She fucking was, she couldn't look me in the eye, but I couldn't prove anything. She would stick to her story until she dropped dead if necessary.

"You understand how awful this is for Sarah?" said Mrs Danes.

"We do, Helena," Roger said, surprising me that they were on first name terms. "I, *we*, can't tell you how sorry we are about it. We also have to consider Adam in all of this though."

My head almost twisted off as I shot my gaze to my stepdad. "Me?"

"Yes, Adam, you. He's your dad and you're bound to be curious considering you haven't seen him for so long. And your mum, well both of us, understand that. But I'm sorry, we are also concerned about you spending time with him."

I pulled my hand from Sarah's and leaned forward. "Why, he's a rapist, not a paedophile?"

Sarah gasped and my mum burst out another sob, but I stared at Roger waiting for his reply.

"No one is saying that," he replied steadily. "But—"

"He's both," Mrs Danes spat out. "Sarah was sixteen, she wasn't an adult. He's both as far as I'm concerned, and I want him away from her. If there's nothing you can do or say to help us to force him to leave, maybe we will have to leave instead." She shrugged and I knew she would do it to protect Sarah.

"Mum, no," Sarah cried.

With my heart hammering I reached for Sarah's hand. The thought that she might leave made me feel weird, like a slab of concrete lay on my chest and it was pushing down on me, making it difficult to breathe. She couldn't leave, we were just getting started, but then I didn't want my dad to go either. There was a tug-o-war going on in my heart and I had no clue who I wanted to fucking win.

"Maybe I could speak to him," I spluttered out. "Maybe if I asked him to leave." Sarah's hand instantly felt sticky with sweat and I turned to look at her. The colour had drained from her face. "He might not even stay," I continued, more to Sarah than anyone else.

"If I don't show any interest in talking to him, he'll go, I'm sure he will."

Sarah's eyes told me that she knew I was conflicted. Sadness reflected off the tears pooled in them and her normally full lips were pulled into a thin line. I lifted my hand to push her hair from her face and she leaned into my touch.

"I would never tell you what to do, who to talk to, or who to believe, Adam." Her voice was soft and the way she looked at me it was like we were alone, like our parents weren't in the room. Her eyes were dark and soulful, and I could see she was fighting against pleading with me.

"I know," I replied.

"But he's manipulative and clever. He will say things that will make you feel at ease with him. He will tell you lies, and then he will domineer you until you have no choices left."

I drew in a sharp breath, because at that moment I wasn't sure whether she was talking about me or my dad.

4

SARAH

Adam clutched my hand tight as we walked up the path into school. He'd insisted I call Alannah and tell her he was going to bring me in and that I wouldn't need a lift. Obviously, it being Alannah she'd argued and wanted to know what the problem was.

"Why didn't you call me after your appointment last week? And where the hell was Adam for the match? And Chanelle Dickson said she saw you and Adam in the car park, and you were crying. What the bloody hell did he do to you, Sarah?"

I'd closed my eyes and taken a deep breath. "I'll tell you at school tomorrow, I promise, but Adam and I are fine."

At least I thought we were, everything seemed fine, but how could the situation not have affected him, and us?

When he picked me up for school though, I'd been greeted with a gorgeous, long, sexy kiss, which almost made me suggest we bunk off. Then on the drive in he seemed almost back to normal, except we couldn't be, not with his dad still being around.

"You okay?" he asked as he pulled me closer.

I looked up at him and smiled wide and hopefully believable. "I just don't know what to tell Alannah."

"It's up to you. Tell her everything or we can come up with some story."

His shoulders were stooped and there were dark rings under his eyes. He hadn't been sleeping well, I knew because he'd been calling me at all times during the night, we'd been calling each other, just to chat. We were a team of two, working to get through it, and maybe it was strange, but it had brought us closer to each other. At least it seemed that way to me, I just hoped it did to Adam too.

"I think perhaps it would help to tell her, but it's your story too, Adam."

He pulled to a stop and pinched the bridge of his nose. I held my breath. I knew how much this was hurting him and I knew he was conflicted; it would be strange if he wasn't. I was his girlfriend of just less than a month and Mr Mills was his dad, the man who he'd been desperate to find for the last thirteen years.

"I don't know, Sarah." He dropped his hand to his side and exhaled unsteadily. "I want you to do what's best for you, but..."

I waited patiently for him to continue as kids pushed past us, one almost shoving me off the path into a tree, which surprisingly Adam didn't respond to.

"I won't tell her," I finally said. "I'll make something up. I don't know, maybe I'll say I had a shitty text message from a friend at my old school."

Adam's whole body relaxed.

"Yes," I continued. "I'll tell her that Harley my friend from my old school had posted some nasty comments about my dad."

"Like what?"

I thought about what would have made me react in such a way.

What could she have possibly posted to make me scream and sob like that?

"How about I say she posted a copy of the flyer that the boys made."

Adam's eyes darkened and his nostrils flared. "I could still fucking kill them for that."

"Forget about it, it's done." I took a deep breath and then gave him a hopeful smile. "What do you think?"

Momentarily closing his eyes on a deep sigh, Adam nodded. "Harley," he repeated. "Okay, let's go with that. As long as you're sure."

I wasn't, but this wasn't just about me any longer. I nodded and stood on my tiptoe to kiss him.

I gasped when his hands went to my bum and he lifted me up, we were in the middle of the path, surrounded by people, but I quickly wrapped my legs around his waist and took everything that he wanted to give to me in his kiss.

It was pain wrapped up in pleasure, and it was Adam Hudson begging me to understand him.

"Get a fucking room," someone shouted.

Adam stopped kissing me and grinned against my lips. "I suppose they have a point."

"Hmm, maybe."

I moved to drop my feet to the floor, but Adam held on tight. "I don't think you can move yet," he groaned, dropping his forehead to mine. "These trackie bottoms don't actually hide much when you're half mast, never mind when you've got a full lob on."

I started to giggle and held on tight to my backpack as Adam walked us into school and deposited me outside my locker. "Okay, I'll see you later," he said as he kissed my temple. "TJ's after school?"

"Yeah, that'd be good. And try not to worry, okay?"

He gave me a sad smile and walked away to go find Mr Jameson before P.E.. I wished I knew what was going on inside his head.

"You're back."

Alannah's voice surprised me as I continued to watch Adam.

"Oh, hiya. Yes, I'm back." I flashed Alannah a smile and looked over her shoulder. "No Amber?"

"No, she's got a dental appointment. I'm quite glad actually." Alannah leaned closer and lowered her voice. "It's so draining pretending to be as miserable as her all the time."

I burst out laughing and it felt good. For all Adam and I had tried to be normal over the last few days, and as much as we'd talked and laughed, a dark shadow had still loomed over us both. At least Alannah's behaviour was natural, maybe Adam was right in not wanting to tell her, this way I could be as normal as I could with her too.

"So come on," she urged as we began to walk to our French class. "Tell me why you were crying in the car park."

"Well, I've told you about my friend Harley from my old school, right..."

"What happened with Mr Jameson?" I asked Adam as we pulled into TJ's car park.

"He already knew what happened, and he was sympathetic, but I still got dropped for a game."

"What?" I cried. "That's not fair. You were supporting me, not to mention the shock you'd had. That's so wrong. I'm going to see him tomorrow and tell him."

Adam started laughed and manoeuvred his car into a space. "Fucking hell, you're even sexier when you're mad and while I appreciate you sticking up for me, it's not necessary. I'll take the one game on the bench, it's fine."

"It's not fine, Adam. He shouldn't have done that."

I folded my arms over my chest and pouted, only for Adam to capture my bottom lip between his teeth and to thread his hand through my hair. I let out a little whimper as my nipples hardened and a pulsing started between my legs.

"So, fucking sexy," he said his voice quiet and controlled. "I think we need to find somewhere to go after we've eaten. I really need to have sex with you."

I was wet and desperate for him and yet he'd barely touched me.

"Adam," I groaned. "Let's skip food."

He pulled away; eyes dark. "Can't sorry, I'm starved, and I promised Lori I'd take her a milkshake home." He grinned. "Stop pouting like you're five."

"Ugh."

He laughed loudly and it was the best sound I'd heard in days.

Once he'd rearranged himself and I'd stopped pouting, we walked into TJ's with Adam behind me, wrapping his arms over my chest. He stopped occasionally, pulling me back so he could nibble at my ear and making me giggle and I wondered how long my care-free mood would last. Adam still hadn't seen his dad since that day in the car park and he had to come out of hiding soon; my bet was his first stop would be his son. I had no idea what Adam thought about that because I hadn't dared ask him. The answer he might give scared me to my core.

As we walked towards the football team's table, I heard my name mentioned by someone. I turned to my right but the three girls and two boys in the booth just smiled at me and carried on eating their food. They seemed too innocent though and one of the girls definitely nudged one of the boys. Ignoring my instinct, I followed Adam to the table. As I sat down, Kirk moved up a place to leave a seat between us.

"For you," he said when Adam frowned. "Thought you might want to sit next to Sarah."

Adam gave him a chin lift. "Cheers."

Things still seemed off between them, but at least they were talking. Flashing Adam, a smile, I unwound my scarf from around my neck, slipped off my pink Borg coat and picked up the menu.

"I suppose you all know exactly what you're having." I looked up at Adam, Tyler, Kirk and Ellis. "So, what should I have?"

They were a tight group of friends, or had been, and I was under no illusion that me being at their table was weird for them. Ellis didn't seem to care one way or the other, but Tyler was watching me with an open mouth like I was Taylor Swift and I'd just popped into the café unannounced. I smiled at him hoping he edged closer to Ellis' attitude towards me rather than Kirk's. He twitched a smile back and then turned to look at Adam, who was watching me.

"Mum's chilli burger is good," Kirk said, gaining my attention. "It's the only thing Dad can't make."

I nodded. "Okay, that's what I'll have."

Adam's eyes twinkled as his lips twitched into a smile and then turned to his friends. "Did Mr J tell you I got dropped for Wednesday's match?"

"Yeah, fucking sucks, lad," Tyler groaned, and glanced at me. "We could do with you as well. Dingley High are pretty good at the moment."

Adam shrugged. "You'll be okay. Dylan will step up, won't you mate?"

Dylan Dickinson, Adam's cover on the team, grinned. "You'll have to fight to get your place back."

"Whatever." Adam gave him the middle finger and turned back to me.

"Hey, Hudson."

I groaned, recognising the voice as Seth Davies, the boy Adam had fought with in the gym. He'd given Adam and I quite a bit of shit over the last couple of weeks; usually shitty comments, coupled with crude hand gestures about us being together. None of it was funny, but Davies hadn't realised that.

"What?" Adam showed no interest.

"How's it feel to have your dick in the same place that your dad did?"

Agony hit in an instant. I winced, like a knife had sliced through my stomach. First pain hit and then a cold sweat enveloped me. I froze with my hands gripping the sides of my chair. My head began to spin as his words jumbled with images of Mr Mills approaching us on the car park.

How did he know? He couldn't know, no one did.

Immediately, Adam was up and out of his seat like a jaguar pouncing on its prey.

"Adam no," I screamed.

"What the fuck?" Ellis cried.

"Shit." Tyler pushed his chair back and waded into the melee that had started two tables down.

Adam was punching Davies, while Davies' friend was kicking at Adam's legs.

.   .   .

You are my sunshine, my only sunshine,
You make me happy when skies are grey...

"For fuck's sake." Kirk jumped up, Ellis hot on his heels.

They rushed over to get Adam away from Davies, and to throw a few punches, but Adam was angry, hurt, and his strength was staggering; he wouldn't be deterred from launching punches at Davies.

While the fight grew in front of me, adrenalin rushed around my body, lighting up every nerve ending, and I began to shake. I didn't know what to do, except watch as my heart beat loud in my ears. Adam was still getting punches in, but now another of Davies' friends had joined in and was landing his fist on the back of Adam's head. Desperate for it to stop, I opened my mouth to scream, but nothing came out. I couldn't make a sound while fear of what was happening gripped me.

Tears began to crawl down my cheeks as I silently begged for help. I scanned the room, but everyone was focused on the boys hitting and kicking each other. A girl I knew from history, Charlie Douglas, took her eye off the fight and turned towards me. When she shifted in her seat, I thought she was going to come and help me, but she leaned across to another girl and pointed. The other girl turned and laughed before whispering something into Charlie's ear.

Vomit rose in my throat as Kirk screamed for his dad, and when Tony appeared from around the back of the café, with a cricket bat in his hand, I couldn't help it, I retched and puked all over the table.

The people closest, momentarily stopped watching and muttered about it being gross, but no one helped me. I started to cry and hung my head, puke dripping from the corners of my mouth and my nose, when I felt a hand on my shoulder.

"Oh my God, Sarah, are you okay." It was Alannah. "Come on let me get you to the bathroom."

My cries turned to loud sobs as she wrapped an arm around me and helped me up from my seat.

"Adam," I managed to choke out.

"Tony is breaking it up, he'll be fine."

She started to lead me towards the back of the café, but as most of the sixth form were there, it was a struggle to get through the gaggle of people standing on tiptoe to watch the fight.

"Move out of the damn way." Alannah pushed a boy to one side and then two girls. "Can't you see we need to get through, you idiots."

Eventually we reached the door to the bathroom and Alannah managed to push us in, just as I heard a loud crack, which sounded like wood hitting something.

"Shit, Sarah, what the hell happened?" Alannah pulled paper towels from the dispenser on the wall and handed some to me, before turning on the tap and soaking one under the water. "Lift your face to me," she said softly, beginning to dab with the wet paper towel. "Just wipe that off your top."

I looked down to see I had some vomit on my shirt. "Oh God."

"It's okay, we'll get you cleaned up, don't worry." She smiled gently and continued to wipe my face as I dabbed at my chest. "So, are you going to tell me?"

I chewed on my lip and nodded.

I wanted to tell her, and I knew I needed the support of my friend, after this I didn't know if I could rely on Adam. If people knew, and how the hell they knew I had no idea, but if they did, then this was going to hurt him too. His recent reaction told me he would be just as pained and tortured by it all.

My chest shuddered to a halt as I opened my mouth to catch my breath.

"Adam's dad was my teacher, at my other school..." I could barely find the words "... And he raped me."

Alannah's mouth dropped open. The wet paper towel in her grasp fell from her fingers to the floor. "S-say that again."

I let out a sob. "I-I-I was raped by Adam's dad, his real dad. He was a teacher at my old school." Repeating it didn't make it any easier to say.

My palms were sweating, and I thought I might be sick again as my mouth filled with water. I ran into a cubicle and hung my head over the toilet, but nothing came out, so I waited for a few seconds until my stomach settled. I spat the spittle from my mouth into the bowl and then stood up to face Alannah.

She stared at me with her arms wrapped tightly around her waist, her glasses perched on the end of her nose. She opened and closed her mouth like a fish in a bowl.

"Neither Adam or I knew," I said as I pushed down the toilet seat and sat on it. "He hasn't seen him for thirteen years and his dad changed his name."

My voice echoed slightly around the white tiled bathroom and I suddenly felt cold and started to shiver. Alannah came into the stall and crouched down in front of me.

"You're sure Adam didn't know?" she asked as she rubbed my arms.

I nodded. "He was as shocked as I was when he turned up."

"The car park." Realisation dawned and she blinked slowly. "Why didn't you tell me earlier?"

"We didn't think we should, and well, it's Adam's secret now too."

She nodded in understanding and then dropped her gaze to the floor. "Did he go to prison."

I drew in a breath and then exhaled it slowly through pursed lips.

"They didn't believe me. He told them we'd been in a relationship and I really messed up in court. I got flustered and... well, they believed him."

Alannah's head shot up and her eyes flashed behind her glasses. "*Fucker.*"

I let out a tearful laugh and grabbed her hand. "Thank you, Alannah. For being my friend, for believing me."

"Why wouldn't I?"

"Because my old friends didn't. They believed him and called me a slut and a whore."

"Well they're fuckers too."

We both grinned but there was no happiness behind either of our smiles, then as the bathroom door slammed open and smashed against the wall, we both startled.

"*Sarah.* Sarah, are you in here?"

It was Adam; his voice high and broken.

"She's here."

Alannah stood up and moved out of the stall and her body was soon replaced by Adam's tall, broad frame.

"Shit, babe, are you okay?" He fell to his knees in front of me and reached up a hand to cup my cheek. "Katie Brown said you'd come in here."

"Yeah, well," Alannah snapped from behind him. "Maybe Katie Brown should have bloody helped her."

Adam glanced over his shoulder. "Thanks, Alannah. You're a good friend."

"I am, which is why *we* all need to talk, but I'll leave you for now. I'll wait outside, that's if there's any café left to sit in."

Adam sighed. "Yeah, there's more damage to Davies and his dickhead mates than there is to this place."

He looked at me and smiled and I noticed the huge bruise on his cheek. "Oh my God, Adam. Your cheek."

"I'm fine. I've told you before, that knob can only manage to get lucky punches in."

He leaned his forehead against mine and I heard the bathroom door close. "How did he find out?" I asked tentatively.

"No idea, but I'll find out."

"No more fighting, please," I begged. "I couldn't stand it if you got badly hurt."

"I won't, but I will do what I have to do to find out."

"Okay."

Adam leaned in to kiss me, but I pulled back. "I stink of vomit. I puked all over the table."

"Yeah I know. I'm so sorry."

I was then in his arms, his nose in my hair and his mouth against my ear.

"So very sorry," he repeated.

I didn't reply but let him hold me tight.

5

ADAM

"I understand," Roger said. "But you can't just respond with punches all the time. This is the second time you've had problems with the same boy. You're just lucky it wasn't on school premises and that Kirk is your friend. The consequences could have been so much worse than you having to wash dishes at TJ's for a week."

"He started it, I told you what he said," I replied as I passed him the plate I'd just washed.

Watching Roger as he dried, I knew he was right. Me laying into Seth-fucking-Davies only did one thing, and that was to stoke the fires of gossip. If I'd ignored him and made him out to be a lying prick, everyone would have forgotten by lunchtime the next day. I hadn't though, I waded in and punched the fucker. At least his eye, which had only just got back to normal from the last thumping I gave him, was black again.

"How did he find out? Do you know?" Roger asked.

I shook my head and drained the water from the sink. "No idea, but I'm going to find out."

"Adam," he groaned my name, a frustrated sigh, and dropped his head back to look up at the ceiling.

"I can't let it go, Roger."

His surprised gaze snapped back to mine, evidently shocked I hadn't called him 'Roge'.

"No more fighting. Please."

He placed a hand on my shoulder and looked me square in the eye, his stare never faltering, until I finally nodded.

I was just about to shrug him off me, when Mum and Lori came into the kitchen. Mum looked at my face and shook her head.

"What?"

"How many times do we have to tell you, you can't resolve things with your fists?"

I wanted to point out that she never had, it had always been Roger, but I couldn't be arsed to argue with her. Instead, I looked down at my little sister who was dressed ready for a party, complete with a netted skirt, pale lemon dress and a bow on the end of each of her plaits.

"Where you off to, Munchkin? You look very pretty."

Lori grinned and twirled from side to side, her tiny hands holding out her skirt.

"Sophia is having a party for her birthday and we're having Karaoke."

I stifled a laugh and grinned at her. My little sister was tone deaf as well as lacking in dancing skills, so I wasn't really sure how her choice of future career i.e. West End performer, would pan out.

"On a school night?"

"She's going to see her grandad at the weekend, so that's why she's having it tonight. And," she said, her eyes shining with excitement, "we don't get picked up until half past seven."

"Wow, cool."

"I know." She nodded, looking at me with big, round eyes. "I think I'll sing Bohemian Raspody."

"Rhapsody," I corrected her.

"Yep, that's what I said, raspody. So," she said with a frown, "do you think that's a good choice? Or I could do that song you like about the Gorillas, what do you think?"

I almost choked on her second choice of song. It was Bruno Marrs' *Gorillas* and it had become a song Sarah and I played a lot at her house, usually to drown out the noises of us getting each other off while her mum watched the TV down the hall. I'd now taken to playing it in my room while I wanked off thinking about Sarah.

"No, Munchkin," I replied through a cough. "Stick to Bohemian Raspody, it's much better."

"Hmm and longer, so I'll get more time to sing."

"Thank God parents aren't expected to stay," Roger muttered under his breath and I found myself laughing.

Mum looked at us both, her face sullen, and then gently pushed Lori towards Roger. "Okay, Daddy is taking you."

"Oh, I thought you were? I've got those shelves to put up in the hall."

Mum turned her back to us and opened the fridge. "Well you can do it when you get back. I've got a headache."

It didn't escape my notice she pulled out a bottle of wine; her head wasn't that bad.

Roger scratched the side of his face and then with a sigh picked up his car keys. "Okay, princess, let's go."

Lori reached on tiptoes and offered me her pursed lips, so I bent to give her a kiss and a hug.

"Have a great time and knock them dead with the singing."

She frowned and shook her head. "You are so weird."

Without saying bye to Mum, she swivelled around on her cute little black Dr Marten boots and strode out behind Roger. It was only as she got to the door that I realised that the boots were miniature versions of Sarah's, and it made me grin. Lori thought Sarah was amazing for finding her in the shopping centre the other week when she got lost, and because she was one of her dance teachers. Now she knew that Sarah was my girlfriend, she'd gone up a whole new level of superstardom according to my sister, who was now even dressing like her.

The front door banged shut after them and I started to make my way out of the kitchen, but Mum stopped me in my stride. "Have you heard from your father?"

"No. Have you?"

Something deep in my head warned me she knew more than she'd been letting on. The weeping and wailing she'd done when Sarah and her mum had come over, had continued for an hour after they'd left, but as soon as Roger led her upstairs and got her to get into bed, it'd stopped like he'd plugged a dam.

Mum opened up a cupboard and stood looking at the rows of wine glasses on the bottom shelf.

"Why would I?" she finally answered as she pulled out a glass.

"Don't know, Mum. I thought maybe seeing as you knew where he'd been all this time?"

I was calling her bluff and I doubted she'd fall for it, but I was fucking sure she was lying to me.

"I didn't, I told you that."

She still didn't look at me while she poured herself a half glass of wine. It wasn't even half past five and she was drinking, which proved to me she was hiding something. She didn't drink a massive amount, but when she did it was for one of two reasons; she'd had a row with Roger, or she felt guilty about something. Her and Roger had seemed okay when he'd left, so guilt it was.

"I don't believe you. You must have had some idea to be able to get divorced."

"We only had contact through our solicitors." She spun around to face me. "I had no idea where he was. I've told you now drop it. If I know Glen, then he'll have left already."

My heart plummeted and I had to swallow hard to speak around the ball of emotion in my throat.

"You don't think he'd try and talk to me first?"

"I doubt it, sweetheart. He's always been a waste of space."

"So why come back in the first place?" I cried, throwing my arms into the air. "If he didn't want to speak to me, why did he come here?"

Mum's red fingernails drummed on the side of the glass. "Sarah obviously." I flinched at the pain her statement caused within my chest. She gave me one of her sympathetic smiles. "Sorry sweetheart, but that's all it can be."

She moved past me out of the kitchen and when she was halfway down the hall glanced over her shoulder.

"Make sure you do your homework and maybe do some studying. Not long until your exams now and just because you're not going to university, doesn't mean you can't try and get good exam results."

As I watched her disappear into the lounge, humming to herself, I knew that homework and revision would be the last thing I'd be able to concentrate on. I wanted to go and see Sarah and make sure she was okay after what had happened at TJ's. Plus, I had a whole load of things running around in my head, not least the sadness I felt that Dad hadn't come here for me at all. Which not only proved he was a shit dad, but also that he really was guilty of raping Sarah. It wasn't that I didn't believe her, I did, but something inside of me was hoping that she was wrong, and it wasn't him but rather someone else. I knew it was a stupid idea, but he was my dad and I had to cling onto something.

Without saying anything to my mum, I took my keys from the hook on the wall and slammed out to my car.

I was about to open the door, when I heard my name being called. I spun around to see my dad leaning against the wall that ran along the bottom of ours and next door's driveways.

"Hi, Adam."

A need to punch him and make him pay for ruining Sarah's life buzzed through my veins as I thought about the pain he'd caused her, and how tortured she'd been in the school car park. This man needed to be taught a lesson, but as I stretched my fingers, clenching them in and out of fists, conflict had me struggling with staying on my spot next to my car. All I really wanted to do was run to him and beg him to hug me and make everything okay.

When he took a step closer to me, I took one back, watching him in his thick smart wool coat, with a scarf wrapped around his neck with some fancy knot.

"What are you doing here?"

"Well I haven't had chance to see you since the day in the car park."

"No, not here, now. But here, in this town." I pointed to the ground and took a deep breath.

He took a step closer and shrugged. "I thought that would be obvious. To see you."

Dragging a hand through my hair, I closed my eyes against

looking at him. If I saw the lies in his eyes, I wasn't sure if I'd get over it... having him and losing him again.

Fuck, what was I thinking, he raped my girlfriend?

"I don't want you here," I grunted and pulled open my car door. "Just go and leave me and Sarah alone."

"She's a liar you know, Adam," he shouted as I put one leg inside the car, causing me to pause. "She agreed to sex. We had consensual sex, twice, son, that's all. Twice and I called it off and she cried rape because of that."

I breathed heavily, my anger pushing out through my nostrils, and got back out of the car.

"You're a liar. You raped her. She told me."

"She told you a lie, Adam. She told you the same story she told the court and they didn't believe her either. *She* asked me to help tidy up my art room. *She* asked me if we could have pizza afterward. And *she* kissed me first. *She* had been flirting with me for weeks. Why else would she spend her own time cleaning up paint?"

"Did she ask you to rape her too?"

I could hardly breathe as I stalked towards him. The thought of what he'd done made me feel sick. With my fists clenched at my side I leaned into his space while a wave of sadness cracked my chest.

I was close enough to touch him.

My dad was here.

"I didn't," he said steadily, shaking his head. "She's lying."

"Why should I believe you." My chin trembling.

He took a deep breath and looked me right in the eye.

"Because I'm your dad, your flesh and blood. Why would I lie to you?"

I couldn't help it. I tried not to, but I fell forward into his arms, wrapping mine tightly around him.

"You left me. You went away and left me. I needed you."

I drew in a pained sob as his big hands landed on my back and rubbed gently. "I'm so sorry, Adam," he whispered against my ear and my lungs jerked out another pitiful cry. "But I'm here now. I've got you."

Even though I knew it was the wrong thing to do, and it was betraying Sarah, I hung on to him like he was a lifeboat and he was the only thing that could save me from drowning.

6

SARAH

I hadn't had the best of mornings. It had got off to a shitty start with a text from Adam saying he was running late and would see me in history. This meant I'd had to walk in with Alannah wondering whether people were gossiping about me.

A couple of people had stared at me and then quickly turned away, but no one actually came up to me and said anything about what had happened in TJ's. I mentioned it to Alannah as we unpacked our stuff into our lockers.

"Can you believe no one has said anything," I whispered as my eyes flicked around the corridor.

"Ellis cut it off while you and Adam were in the bathroom." She shrugged. "It's standard."

"He can't warn everyone to keep quiet. Someone is bound to say something."

"I doubt it. He made out that Davies was lying because he had it in for Adam, and that if anyone repeated it there'd be consequences."

I stared at her wide-eyed. "And they'll take that? They'll do as he said?"

"There's always a first time, but yeah, pretty much."

She sounded so casual about it, I was a little shocked. I knew Adam and his friends had a hold over the girls of the school, but to be able to keep a whole sixth form quiet made me wonder what consequences there'd been in the past.

"Don't think too much about it," Alannah said as she linked her arm with mine. "For once just be grateful that they have the authority to shut it down. How are you feeling anyway? Did Adam stay with you for long after he dropped you home last night? Or did you have one of those middle of the night conversations that you enjoy having? You look knackered."

I gave her a small smile. "No, he went home after about an hour, and I didn't hear from him until my text this morning."

Alannah halted in her step momentarily but then continued. "All that fighting must have worn him out."

"Yeah, maybe." I didn't think so, but Alannah was still finding it difficult to trust Adam, so I kept my thoughts to myself and went off to English.

When I finally saw Adam, it was in our second lesson of the day, history. When he walked in though it was evident that he was not in a good mood. He wore his baseball cap pulled low, but the scowl beneath the peak was plain to see.

"Morning." He flashed me a smile and dropped a quick kiss on my lips. "You okay?" He exhaled, pulled his hat off his head, mussed up his hair and then replaced the cap.

"Fine, what about you?"

When he didn't answer, but started to search inside his bag for something, my stomach twisted. His shoulders were tense, and he kept sighing heavily. When he sat up straight and thudded his text-book onto the desk, he didn't even look at me, but stared straight ahead to the front of the class where Mr Raymond was talking to a boy called Daniel.

"I thought you might call me last night."

"I was knackered," he replied, with only a quick glance in my direction.

"Fine." Call me a child but I pouted and shifted my chair.

I got that everything happening was difficult for him, but there was no reason for him to be salty with me. We were supposed to be helping each other through the pile of shit that had landed on our laps, not act all sulky when we were together. I was entirely sympathetic to how he must be struggling with his emotions, but I didn't want be treated as though it were all my fault. He could stew on his mood if he wanted to, but there was no way I would allow him to make me feel isolated or uncomfortable.

I leaned forward and poked Shannon. "Did you hear from Liverpool uni?"

"Err, yeah," she replied, blinking rapidly. "I need two B's and an A."

"You think you'll get them?"

Shannon tucked her hair behind her ear and studied me. We'd barely spoken in the couple of months I'd been at the school, apart from the odd conversation during our history lessons, but I needed to make more friends, plus part of me thought it might piss Adam off because when we were together my attention was usually on him.

"I hope so," Shannon replied, curling her lip. "I'm struggling with English lit though. I just don't dig deep enough with my essays apparently."

"I can help you, if you like." I leaned over the desk. "It's one of my better subjects."

"You wouldn't mind?"

I shook my head and, in my periphery, noticed Adam shift his chair a little closer.

"Catch up with me later and we'll sort something."

Shannon grinned and was about to say something else, when Mr Raymond barked at us all to be quiet.

I sat back in my seat and felt a warm hand on my leg.

"I'm sorry," Adam whispered. "I'm a dickhead and I shouldn't take my bad mood out on you, especially not at the minute."

"No, you shouldn't." I looked straight ahead.

"Can we talk before the next lesson? We need to, about what Davies said at TJ's."

I turned to him and nodded. "Yes, I think we should."

Adam smiled and leaned in to kiss my cheek. "I am sorry, more than you know."

"I know." I sighed and smiled back.

Adam pulled at a strand of my hair as I stood in front of him where he sat on the wall which surrounded the yard. He'd told me that sixth formers rarely visited it, leaving it to the younger kids to congregate, gossip and bitch in, and as most of our year group were gathered in the dining room, he'd thought the yard the better place to talk.

"Has anyone said anything?" he asked and dropped my hair, taking my hand instead.

"No, I had some strange looks, but nothing else."

His nostrils flared and his eyes darkened. "Tell me who the fuck it was, and I'll sort it."

"No, you won't," I replied with a shake of my head. "I can cope with a few side eyes. If you say anything it'll just fuel the fire, anyway Ellis shut it down apparently."

"Yeah he said, but there's always some dickhead who thinks they're a fucking joker."

"Has someone said something to you?"

"Davies. He thought he was fucking hilarious in maths. Mrs Baker was talking through a problem and he shouted, 'sorry to be *sloppy,* Miss, but can I have a few *seconds* to write the problem down. I want to try the pen my *dad* bought for me, just because we're really *close'.*" Adam pulled me closer and rested his forehead on my shoulder. "Then the fucking knob said, 'are you *close* with *your dad*, Hudson?'. Kirk had to hold me back. I don't know whether the stupid prick has a death wish or something, but he won't get away with it."

I let out a long, exasperated sigh, wishing I had the nerve to kick Davies in the bollocks myself. I didn't want Adam to be getting into fights over me all the time. "How the hell did he even find out?"

Adam grunted. "No idea."

Silence fell between us and I wondered what had happened to his desire from the night before to stop at nothing to find out how Davies found out. Something had changed in him since he'd held me tight in the bathroom at TJ's.

"Are you okay?" I asked, moving back so that Adam had to lift his head. "I get it, if you're pissed off by everything, but I thought we were in this together."

"We are."

His words were sharp, and as he looked over my shoulder my

stomach and heart drummed an erratic beat in unison. Everything had seemed a little bit easier since Adam and I had been together. With the robbery at the Tesco Express, him saving me with the EpiPen and then holding me together when Mr Mills arrived, I'd felt like we could become indestructible together; but now something was gnawing at my nerves causing me to doubt everything.

"You just seem distant that's all."

I didn't want to sound like some pathetic little girl, who needed her boyfriend to hold her hand, but I couldn't help being fearful. If he ended things and went back to being horrible and mean to me, I wasn't sure I'd be able to cope. Alannah was a good friend, but Adam got it, he knew about having sadness smother you until it took your breath from your lungs. He knew how it felt to face every day with a blackness shrouding your soul.

"I'm just worried, that's all," he replied, finally looking at me.

"Okay." I studied him carefully and watched as his eyes flickered around, looking everywhere but not seeing anything.

"How come you offered to help my dad... him, to clean up the art room?"

Adam's question shot sudden and unexpected. It punched me in the stomach and physically knocked me back a step.

"W-what?" My mouth went dry as instinctively I pulled my hand from Adam's and pushed it up the sleeve of my jumper, rubbing at the raised skin on my wrist. Adam finally looked at me, really looked at me, and took a deep breath. I waited for him to let it out, but his chest remained still as his gaze stayed pinned to me. Finally, and very slowly, he exhaled.

"What made you offer to help him clean the art room? Didn't you feel uncomfortable being alone with a teacher?"

I shook my head and rubbed furiously at my scar. "He was my

teacher. He was supposed to protect me, of course I felt comfortable with him. W-w-why are you asking this?" My chest started to move up and down with erratic breaths as I stared at Adam.

"I'm just trying to get the facts," he replied and jumped down from the wall.

"The facts? The fucking fact is that he raped me." I hissed out my words, chancing a look over my shoulder to check we weren't being overheard. "What other facts do you need?"

"I'm trying to..." he paused and ran a hand through his hair, a pained look crumpling his handsome features. "Build a picture. I'm trying to build a picture."

I shook my head and took another step away from him. "No, I don't want to help you build a fucking picture, Adam. I don't need to build a picture, because I still have them whirling around in my head every minute of every day. I see them at night when I'm sleeping too. They never go away, Adam, so if you want a picture go and ask your fucking dad."

I ran from him, stumbling against groups of kids, pushing through them. I had no idea if Adam was following me. I didn't care, I just needed to be away from him so that I'd be able to breathe.

The door back into school slammed against the wall as I shoved it and ran into the corridor which led to the sixth form part of the building.

"Watch it," a boy carrying a stack of chairs cried as I almost sent him toppling over.

I didn't respond but kept running. I was going to get my stuff from my locker and go. I couldn't sit in a classroom and pretend I was fine; that my boyfriend wasn't a dick.

With the bell only a few minutes away, the corridor where our lockers were heaved with everyone grabbing their books for their afternoon lessons. As I moved past them, I sensed that I'd grabbed their attention; I was running, was close to tears, and I was desperate to go home.

"Sarah." A large hand grabbed my elbow. "I'm sorry, okay?"

I swung around to face Adam and pushed both my hands against his chest. "I don't want to speak to you, or even see you right now."

"Babe, please."

"No." I shook my head. "You're supposed to believe me, but you obviously don't."

"I didn't say that. I was just—"

"Yeah you said." I turned away from him to see most of the people in the corridor had now stopped what they were doing and were listening to us. "*Seen enough?*"

A few people rolled their eyes or laughed but most continued to stare as Adam reached for me.

"Sarah."

"No. I don't want to talk about it. I'm going home."

"Let me take you," Adam offered but then turned on a girl who stood whispering behind him. "Why don't you fuck off and get a life."

I took the opportunity to move away from him and quickly open my locker and pull out my backpack.

"Sarah, just wait. I'm sorry." Adam sounded desperate

Pushing past him, letting my bag smack him in the stomach, I marched out of school and once I was outside, I let the tears roll.

7

ADAM

"Happy birthday, mate." Ellis slapped my back and pushed an envelope against my chest. "It's from my mum and dad, so don't start thinking I've turned into a girl."

I forced out a smile and glanced down at the card. "Tell them thanks."

"So, plans for tonight? You have to have one because having your eighteenth birthday on a Friday night is pretty fucking lucky, if you ask me."

I shrugged.

"Don't tell me that because you're all wifed up that you're not having your first legal drink with your mates."

"No," I protested. "I'm just not in the mood to do anything to be honest. Like you said, it's not like we haven't been in a pub before."

I looked over Ellis' shoulder when I felt the breeze from the main door into school opening. My heart jumped when I saw a flash of blonde hair, but it wasn't Sarah. I hadn't seen her since she'd stormed off home two days before. I knew she'd been in school, but she'd somehow managed to avoid me as we hadn't had any lessons together. The only one we did have normally had been history, but Mr Raymond was off sick and so Miss Daniels had given us a study session instead of bringing in a substitute teacher—as usual no fucking expense spared at Maddison High School. Apparently, Sarah had studied in the library rather than the classroom like the rest of us, but by the time I'd got there she was nowhere to be seen.

I hadn't seen my dad again either. After I'd cried on his shoulder like a big fucking baby, I'd pushed him away and then gone back into the house yelling at him to stay away from me. The problem with that was that he had kept away, and I was kind of missing him too, despite barely knowing the man.

"What the hell is wrong with you?" Ellis groaned, bringing me back from my thoughts. "Has Sarah told you you're not allowed out? It's not that crap that Davies was saying is it? I told you, I warned everyone not to repeat the shit he comes out with."

"No, none of that." My head snapped up and I faced him with narrowed eyes. "I just don't want to go out drinking."

Guilt rolled around my stomach at the fact I hadn't told Ellis about Sarah and my dad. He was my best friend and I didn't want to tell him that Davies wasn't talking shit, everything he said was true. What made me feel even more guilty was that I hadn't told him to protect Sarah. He'd shut things down for me, not because I'd demanded it for my girlfriend.

As I contemplated how crap I felt, we started to walk down the corridor towards the IT & Science block where we both had Chemistry, but there was none of our usual joking and talking shit. I couldn't bring myself to even muster a smile, I was so miserable about the situation with Sarah. I'd called her numerous times and sent text messages, but not one of them had been answered, even though I knew she'd read them and listened to my voice messages. Not seeing her had knocked me off kilter and I felt as though I was wading through mud. My soul would be in danger of turning black again if I didn't get to touch her soon, that realisation made my nerves bounce like a series of live wires sparking off each other.

How could I feel so lost without her after only three weeks of being together – well two and a half, because my heart felt as though she'd actually dumped it.

As we reached the labs, I noticed Tyler and Kirk. Kirk was looking at his phone, while Tyler kicked a football against the wall.

"Have you actually had sex with that thing?" Ellis asked Tyler as we approached them. "Because I see you with that more often than I see you with a girl."

Tyler gave a sarcastic smile and volleyed the ball at him. Ellis, with the lightening reflexes which made him a great keeper, caught it and pulled it to his chest.

"Aren't you supposed to be in IT?" I asked.

"We were waiting for you." Kirk thrust an envelope at me, which was closely followed by a smaller one from Tyler. "It's cash from all of us and our parents. It was Tyler's mum's idea."

When Kirk waggled his tongue and circled his nipples with his fingers, I couldn't help but laugh.

"Stop sexualising my mum," Tyler said, nudging Kirk in the ribs. "Otherwise I'll tell you what we all say about your mum's arse in her uniform."

Ellis and I burst out laughing but Kirk made a gagging sound.

"Yeah, it's gross isn't it, so shut the fuck up otherwise I might have to tell my dad."

We all went silent. Tyler's dad was fucking huge and was pretty scary. Looking at each of us in turn, Tyler grinned knowing that he had us.

"I'll open them later," I said. "Thanks a lot. Appreciate it."

"No problem," Tyler replied. "We figured you could get whatever you want rather than us get you some crap you don't need."

"Yeah," Kirk added. "My mother wanted to buy you a suitcase, because she reckons everyone should have a decent one." He rolled his eyes which made me laugh and a little light flickered my soul back to life. We still weren't back to normal, and I wasn't sure I wanted us to go back to being that group of dickheads again, but not many lads had a group of mates who along with their parents clubbed together for a birthday present.

"What did your mum and Roge get you?" Ellis asked.

"Gave me cash."

I thought back to the big drama Mum had made at breakfast about her baby becoming a man and then handing me an envelope with a hundred quid in it. I was really grateful for it, but I had to bite my tongue not to say a better present would have been that she had filled in my university grant forms. Not being able to continue my education like I wanted, just because they couldn't afford it, made me fucking angry, especially as all I'd asked her to do was give me some time to fill in a few damn forms. New sofas were essential to Elouise Crawford, further education not so much.

"So, plans for tonight?" Tyler asked.

"He doesn't have any. Doesn't feel like going out drinking." Ellis threw the ball back to Tyler.

"What nothing at all?" Tyler glanced between them both before bringing his shocked gaze to me. "But it's Friday and you're eighteen."

I shrugged. "I know, I just don't fancy it."

Kirk was particularly quiet, and I guessed he had a lot to say, but it probably meant disrespecting Sarah, so he'd decided not to bother.

"Can we at least go to TJ's after school?" Tyler asked. "We can get Rebecca to sing Happy Birthday to you."

"No way," Kirk cried. "You are not getting my mum to sing. She's awful."

"Okay," I replied with a laugh, realising I was being a bit miserable. "Let's do that, but Kirk's right, no singing."

"I suppose it's something," Ellis complained. "Come on then, birthday boy, let's go otherwise we'll be late."

We all said our goodbyes and I followed Ellis to our classroom. When I got to my desk, Alannah turned in her seat to face me.

"That's from Sarah." She threw an envelope towards me and I just managed to catch it before it skidded to the floor. "I've no idea what's going on with you two, but I can't say I didn't warn her."

I leaned forward and narrowed my eyes. "For your information, Alannah. She's the one not speaking to me."

Alannah rolled her eyes. "Exactly, so what did you do to upset her, Adam? She's going through enough at the moment, so try being a decent human being and a good boyfriend."

"I'm not even sure I still am her boyfriend," I muttered.

"Well personally I think that would be a good thing," Alannah whispered, her eyes watching Ellis as he approached his desk next to mine. "But she seems to think you can change, so bloody well show her she isn't wrong."

With that the conversation was evidently over, because she turned her back to me.

"Okay?" Ellis asked.

"Yeah." I nodded down at the envelope in my hand. "It's a card from Sarah, I didn't realise she even knew it was my birthday."

Ellis pulled out his textbook from his bag. "I asked her if she wanted to club in with us. She hadn't known, but said she'd rather get you something on her own." He grinned. "Do you think you'll get something special in the shagging department?"

It was very doubtful, but I smiled and shrugged.

"Maybe, who knows?"

As he tuned into Mr Kettle's lesson, I undid the envelope and pulled out Sarah's card. As soon as I saw it, I burst out a sharp laugh. It said now you're 18 do you feel like an adult with a check box for yes and no, but in the 'no' box was drawn a cock and balls and a 'b' had been added to the end of the word no.

I opened it up and took a deep breath, wondering whether she'd written a note to say have a great birthday, but you're dumped. I was happily surprised by what she'd written.

Happy 18th Birthday, Adam
    Hope you have a great day
    I know things have been difficult, but I know you'll get through it
    Sarah xx

I put the card back in the envelope and dropped it into my bag, determined to call her and sort things out. First though I had to figure out why nitrogen had a larger ionisation energy than oxygen.

"Burgers are on us tonight," Rebecca said as she pulled me in for a hug. "It's not every day one of my boys turns eighteen."

"Thanks, Rebecca, and thanks to you and Tony for the money as well."

I'd finally opened the envelope to find a hundred and twenty quid in it. I was shocked but buzzing at what they'd done.

"Our pleasure, love. Now take a seat, boys and I'll get you all the usual. Kirky, you doubling up?"

"Of course, I am."

He grinned at his mum and when she pinched his cheek, I felt a stab of jealousy at their closeness. I'd never had that with my mum, not that I wanted it. I didn't even like her particularly so certainly wouldn't want to joke and banter with her.

"So, is Sarah meeting us?" Tyler asked while he read the menu, despite knowing it off by heart.

I shifted in my seat and glanced at the door. I'd sent her a text, asking her to come, but wasn't hopeful. Alannah had mentioned earlier that Sarah was off for the afternoon for a therapy session. Thankfully mine were done with because Alex, my therapist, had told Roger I was handling things well, but then I had less shit to deal with than Sarah.

"Not sure, she had an appointment."

"What sort of appointment?" Kirk immediately winced. "Sorry, none of my business."

"Grief counselling."

I said the words with bite, hoping they realised I was still pissed off with the stunt they'd pulled over the flyers about her dad.

Tyler cleared his throat and put the menu back in its wooden stand.

"Oh well," Ellis said. "Maybe you'll get your present later." He smirked and winked, but I wasn't in the mood.

"I'm just going for a piss." I pushed my chair back with a

screeching sound. "No nicking my chips if they're here before I get back."

As I pushed open the door of the hallway that led to the bathrooms, I heard Kirk groan about this being a lame eighteenth, and I had to fucking agree.

I'd barely washed my hands after taking a pee, when the bathroom door swung open. I expected one of the lads to tell me our food had arrived, seeing as there was barely anyone else in the café – it was Friday night, most sane people were in town in the pubs. I did a double take to see Mackenna White leant against the doorway, smiling what I guess she thought was a seductive smile.

"Happy birthday," she said breathily.

I fought the urge to roll my eyes and nodded. "Cheers. I think you picked the wrong door by the way. You're supposed to be in the one with Sandy on it." I pointed at the picture of Danny Zuko from *Grease*.

"No, I'm in the right place. I came to give you your birthday present."

Before I could even respond, she took a step forward and wrapped her arms around my neck.

"Mackenna, fuck off." I reached up and grabbed her wrists, pulling at her arms. "I'm not interested."

She managed to get one hand free of mine and landed it straight on my dick, rubbing over the top of my jeans.

"You know you want me, Adam. You know I give you the best blow jobs you'll ever have."

I instantly thought of Sarah and the fact she hadn't gone there yet. Of course, I wanted my dick in her mouth, but what we had was so much more than her knowing the right suction and what to do to my fucking balls while she was sucking me off.

Mackenna's hand stayed firm, stroking, and I hated myself for the fact I started to get hard. An involuntarily groan came from my chest. My eyes closed and Mackenna's mouth landed on mine. Reality hit fast. It took a millisecond for me to realise that the thought *I was eighteen and I was almost sure my girlfriend had dumped me, so who was I hurting?* was actually the wrong fucking thing to think. I grabbed Mackenna's forearms and pushed her away.

"Get the fuck off me, I'm not interested."

Whether I was with Sarah or not, was irrelevant. Looking at her and seeing the smug look on her face, the press of her obviously braless tits in her tight, white, top instantly made anger pulse through me. The fact she'd touched me repulsed me, but that I'd let her get to that point made white hot fury burn through my veins. I should have pushed her away or left the bathroom before she'd even taken a step towards me. The fact that my fucking dick had responded to her made me angrier.

"She's not even here," Mackenna said, pouting her lips like she thought it was sexy. "She wouldn't even know."

"The fact that you know I'm going out with Sarah makes what you've just done even worse." I shoved her to one side and pushed past her. "Stay away from me, Mackenna; you know what I can do if you don't."

She gasped low but I ignored it as I pulled open the door and stormed off down the hallway, back into the main part of the café.

When I got back to the table our food was already there and the lads were all about to tuck in. Tyler had a handful of chips, about to shove them into his mouth, when he looked up at me and grinned. "Fucking hell, you been having a dump? You've been ages."

"No," I growled out. "Fucking Mackenna. She thought it was okay to come into the men's bathroom and lay it on me."

Kirk shrugged and looked at me quizzically. "And?"

Ellis slapped him in his stomach with the back of his hand. "He's going out with Sarah now."

"And?"

I sighed heavily, knowing that it was partly my fault Kirk was a prick. A couple of months ago I'd have agreed with him.

Flopping down onto my chair, I picked up my burger and took a huge bite forcing it down with a swig of coke. All three of my friends were watching me while we ate. I had no clue what they were expecting me to do or say, but I continued to eat in silence.

"Listen," I eventually said, pushing my empty plate away. "I'm going to get off. I forgot my mum wants to do cake and all that shit."

Tyler and Kirk exchanged a glance, while Ellis sighed and then plastered on a smile.

"Okay mate," he said, grabbing the chips from my side plate. "Enjoy the cake. Maybe we can do something tomorrow?"

Inwardly I sighed with relief, grateful that he wasn't going to make a deal out of me leaving.

"Yeah, sounds good. Maybe go into Manchester, if you're all up for it?"

It was the least I could do seeing as I'd spoiled their plans to get me pissed on my actual birthday.

"Yeah," Tyler replied around a mouthful of chips.

Kirk nodded and Ellis punched me in the ribs.

"I'll speak to you in the morning."

I nodded and started to walk away. When Ellis shouted my name, I glanced over my shoulder.

"If Sarah doesn't give you the best fucking birthday present ever, then I want to know why."

They all started laughing and feigning amusement I left, determined to sort things out with my girlfriend.

When I got to the bungalow Sarah lived in with her mum, I could see the light of the TV flickering in the lounge. The curtains weren't closed properly, and I could see Mrs Danes sitting in an armchair watching television, drinking from a mug. I didn't know if Sarah was in there with her, but I decided to go around the back and try the doors at her bedroom. If I knocked at the front door, there would be a good chance she'd tell her mum to tell me she wasn't home, and I needed to see her.

The side gate was locked, but it wasn't so high that I couldn't get over it, and thankfully the path down the side of the bungalow was lit up from the streetlamp at the end of their neighbour's driveway.

The kitchen was in darkness, but I ducked below the window just in case. Thankfully, light was shining under the blinds at the window and the curtains at the patio doors that led onto the garden from Sarah's room.

I took a deep breath and tapped out a text message on my phone; I didn't want to knock in case it scared her.

Adam: I'm outside in the garden. Can I come in?

Pushing my hands into my jacket pockets, I waited as my breath floated in the cold February evening. A shadow appeared under the small gap below the curtains and then they were pulled back to reveal Sarah. As soon as I saw her, I inhaled sharply. She looked fucking beautiful; her hair was piled on her head and she was wearing short, silky pyjamas in pink with a thin black stripe.

She hesitated and I thought she was going to tell me to go away, but after the longest seconds of my life, she unlocked the bolts and lock and opened up one of the double doors.

"What are you doing here?" she asked as she wrapped her arms around her body.

"I wanted to see you." I shivered and pushed my hands further into my pockets. "Can I come in?"

Sarah blew out her cheeks and stood to one side. "Quick before all the cold air comes in."

I moved inside and was immediately grateful for the warmth of her cosy bedroom. The door was quickly closed and bolted and then Sarah drew the curtains against the darkness.

Music was playing from a Bluetooth speaker and there was only her cream coloured lamp on. Books were scattered over her desk and on her Mac was a web page all about the French Revolution.

"You started on the homework for next week?" I pushed one of the textbooks with my forefinger and then looked up at Sarah. "I thought we were going to do it together?"

"I was just taking notes," she replied, crossing her arms over her chest. "Thought I'd give us a head start."

I felt a hint of hope at her words. "So, are we still going to do it together. You haven't persuaded Shannon to swap partners?"

Sarah's eyes narrowed but her mouth twitched at the edges as she shook her head. "No. Just because you're an idiot I do know that you're the best person to do the project with. Seeing as you're the history guru."

"That the only reason?" I asked. I took a step closer to her, my fingers itching to touch her.

"What do you want, Adam?"

She moved to sit on the edge of her bed. The duvet crumpled

into soft creases, and I couldn't help but think about her lying in it, naked.

"I wanted to see you and to apologise for being a dick the other day. Everything... everything was getting on top of me. I took it out on you, when you're the last person I should be taking it out on." I looked down at the floor and sighed. "I'm so fucking sorry, Sarah."

When I looked back up, she was watching me with tear filled eyes. Every drop against her lashes pounded into my heart.

"You really hurt me, Adam."

Sarah's hand went to her wrist, but then she cleared her throat, straightened her shoulders and dropped her hands to lap. She was trying to be brave again and it made my stomach turn over to think she felt she had to be that way with me. We'd come so far in such a short space of time, that wasn't us anymore. I wasn't meant to be the person who scared her or made her feel insecure. I was supposed to be the one person she could rely on to have her back and to support her through all the bad things that she was battling with.

I moved closer and dropped to my knees in front of her. I wanted us to be eye to eye, but I also wanted her to know I'd fucking beg for forgiveness if that was what she wanted.

"This, with him coming back," I said as I cupped her face. "I don't know how to deal with it. My mum is useless, she just puts on the drama when I mention him. And... well, I can't talk to you about him."

Sarah let out a little gasp and her eyes went wide.

"I know what he did, but I'm so conflicted. I hate him for what he did to you, but he's my dad. I have all these feelings whizzing around in my head and in here and..." I patted my chest and took a deep breath. "...I don't know how to separate them."

Sarah closed her eyes and leaned into my touch, her face so

pained, I felt sure she was going to dump me. I could understand if she did. Now I was a constant reminder of what had happened to her.

I had never wanted anything so much in all my life as I wanted what we had, but at the same time I wanted my dad too.

I knew I couldn't have both.

"How do we do this?" she finally said. "How do we be us and not let him get in in the middle?"

"I don't know. I just know that I want to try." I licked my lips and waited on a desperate breath for Sarah to answer.

"Okay, let's try." She reached up and held onto my wrists. "I like you Adam, *a lot*, and I know we could have something special. But if you're not into this as much as I am, then let's finish it now."

Was I as into it as much as she was?

Was I able to have just one girl in my life?

Was I capable of being a good boyfriend?

For Sarah Danes, no fucking doubt about it.

"Yes, I want this just as much as you do," I whispered against her lips. "I can't believe how much, but I do."

Sarah kissed me back, slowly and gently, painting a picture with her lips of what we could be like. When she pulled away, her smile shone with brilliance.

"What?" I asked.

"Just surprised and pleased that you came. I was sure that you didn't care."

I frowned. "I care more than you will ever realise."

She nodded, clearing her throat, and then quickly glanced at her chest of drawers. "I bought you a birthday present, but I'm not sure it's appropriate really."

"You did?"

Without saying anything she reached for the blue and silver wrapped parcel and handed it to me. "I feel a bit stupid now," she groaned and dropped her face to her hands.

I grinned and ripped at the wrapping paper, to find some lacy red knickers and bra. The tiniest, sexiest underwear I'd ever seen.

I swallowed and instinctively cupped my dick when it twitched at the realisation that Sarah had planned to wear them for me.

"*Fuck*," I ground out as I held up the thong and examined it.

Sarah made a grab for the parcel. "Give it back to me, it was a dickhead idea."

I moved out of her reach and grinned. "No way, you can't take back a present once you've given it to someone." I dangled the bra from my finger. "You do know it's still my birthday."

"Of course, I do." Her face was a deep shade of pink as she rolled her eyes.

"Well, maybe I want my present on my birthday."

The image of Sarah in the red underwear made me rock hard and I couldn't wait another second to touch her. I flung the lacy bra and thong on top of her chest of drawers and scooted forward on my knees until I was eye to eye with her again. Pushing my hand into her hair, I pulled her mouth to mine and took it in a kiss. Sarah's lips immediately opened up for me, her tongue responding to mine, instantly causing the nerve endings in my lips to come alive. She gripped my t-shirt with one hand and pushed my jacket off my shoulder with the other, thrusting her hips up from the edge of the bed. Shrugging my jacket off my other arm, I flung it across the room and groaned as Sarah's hand travelled up the back of my t-shirt.

Her cool fingertips dug into my muscles, and I scrambled onto my feet so I could push her back until she landed on the bed. Instinctively, she opened her legs and allowed me to climb on top of

73

her, resting between them; our lips never breaking. My tongue stroked against Sarah's and hers responded, welcoming the passion I was offering. There was nothing curious about the kiss, we both knew what we wanted and were desperate to take if it wasn't offered. It was slow and intimate, not hurried and with every second my dick grew harder.

Sarah's hand moved from up my t-shirt to the front of my jeans where she reached for the button on the waistband. I lifted my body from hers to give her the space she needed. With quick, small fingers, my button was soon open and my zip down, giving my dick room to move.

"Babe," I gasped. "Need you so fucking much."

Sarah reached inside my jeans and boxers and wrapped her had around me, giving a gentle squeeze before slowly pumping me.

"I want to see you in the underwear," I groaned. "But I can't wait."

"Later," Sarah whispered and continued to pump me.

I moved my hand up her smooth leg, until I felt the hem of her silky shorts. My hand went up to cup her arse and the fact that she was bare underneath ramped up my need to be inside her. It was too much and I couldn't wait any longer. I pulled away from her and reached for the waistband of the silky fabric.

"Is your mum likely to come in?" I mumbled into her mouth.

"No. I've locked the door and she thinks I'm alone in here."

I looked over my shoulder to see the small silver bolt had been pushed across. "Were you expecting me?"

Sarah shook her head as she looked up at me through her lashes, while chewing on her lip.

"What?" I asked stooping down to nibble at her earlobe. "What aren't you telling me?"

"I was..." her eyelashes fluttered closed as she breathed out, "I was touching myself."

My dick went from rock to diamond hard in an instant. The thought of Sarah's fingers, touching her beautiful pink pussy and circling her perfect clit was too much. I ripped down her shorts and pushed down my jeans in almost one movement. I was about to thrust inside her when I remembered the condom.

"Shit let me get my wallet," I gasped. I moved to reach for it, but Sarah pulled me back.

"Have you ever had sex without a condom before?"

My heart faltered at what I thought she was about to offer. "N-no."

"I don't need you to use one, if you don't want to. It would be perfectly safe... in all ways." Her head moved as she looked towards her chest of drawers where the red underwear lay.

Nudging my nose against hers, I brought Sarah's gaze back to mine, understanding everything she said without saying the words. "Are you sure?"

Perfect lips parted slightly as she nodded, and when her tongue flicked out to slowly lick them, I thought my balls were going to explode.

I didn't have to think anymore, I jumped off the bed and practically ripped off my remaining clothes, leaving them in a pile. As I'd hastily got myself naked, I hadn't been watching Sarah, but when I looked over to her, she had stripped off her pyjamas and was lying back on her elbows, baring all of her beautiful creamy skin to me. Her nipples were hard, and goose bumps feathered over her skin. I'd never seen anything more beautiful or sexy in all my life.

As I moved towards her, Sarah's breathing sped up and she opened her legs, her body responding to me before I'd even touched her. Sucking on my bottom lip, I couldn't believe that she was mine. I'd been so stupid to hurt her. The feelings that she evoked in me battered my head. If this was how I felt about her now, my future would be torment if I didn't become the boy she needed me to be. I knew she was too good for me. She was too good, too beautiful, and I was too undeserving.

"You are so fucking stunning," I whispered as I bent down and took one of her nipples into my mouth and sucked it.

Sarah moaned and thrust up her hips, grabbing my wrist and pushing my hand towards her pussy. I smiled around the hard nub in my mouth and parted her lips. She was really wet, and I slid two fingers easily inside of her, instantly feeling her inner muscles tighten around them. As I swirled my tongue around first one nipple and then the other, I pumped in a gentle rhythm until she moaned against my mouth.

"Adam, I need *you*," she urged.

I pulled out my fingers and moved them to my mouth and sucked them clean, her desire popping against my taste buds. When I reached down for her hand, Sarah's legs widened, and I knew I was going to fuck her hard. I wouldn't be able to hold back. I had to brand her as mine and make sure that this moment was etched indelibly into her brain forever.

"Turn the music up," I whispered, as I knelt on the bed.

Sarah didn't question me but reached for her phone and pressed at it until the sound of Dua Lipa's 'One Kiss' drowned out our heavy breathing.

Unable to hold back any longer, I lifted Sarah's leg above my waist and pushed inside of her in one swift thrust. The moment I felt her muscles contract, the touch paper was lit, and my hips started a race with the pressure building in the pit of my stomach.

Sarah's legs wrapped tightly around me, and her fingers pushed against my skin as she bucked, taking each of my harsh, quick thrusts and matching them with her own. The sensation of being inside her without anything between us made me feel like I'd been hit by lightning. Every single part of my body shook with the sensation.

"Oh my God, Adam." Sarah's head fell back against the pillow and her mouth parted on a silent moan.

I reached a hand up to palm Sarah's tit, and pinched her nipple, it brought a sharp gasp from her and when her inner walls clenched my dick, I couldn't hold back any longer. I roughly pulled out and then pushed back in, hard and fast, causing Sarah to move up the bed as her silver headboard banged against the wall. I drilled and drilled until I exploded, and just as I groaned out Sarah's name against her mouth, she let out a shocked whimper and dug her nails into my back.

Her keening cry collided with my heavy breath and I looked down, taking in the beauty of her orgasm.

Slowly, we stopped moving, but I stayed inside of her, not wanting to break our connection. When she reached up to kiss me softly, I felt like I was dropping from the sky, weightless and free.

"That was amazing," Sarah whispered against my skin as her lips caressed my cheek.

"Every time with you is amazing and better than anything that's gone before."

I'd made the mistake once before of not telling her that, I hadn't wanted to tarnish us with my previous experience, but now was the time to say it. I'd never experienced anything like it in my life before. The pleasure and euphoria were bigger and better than I'd imagined possible.

Sarah's fingers brushed through the mess of my hair, and she smiled up at me. When her eyes twinkled, I felt my heart jump at the depth of my feelings for her. She was fucking perfect and she was mine.

"Happy birthday, Adam."

"Best birthday ever," I sighed. "Best fucking ever."

As we lay together in the stillness of her room, listening to the music while I stroked her hair and she rested her head on my chest, I couldn't help but fear that one day she'd realise that I was no good for her. But, until that day, I knew I would do whatever I could to protect her.

8

SARAH

Lori ran into the dance studio with a huge grin on her face; her plaits flapping behind her.

"I'm ready."

"Okay, let's go." I grinned and grabbed her hand as she skipped along beside me.

Adam had gone into Manchester with Ellis, Kirk and Tyler as a birthday celebration, so I'd gone into the studio to help Clarice out, even though it wasn't my day for Street Dance lessons. Once we finished the lesson, I'd planned to spend some time looking for a job for my gap year, but when Mrs Crawford had dropped Lori off at class, her face had lit up when she'd seen me there. She'd asked if I'd mind taking Lori for a couple of hours afterwards. Apparently, she had a hair appointment and Roger had been called out on an emergency for the IT company he worked for. I didn't actually mind because Lori was very cute and funny, but I knew when Adam found out he would be annoyed that his mum had asked me.

"What are we going to do?" Lori asked excitedly.

"What would you like to do?"

I was surprised she had the energy to do anything; she'd just spent the last hour and a half dancing around and pretending to be a Water Buffalo – Clarice had told them to pick an animal and that's what the petite, blonde-haired cutie had gone with.

"Can we go to TJ's?"

Her eyes shone as she gave me the biggest smile, so big and sweet that I couldn't possibly say no. I wasn't sure how I felt going back in there, but I had to at some point, maybe having Lori come along would distract me. Plus, Adam's mum had given me twenty pounds to use to entertain her daughter.

"Okay, let's go and when we get there, we'll call Adam and make him jealous that we're having burgers and milkshake."

"Yes," she cried, "that would be so funny."

I doubted Adam would be bothered he was missing out on lunch at TJ's, but it made Lori giggle, and making her happy was my aim for the afternoon.

When we entered TJ's, I'd been pleased to see only a handful of people in there, and none of them were from school. Neither Rebecca nor Tony were working, so there wasn't actually anyone there who had seen the drama from a few nights before. Calming myself down, I breathed a little easier and ordered us both a burger, chips and milkshake. While we waited, I played with my phone and listened to Lori talk my head off. We'd tried to facetime Adam, but he hadn't answered. I guessed he was probably in some bar or pub having a few afternoon drinks. I wasn't worried because I knew he would call me back once he saw the missed call.

After we'd had sex in my bedroom the night before, we'd fallen asleep and it was my mum knocking on my door to say she was going to bed that woke us. I had quickly pulled my pyjamas back on and gone to the door to say goodnight and thankfully she hadn't wanted to come in. I think because I looked genuinely sleepy, she didn't think twice about there being someone – Adam - in there with me.

Once we'd heard Mum shut her own bedroom door, Adam and I had sex again. That time was slow and quiet, and I didn't think I would, but I came even harder than before. Adam eventually left at almost two in the morning and when I bolted the door after him, it took every single ounce of restraint I had, not to text him and ask him to come back.

"When we do street dance next week, can we try being robots again?" Lori asked, her mouth chasing the straw in her milkshake. "I think I'm really good at it."

I had to admire her confidence, if not her skills, so I nodded. "If you want to, but I do want to show you how to do a running man."

Her little brow furrowed and with a huff of impatience she grabbed at the red and white paper straw.

"We're going to run?"

"No, we're going to do a running man. It's a dance move."

Lori looked at me with her nose wrinkled and then took a huge slurp of strawberry milkshake. Laughing, I turned back to my own burger and took a bite.

"Oh no," Lori groaned beside me. "I *do not* like her." I twisted in my seat, to see Mackenna White approaching us. "She's skanky."

"Lori," I admonished in a hissed whisper. "You can't say that."

"That's what Tyler calls her." She pouted and then her eyes went huge. "Uh oh."

I looked up to see Mackenna standing next to me, clutching a pale blue hoodie. We stared at each other for a few seconds, until I finally caved and smiled.

"Can I help you?"

Mackenna's eyes flickered towards Lori and her nostrils flared. "I see you've been demoted to babysitter."

"No." I shook my head and then grinned at Lori. "We're having a girl's day." I looked back up at Mackenna who looked distinctly bored.

"Whatever. Just give this to Adam." She threw the hoodie at me and I managed to catch it before it landed on top of my burger.

"It's Adam's?"

I held it up and examined it. It did look like Adam's.

"Why do you have it?" I asked. "Are you returning stuff he left at your house?" The words felt like poison on my tongue. I'd seen Adam in the hoodie before; the night his dad came back. If he'd worn it then, how had Mackenna got it?

"Yeah," she said, flicking her long, poker straight, brunette hair over her shoulder. "He left it in my room yesterday afternoon."

I felt the colour drain from my face as her words sunk in. "Your room?" I screwed the hoodie around my fingers, desperately trying to stop them from shaking.

"Yeah. You know," she said, giving me a smirk. "The room that usually has a bed in it."

I turned to Lori who was watching us with her mouth hanging open around her straw.

"Lori why don't you go and choose which ice cream you want?"

She frowned. "Not you too. Everyone always sends me to do something." Climbing down from her chair, Lori rolled her eyes and ran off towards the ice cream counter.

"What are you doing with Adam's hoodie?" I asked, clearing my throat to stamp down the waver in it.

"I told you. He left it in my bedroom yesterday after school." She reached forward and picked something from my shoulder and flicked it to the floor. "He left in a bit of a hurry. I wasn't even dressed."

My heart rushed at a hundred miles an hour as I tried to wade through the thoughts in my head. The way he'd been with me the night before and we'd had sex, it had been sweet and caring. He was genuinely sorry for what he'd said; he'd told me I was beautiful.

"You're a liar. He was with me."

If I'd thought I'd called Mackenna's bluff, I was wrong. She scoffed and ran a hand down her top. "Maybe later, but he was definitely with me before half past six. He left quickly saying he had to get to your house, so I'm guessing it was about seven when he got to you."

My memory whisked back to when he sent me his text – 19:05.

I drew in a breath and steadied my gaze on Mackenna. "You're a liar. He didn't sleep with you last night. He wasn't at your house at all."

"Oh, you're so sure aren't you." She licked her lips and leaned closer to me. "I'm not lying."

I held the hoodie to my face and inhaled deeply before looking up at Mackenna with a smile. "I know you're lying because this isn't his hoodie."

Mackenna's mouth dropped and her cheek twitched before she pulled her mouth back into a smirk. "Whatever you think. Ask Adam what happened between us yesterday and I'm telling you that's his."

She then turned around and stormed away, and as she did Lori reappeared with a huge bowl of chocolate ice cream.

"That's not Adam's hoodie," Lori said as she climbed back onto her chair.

"How do you know?" I asked, my attention on her.

"His has his name in red pen on the inside. I wrote it." She beamed at me and dug a spoon into her ice cream.

"I knew that it wasn't his too."

"How?"

"It doesn't smell like him." It didn't, it was a familiar smell, but it definitely wasn't Adam's. "Okay," I said, draping it over a spare chair and picking up a spare spoon. "Let's eat this and then try Adam again."

Before we had even had two spoonful's my phone rang out and Adam's name flashed up. I answered it and my heart sped up when his face filled the screen.

"Hey, babe." His smile was big and beautiful as he came closer to the screen and kissed it. "God, I'm missing you."

I giggled and Lori snorted. "Are you drunk?" I asked as he swayed a little.

He closed one eye and laughed. "Maybe a little. It's true though, I'm missing you."

"I'm missing you too," I sighed contentedly and rested my chin on my hand as I stared at my gorgeous boyfriend on the screen. "You're having a good time though?"

"Yep, I am." He breathed out slowly. "It's been good. The lads are making sure."

"Good, I'm glad."

We both stared at each other, our gazes never wavering.

"Adam," a little voice blasted out next to me. "Guess where we are?"

Before I had chance to do anything, my phone was pulled from my hand and Lori had it pushed right up to her face.

"Munchkin, how come you're with Sarah? Dance finished ages ago."

"Mummy went to the hairdresser and Daddy had to go to work, so Sarah brought me to TJ's. We had burgers, chips and..." Lori turned the phone to her bowl of ice cream for a few seconds and then back to her face. "Are you jealous? We're having chocolate ice cream."

I leaned in close to Lori so I could see the screen; I hadn't seen enough of him yet. Adam's mouth dropped in a mock gasp.

"No way. I'm so jealous. So, you're having a good time with Sarah?"

Lori nodded. "Yeah until that girl came over and tried to say she had your hoodie."

"Lori no, don't tell—"

She totally ignored me and when I tried to take the phone from her, she turned away from me.

"She was telling lies though, Adam. It wasn't yours, yours has your name in it. I know because I wrote it. She said you'd been in her bedroom, but Sarah knew you hadn't. Sarah knew it wasn't your hoodie—"

"Lori wait," Adam called. "What girl? Where's Sarah? Put Sarah on."

"Sarah said it didn't smell like you," Lori said proudly as she grinned at me. "She knew it wasn't yours and she didn't even know about your name in it."

"Pass me to Sarah, Munchkin." Adam's voice was soft and cajoling and suddenly sounded more sober.

Lori passed the phone to me and then without a care in the world, went back to her ice cream.

"Who was it and what the fuck did she say?" Adam asked scrubbing a hand across his mouth.

"Mackenna, but it doesn't matter, I didn't believe her." I chewed on my lip. "I might have for one second, but then I thought about last night and I just knew it wasn't true."

Adam closed his eyes and breathed heavily.

"Adam?"

Why didn't he look relieved that I believed him?

Why wasn't he smiling and telling me what a bitch Mackenna was?

He looked over his shoulder and sat up straighter.

"Take Lori back to mine. There's a key in the safe on the wall. The number is 1106. Wait for me there, I'm coming back now."

I felt a cold sweat break out over my back as my stomach knotted and bile rose in my throat.

"Please Adam don't tell me-."

"No, Sarah," he cried. "No, it's not that but I do need to talk to you. Please, wait at my house." His voice was pleading as both his hands moved to grip the phone. "Please babe."

I gave him a single nod and then ended the call. I waited for Lori to finish her ice cream, but I couldn't eat another spoonful, as I felt sick at the thought of what Adam was going to tell me.

9

ADAM

The lights were on in the lounge when Ellis' dad dropped me off at home, but no cars were on the driveway, which surprised me. It was almost half five. I'd wanted to be home much earlier, but by the time I'd persuaded the lads I'd had enough to drink, we'd missed our bus, only to find out the next one had been cancelled because it had broken down. Tyler had insisted we wait in a bar but Ellis as usual had my back and must have noticed I was desperate to get home, so he called his dad.

When I walked into the lounge, Sarah was curled up on the sofa, with Lori and they were watching a film. Sarah was at least but Lori was fast asleep with her head on Sarah's lap.

"Hey," I whispered.

Sarah looked up at me and I couldn't find any light in her eyes, only dread. She let out a long breath and then glanced down at Lori.

"She fell asleep only ten minutes in."

I looked at the screen to see it was Frozen flashing in front of us. "She knows it off by heart anyway."

I moved towards her and sat down slowly, so I didn't disturb my sister. "I'm so sorry that Mackenna gave you shit."

"What's going on Adam," Sarah whispered. "Why did you look so shady when I told you about what happened. I know that wasn't your hoodie, I believed you weren't with her, so why did you look so guilty?"

Sarah's breathing had sped up and she was talking as though she'd just done ten laps of the school field. I grabbed her hand and held it between both of mine.

"It's not bad, well it is, but I don't want you to get mad about it. Come into the kitchen so we don't wake Lori."

She nodded once and gently prised herself from under the Lori's dead weight and placed her down on the sofa. Apart from a little grunt, Lori didn't make any movement or noise.

"She okay?" I asked. "She never sleeps in the afternoon."

"She was a water buffalo at dance," Sarah explained. "That and the excitement of burger and milkshake at TJ's tired her out."

I nodded and took Sarah's hand, leading her out to the kitchen and then pushed the door almost closed, so we didn't disturb Lori.

"Tell me then."

Sarah moved away from me and stood with her back against the breakfast bar. I wanted to move closer, but I knew if I did, she'd probably move again anyway. With her arms firmly crossed over her chest and her neck stretched, I knew she was thinking the worst. She wasn't in the mood for me to try and charm her.

"Mackenna kissed me yesterday while we were at TJ's." I rushed out the words, wincing as they registered with Sarah. "She came into the men's toilets and kissed me. I kissed her back for like half a second and then pushed her away and told her to fuck off. That's when I left and came to your house."

My breath was patchy having rushed out the words, but when I looked at the anger on Sarah's face, I knew I should have probably taken my time and explained things properly. Her nostrils were flared, and she was exhaling hard, thankfully though her hand wasn't rubbing at her wrist which meant she was feeling strong.

"You kissed her back?"

"Yeah, but hardly."

"How long is hardly, Adam? Half a second, one second, two minutes, half-a-fucking-hour? Exactly how long?"

I cringed as I remembered the shortness of the kiss but the fact that it had been coupled with Mackenna's hand on my dick.

"Okay, a second, maybe two," I replied with a wince.

"What or maybe three or four, or maybe one thousand eight hundred."

I blew out a breath. "Shit, that was quick mental arithmetic, babe."

Sarah's nostrils flared. "This is not fucking funny. Not one little bit. Now tell me the truth and don't even think about lying to me."

Fuck.

"Yeah, it was definitely only a second, I swear." Her shoulders relaxed but I knew I had to tell her everything.

"But there is something else."

Sarah's eyes gleamed with anger and then narrowed on me. "What?"

"She felt my dick. She put her hand on it when she kissed me, but I pushed her off after a second, I fucking swear to you."

She fell silent, chewing on her bottom lip as she watched me. I didn't dare move or breathe in case it made her think I was lying.

"Mackenna White not only kissed you, but felt your dick too?" she asked, her tone surprisingly calm and low.

"Yes." I let my head drop back as I groaned. "But I swear to you, both were for about a second, then I pushed her away."

I knew Sarah had demanded I didn't lie, but there was no way I was telling her that Mackenna had actually made me a little bit hard. That was something she *wouldn't* accept, plus it would be a shitty thing to tell her. She didn't need to know.

"Why didn't you push her away before she got that far?" Her tone had changed, now it was hard, and I couldn't say I was surprised. If she'd told me some lad had kissed her, even if it was only for a half a second, I'd have to fucking plant him one in the face *and* kick him in the bollocks.

"It just happened so quickly. One minute I was telling her to get lost and the next she was kissing me. I swear, Sarah, I didn't want it, or her. I didn't respond and I pushed her away, walked out and then came to you."

"So, you kissed her and then came and had sex with me. Wow, lovely, Adam, really lovely."

"It wasn't like that," I protested. "You were angry with me and after she—"

"Oh, so you kissed her because I was angry with you. You kissed her and then thought oh maybe I'd better make it up with Sarah, oh I know I'll go around to her house and shag her into forgiveness."

My heart thud, thud, thudded in my chest wall as Sarah stared at me with a murderous glare. She took a step away from the breakfast bar and I thought she was going to leave but I couldn't let her do that, she had to believe me. I moved to stand in front of her.

"I swear, Sarah, it was just the tiniest moment and then I pushed her away. Now today, bringing you that hoodie, which isn't fucking mine by the way and I can prove it, she's just messing with us. She's trying to cause trouble because she knows me and her are finished and I'm with you now."

"Are you though, Adam," she hissed, "or are you still messing around with her and pretending that we have something special, because call me stupid, but I thought we did. You're known for being horrible to girls who piss you off, so why is Mackenna so damn brave all of a sudden?"

I had wondered that myself but had no idea or clue to the answer. "I don't know." I shrugged. "Maybe she's realised I'm changing, and that you have me by the bollocks."

"Don't try and be funny, Adam. I told you, there's nothing amusing about this." Sarah's voice broke and her chin trembled as she stared at me. She looked so sad and hurt and all I wanted to do was wrap her up in my arms and tell her how much she meant to me.

I strode forward and pulled her against me. "I'm so sorry. I swear it was all her." I kissed Sarah's forehead, leaving my lips on her skin and breathing in her soft, flowery smell, determined to always remember it. "Honestly, I only want you."

As she looked up at me, her gaze full of doubt, I considered telling her how I really felt. That I wasn't sure I'd ever want to be without her ever again. That I couldn't imagine my life without her in it. That she was burrowing herself deep into my soul more and more each day, so that I couldn't even remember what I did before she came to Maddison Edge.

"I'd rather you tell me if it was more than you're saying," Sarah whispered. "I'd much rather the hurt now than further down the line when..." her voice tailed off and she looked down at the floor, the crown of her head resting against my chest.

"Sarah, look at me." She took a few seconds, but eventually looked up so I could look her directly in the eye. "I swear to you,

Mackenna White means nothing to me. She kissed me and I pushed her away. I came to you because her lips on mine again made me realise they didn't feel right. The only kiss that feels right is yours. I knew I had to apologise and make you see how sorry I was. I had to make you give me another chance, and I couldn't wait another minute. Last night at yours, in your bed, with you, was the best night of my life and I'll never forget any of it."

She inhaled slowly and then gradually let it out as though with her breathe she pushed out the pain and anger she felt. Then when it had gone, she reached up to cup my cheek.

"Please don't hurt me, Adam. I'm not sure I could stand it."

I didn't answer, I couldn't answer because I'd promised myself that I'd never lie to her. I would try my best not to, but the blood that flowed through my veins was black and twisted, it was weak and undependable, it was my mum and dad's blood and it wasn't to be trusted.

My mum finally arrived home at about six, when I'd already fed Lori and sent her up for a bath. Apparently, the hairdressers were rammed, but I didn't fail to notice that she had a few shopping bags with her. She'd tried to insist that Sarah stay for dinner, but even I didn't want to sit down with her and Roger, never mind have my girlfriend suffer it too.

We'd finally escaped, just as Lori came running downstairs shouting excitedly that Roger was home and she wanted to tell him all about having burgers with Sarah and being a water buffalo.

"I really don't know why you don't like Roger," Sarah said as she drove my car through the streets of Maddison Edge towards the new Chinese restaurant that had recently opened up. "He's lovely."

I gave her a sideways glance and chuckled. "I notice you didn't include my mum in that statement."

"Well, she's, she's…" Sarah let out a nervous giggle. "I mean it's not that don't like her, but Roger is just… well he's lovely and your mum-."

I grabbed her hand and pulled on it. "It's fine, I don't think much of her either."

"But you didn't say you hate Roger either, so that's a change."

I rolled my eyes. "Yeah well, he's been okay recently."

"Whatever." Sarah's tone was full of humour and I was glad that we appeared to have got over the Mackenna issue. "So, what's this place like? Do you know anyone who's been?"

"Yeah, Tyler's mum and dad went last week on the opening night. They said it was really nice."

Sarah indicated to turn at the upcoming junction, but I noticed a familiar figure leaving the shop on the other side of the road.

"Fucking bitch," I yelled and grabbed hold of the steering wheel. "Do a U-turn quick."

"Adam," Sarah cried checking the mirrors for traffic. "What the hell are you doing?"

"Mackenna is coming out of that shop."

Sarah screeched to a halt at the side of the pavement and within seconds I was out of the car and standing in front of Mackenna.

"What the fuck did you think your little stunt earlier would achieve, Mackenna?" I yelled at her.

Mackenna smirked and cocked her hip. "Oh, stop being such a baby. You know and I know you won't be with her for long and that you'll come running to me."

Anger boiled up inside my head. It's like I could see her clearly, clearer than I had in TJ's the afternoon before. She was hard faced and looked like she had a constant smell under her nose. She never said anything nice about anyone and was a bitch to every girl that hung around with her – fuck, she was the female version of me. Or rather how I had been before Sarah.

Mackenna lifted her hands and I knew immediately she was going to touch me, this time though, I would stop her before she managed it.

"No," I snapped harshly as I grabbed her wrists and pushed her arms behind her back. "I don't want your hands on me. Get the message, Mackenna and stay the fuck away, or I swear I'll fucking ruin you in school."

"What the hell do you think you're doing?" We both startled at the sound of Sarah's voice, which was loud and, even though there was a slight waver to it, explosive. "Get away from him."

Mackenna gasped and swung her head in Sarah's direction. She didn't speak but just gawped as my girlfriend strode towards us and positioned herself between me and Mackenna.

"Back off, Mackenna and don't even think about coming near Adam again. Your stupid little trick didn't work. I knew it wasn't his hoodie, so I'm not really sure what you thought you might achieve. And before you try and tell me about the kiss in the men's toilets, which is real classy by the way, I know all about it. I know how you not only put your lips on him but also your hands, so don't even try and cause any more trouble."

Sarah's chest heaved with the exertion of her tirade and I actually found myself getting a little turned on by it. This girl who had been through some awful shit in the last year, had stood up for herself against a girl whom I'm sure in her old school, would have been one of the bitches who taunted her.

She tipped her head on one side waiting for Mackenna to reply, but she seemed to have no clue what to say. Sarah had called her bluff about the kiss and I'd proved it wasn't my hoodie because I had got mine from the wardrobe earlier and shown Sarah. It worried me though the length's Mackenna had gone to, getting a similar hoodie to mine just to cause trouble. Whatever her game was, she'd been pretty serious about it.

"Nothing to say?" Sarah asked.

Mackenna curled her lip and flicked her dark hair over her shoulder. "Believe me, new girl, he really isn't worth the effort."

"Well in that case you won't want to come near him again, will you? So, I suggest you..." Sarah leaned close to Mackenna, her mouth right up against her ear. "Fuck off."

Mackenna opened her mouth, but evidently thought better of it because she stormed past Sarah, bumping her with her shoulder. We watched as she sauntered past, her carrier bag bashing into her legs.

"Wow," I breathed out. "That was fucking hot."

"What was?" Sarah cried. "Mackenna's backside swinging in time with her plastic bag?"

I laughed and turned back towards her. "No, you giving her fucking shit. It was awesome."

I looked Sarah up and down and felt my dick go from semi-hard to rock-hard. She had her hands on her hips and her chest was pushed out and heaving. Not to mention that she'd left her coat in the car and her nipples were hard against the soft fabric of her top because of the cold.

"How hungry are you?" I asked, taking a step closer to her.

"Very, why?"

"I really need to be inside you within, like, the next ten minutes."

My balls began to ache as I thought about getting Sarah naked and having her ride me in the front seat of my car. Me with my jeans around my ankles while Sarah's small but perfectly formed tits jiggled up and down.

Sarah cleared her throat and put a hand to her neck as her chest heaved. "Where can we go?"

"Get in the car quick, I know somewhere we can park up."

Up until now I hadn't wanted to have sex with Sarah in my car, I thought she was worth more than that, but tonight *had* to be an exception, otherwise I think we'd both explode.

"Oh shit," I groaned as Sarah made my dream a reality and she drew a figure of eight with her hips. "That's amazing."

She then went back in the other direction, and I thought I was going to blow quicker than I'd ever done before. When she then started to roll her hips in an undulating wave, my palms hit the roof of the car.

"Oh, my fucking God."

Sarah leaned forward and nibbled on my earlobe. "Is that nice?" she whispered.

I wasn't sure I could make a coherent sentence so just nodded and dropped my hands to her slim waist.

She was completely naked while my jeans were around my ankles and my shirt was undone; she'd wanted to lick my tattoo for some reason, which was a bit off the wall, but who was I to complain. Her hair that had been up in a messy bun, was now streaming down her back, almost touching the curve of her fucking amazing arse. I was desperate to tug on it, but I had sensation overload and kept changing my mind on what I wanted to do to her. When she groaned and let her head drop back, my mind was made up and. I instantly took one of her nipples into my mouth and sucked hard.

She'd always been responsive to my touch, right from the first time we'd had sex, but tonight something had turned her confidence up a few notches. I was sure it had been the run in with Mackenna. It must have been a while since she'd held her own with anyone, and I imagined that standing up to Mackenna had made her feel amazing. Shit, she *was* amazing.

The more I sucked, the faster Sarah bounced and thrust, this in turn sent me crazy with need for her. I couldn't get enough of her creamy skin, of her smell, of her fucking beauty. The pleasure I was feeling couldn't stop the doubts though, and with each groan that echoed around the inside of my car another reason of why I didn't deserve her would tumble around my brain.

"Adam," Sarah cried and slapped her hand against the steamed-up window next to us. "Oh God, I'm gonna, oh shit, I'm gonna..."

She didn't speak again but screamed out her orgasm as mine continued to build.

"Keep going," I said, breathing heavily. "I'm so fucking close."

Sarah's eyes peeped open and she gave me the laziest, sexiest smile I had ever seen. She momentarily stopped moving, but when I grabbed her tit and gave it a squeeze, she gripped my shoulders and picked up the pace again.

My balls began to scream for release as the pull in the pit of my stomach built and sparks flew around my body. Sarah bounced and when I saw a familiar red blush creep over her body, I knew she was close to orgasming again. I reached between us and circled her clit with my fingers, while at the same time as sucking hard on the soft skin on the rise of her chest.

"Oh shit, again," she called out breathlessly and bucked above me without any rhythm.

It was enough to finally send me crashing over the edge of oblivion and I screamed out for God and for Sarah. My hips started to piston upward and I grabbed Sarah's hips to still her, afraid that if she didn't, I would blow so hard I might burst a blood vessel.

"Fuuuck."

I came and I came, and I came, it felt as though it was never ending and with each sharp punch of my hips, Sarah took it. She rode with it and then came for a third time.

The car was filled with the heady scent of sex, the windows all steamed up and the air was punctuated with our sighs and heavy breathing as we tried to come down from the primal and fucking hot as hell experience we'd just had.

"Gets better every fucking time," I whispered as I leaned forward and took Sarah's mouth in mine for a sweet kiss. "Amazing."

"I came three times." She dropped her head to my shoulder and let out a contented sigh. "I'm exhausted."

I smiled against the skin of her shoulder and pulled her closer to my chest. "I can't believe how we fit so fucking perfectly."

"Hmm." She snuggled closer and I knew she was about to fall asleep.

"Hey, don't fall asleep. We need to go and eat, unless you want to go home?"

"Nope." She shot up and frowned. "I'm ready for crispy beef and fried rice."

I laughed and slapped her bum lightly. "Okay, get dressed babe and I'll feed you."

"Ah, perfect end to a perfect night."

I couldn't help the huge fucking grin on my face.

Sarah was going to keep my car overnight, and by the time she dropped me off, it was gone midnight. I was surprised to see a light on in Mum and Roger's room. I could hear them talking as I went up the stairs and it sounded like they were arguing. Their room was the other end of the landing to mine, so when I got a few stairs up, I stopped to listen.

"You're being selfish, Elouise. You need to tell Adam at least, then it's his choice what he does."

My ears picked up at the mention of my name, so I held my breath as my mum's softer tone started.

"I told you no. I'm not. It's not necessary."

"Well I think you're wrong. Just like you should have reported that monster that beat him."

My heart beat wildly at the mention of Eric.

Mum hissed something back, but I couldn't hear properly. I wiped my sweaty palms on my jeans and tried to even out my breathing as I continued to listen and tried to ignore the images of Eric in my head. No one said anything else, I heard the bed creak and then the click of a lamp and there was silence. I continued on up the stairs, coughing so they wouldn't think I'd been listening in on them. It worked because as I got to my bedroom door, I heard Roger softly calling my name.

"You okay?" he asked. "Had a good day?"

He scratched at his chest and more thoughts of Eric invaded my head. He'd always been bare chested and wearing grubby tracksuit bottoms that he'd worn for bed when he'd sat at the breakfast table, whereas Roger always wore a t-shirt with his pyjama bottoms and always came down to breakfast fully clothed.

"Yeah it was good thanks," I whispered, aware that waking Lori would be a fate worse than death for us all if she was tired the next day. "I came back early though, to see Sarah. She had Lori with her all afternoon."

Roger scrubbed a hand over his stubble. "Yeah so I believe. I'll thank her when I see her. I was called into work, one of our customer's servers had a power outage and it took nearly all day to get it back up. I didn't realise your mum had a hairdresser appointment."

I studied him and realised how tired he looked. He worked some long fucking hours and still found time to take Lori to all the clubs she insisted on going to. He was also the one who came to all my matches, so how he found time to relax I had no idea.

"Anyway, I'll let you get to bed, I just wanted to check you were okay and didn't need a bucket after a day of drinking." He grinned but when I didn't respond, it dropped from his face. "Did you lock up?"

I nodded, not using my usual snarky response of 'no I left everything open'. "Yeah."

"Great, thanks for that."

"No problem. G'night."

"Night, see you in the morning."

As he padded back to his and Mum's room, it struck me that Roger had been the one to check I'd had a good day, the one who as usual checked to see if I needed anything. The one to parent me.

"Hey, Roger," I called softly.

He turned quickly, his hand at his mouth covering a yawn.

"Thanks again for the money for my birthday. I know it was all from you, so I really appreciate it."

He looked taken aback and his eyes went wide. "N-no problem. My pleasure."

I didn't say anything else but turned and went to my room. When I turned on the lamp, I saw some forms on my desk with a note attached to them. I picked them up and couldn't believe what I was seeing, they were Student loan forms, all filled in and signed at the bottom by Roger.

I looked down at the note and blew out a breath.

Adam,

I know these are too late for this year, but I hadn't realised your mum had them and just not filled them in. I thought she had, and you'd been refused, so sorry about that. I found them yesterday under some magazines. Maybe you should contact clearance and see if they can find a spot somewhere, or at least keep these safe for next year.

Roger

When the tight prickle of emotion, hit the back of my throat, I was surprised. I didn't think I cared about anything or anyone other than Lori and now Sarah, but Roger had caught me unawares and I instantly felt bad about all the shit I'd given him. He was a decent bloke, like Mum had always said, I had just never trusted her word before. Especially as she'd told me Eric was good man too.

I folded the papers up and put them in my drawer, and it was then that I noticed Sarah's notebook. The one I'd taken when she'd left it in TJ's before we got together. I'd forgotten I had it. I ran a finger over the pink and yellow flowered cover and contemplated taking it out and reading it, but somehow it didn't seem right. I should probably give it back to her. I was fucked, because I shouldn't have taken it in the first place. I just wished I'd had that realisation on the day I'd picked it up from the table. Just another of my regrets where she was concerned.

Pushing the drawer closed I glanced over my shoulder at my bedroom door, thinking about Roger a few feet away and wondered if he regretted anything; like marrying my mum. Then I remembered what he'd said to me once, when we first moved in. I'd been playing up and refused to eat dinner with him and he said;

"Push all you like, Adam, but I'm here to stay. I love your mum and believe it or not I love you and Lori too. Whatever happens in this family that's what we'll always be, a family; I'll always be here for you to rely on, so stop acting like an idiot and drop that barrier, because I'm not going to hurt you."

He was right, he was always there for us and I could always rely on him.

He proved it again a few hours later. At around three am, when I had a nightmare about Eric beating me. Roger was the one who rushed in and calmed me down and then sat at my desk until I fell back to sleep.

10

SARAH

My stomach cramped as I walked up to the entrance of the Tesco Express, the scene of one of the worst nights of my life. The cramps weren't just because of nerves at revisiting the place, but also because I had my period. To be honest, although I knew Adam and I were covered with contraception when we didn't use condoms, I'd still been worried. The way my life had gone so far it would be my luck to fall pregnant with my new boyfriend. My new boyfriend who had a dad that petrified me.

We still hadn't really talked about him, his dad, but I knew we'd have to at some point. If only about the fact that while I was trying hard not to live my life in fear, I was terrified. Every day I walked around with my eyes on alert. I was forever watching and waiting but needing to move forward.

That was why I'd gone to the shop alone. I had to move on and going to this particular shop, alone, would hopefully help to dispel more than one nightmare. Pushing my shoulders back, I stepped towards the automatic door of the store. In the brief moments while I waited for it to start to slide open, I took a deep breath and steeled myself. Once I was inside, I didn't feel as anxious as I'd expected to. I didn't feel the need to sing in my head, or even to reach under my jumper for my wrist, what I did do was picture Adam smiling at me. The moment I envisaged his blue eyes shining, the comfort was instant. I felt calmer and braver as I walked around the store, breathing slowly and carefully, not rushing to get what I needed and then get out.

I picked up a couple of chocolate bars, one that I knew Mum liked and one for me as I always needed chocolate when I had my period, I also got a jar of Nutella; I definitely felt the chocolate munchies coming on. As I wandered down the magazine aisle, I felt a creeping sensation and the hairs on the back of my neck stood to attention. Quickly swivelling around, I clutched my basket in front of me like an incompetent shield, but there was no one there, just a little old lady reading the back of one of the paperbacks from the display shelf.

Shuddering, I remembered about the security mirror, so looked up at it. I couldn't see anyone in the next couple of aisles and there was only a young boy at the checkout.

"Stupid idiot," I muttered to myself and blew out my cheeks.

After picking up a football magazine that I knew Adam liked, I made my way to the checkout. I was pleased to see Rita there, the lady who'd been working the night of the robbery. She looked a little thinner than I remembered, and when she smiled at me it barely touched the edges of her mouth.

"Hi, Sarah."

She sounded pleased to see me though, and when I placed my basket in front of her, she reached for my hand and gave it a quick rub.

"How've you been?" she asked, concern filling her gaze.

"Okay, you know. How about you?"

She shrugged and took one of the items from my basket to scan it. "I can't work in the evenings anymore. I'm too nervous. Which is a pain because I've now got to find childcare, whereas my husband is home at night."

"Really, that's awful. Have you seen a counsellor about it?" I contemplated whether I had Eleanor's card in my purse. I knew if anyone could help Rita she could, or at least recommend someone.

"I haven't, but my husband wants me to. Plus, this place and Murray have been very worried. I'm going to be getting a call soon to arrange something; our HR department have sorted it."

I felt a sense of relief for her, knowing she was going to get help. It wasn't any fun feeling anxious all the time, particularly when it wasn't anything you could change. All Rita could do, all I could do, was learn how to cope with the past to be able to move on with the future.

"It'll be the best thing you do," I said as Rita scanned Adam's magazine. "It really helps me."

I was a little taken aback that I'd told her I was in therapy, as I didn't tell many people, but I was sure knowing that there were others in the same boat might help her. Rita nodded and gave me an attempt at a smile.

"I hope so, I really do. Now, is there anything else I can get you?"

I shook my head and reached to my back pocket for my card, but Rita's hand shot out and landed on my shoulder.

"No, it's free still. I just need to get Murray from out of the back, so he can sign for it."

"Are you sure?"

"God, yes. He got the go ahead from head office. He has to sign for it, so give me one minute." She leaned around me to speak to the old lady who'd been looking at the books. "Would you like to go to the next till along, my love."

The old lady smiled and moved past me, and as I watched her, I could have sworn I saw a flash of a navy-blue coat out of the corner of my eye, but it quickly disappeared. My skin prickled with a cold shiver and I had a strong sensation of being watched.

Swallowing hard and wrapping my arms around me, I waited for Rita to come back. The seconds seemed to last for far too long, all I wanted to do was get out of there. Finally, Rita reappeared with Murray following her.

"Sarah, how are you?" he asked, his smile much brighter than the one Rita had offered to me. "How's Adam?"

"He's good thanks, we both are. We've both been speaking to counsellors, which has helped."

Both of us looked at Rita who was listening intently to me.

"I know," she replied with a quiet laugh. "It's going to happen."

I picked up my bag of things and smiled at them both. "That's really kind of you again, for this. We really appreciate it."

"No problem," Murray replied waving me away. "Say hello to Adam for me, I haven't seen him since that night."

"I will do."

"His dad said he was worried about him getting flashbacks, so he's been trying to get anything for him that Adam might need."

"He did?" I smiled as I thought again of what a nice man Roger was.

"Yes," Murray nodded sagely. "I think it's for the best, after all he was the one who could have ended up shot if things hadn't gone right."

My stomach dropped at the thought. Images of the dead eyes of the man who'd been intent on shooting me, formed in my head.

"I'm sorry, Sarah," Murray said slapping a hand to his head. "I shouldn't have said that, I could cut my tongue out."

"Honestly, it's fine. He didn't get hurt, so everything is okay." I gave him a wavering smile and cleared my throat. "Anyway, I'd better go. Great to see you both."

Rita and Murray said goodbye and I left the store, ready to make the mile and a half walk back home. Mum hadn't wanted me to walk, not with Mr Mills being around. She'd said she'd call at the shops on the way back from work, but it was half-term and I'd been cooped up in the house all day and walking helped with the cramps, so had decided not to wait. Now though, after Murray reminding me about Adam almost getting shot, and the feeling I was being watched, I wish I'd waited.

Trying to put all my worries to one side, I pulled my scarf a little tighter around my neck and began the walk back. I was getting a little more used to the routes, having decided to take more notice when Adam picked me up in his car, that and spending half an hour on Google maps before I'd set off. To walk to and from the shop, I'd picked a route that kept me in the open residential areas where possible.

After about five minutes of brisk walking, I was sure I heard more than the echo of my own steps behind me. I didn't dare look in case I *was* being followed and drew attention to myself. I pulled my phone out of my bag as casually as I could and dialled Adam's number.

"Hello, gorgeous," he answered after only a couple of rings.

"Hi."

Normally the sound of his voice would bring a big smile to my face, but I was trying to concentrate on stepping up the pace and when I did, I most definitely heard the steps behind me pick up too,

"Are you back from snooker yet?"

Adam had gone to play snooker with Ellis earlier, and I had no idea how long a game lasted. I just hoped he was back.

"Nope, still playing. Why?" His voice dropped and I knew he could sense something was wrong. I didn't want to come across all needy and spoil his time with his friend, but something felt wrong.

"I'm probably being stupid and paranoid, but I think someone is following me."

"Why? Where are you?" I heard a noise in the background and then muffled voices.

"I don't know," I whispered. "And I daren't look behind me."

"No don't!" he cried. "Just keep walking. Do you think they're still behind you?"

I picked up my step and held my breath but didn't hear the footsteps.

"I don't know." I blew out a breath of frustration with myself for being so stupid. "Adam, forget it really. I'm being stupid. It's broad daylight, nothing is going to happen to me."

"Something scared you so you're not being stupid."

"Honestly I'm fi-"

"Babe," Adam replied, sounding as though he was running. "Just tell me where you are."

"Adam no, I don't want to spoil your time with Ellis. Just stay on the phone with me." My heart hammered knowing I was being an idiot but also hoping that he insisted on coming to pick me up.

"I will, but I'm still coming to get you. Now, *where are you?*"

I looked around me to see if I could see anything distinguishing as I had no idea the name of the road I was walking down. I hadn't learned the street names, just the basic route.

"I don't know," I whispered back shakily. "I went to the Tesco Express and turned right out of there and then the first right."

"You went there?" Adam asked incredulously. "Shit, Sarah. Why the hell didn't you go to that little shop on the edge of your estate?"

"Because I wanted to get going back there over and done with. Plus, that shop near us doesn't sell the real stuff - of anything."

"Were you okay?"

"Yes, at first it was weird, but then once inside I felt fine. Although, I thought someone was following me in there too."

"Please tell me you're joking."

I really wished I could tell him that, but I'd been sure then as well.

"Fuck," he said before I responded. "I'm just going to lose you for a second while I start my car up, then the Bluetooth will kick in, okay."

"Okay."

As the line went quiet, I definitely heard steps behind me. I wanted to check because it wouldn't be fair on Adam if I pulled him away from his friend for someone innocently walking along.

"I'm back." Adam's voice felt like his arms were wrapping around me and I almost sagged to the floor. "Just keep walking and look straight ahead."

"Should I not check?" I asked quietly. "What if I've got it wrong and you've picked me up for no reason?"

"Doesn't matter. Now, I think I know where you are, but can you see anything at all that might give me a clue, or is it just houses."

"Just houses." I didn't want to be too obvious about looking around. "I'm still not sure you should come."

"I'm coming. Just keep walking and look straight ahead, but I think I'll be with you in about four or five minutes... move you dick... sorry." Adam breathed out. "Some fucking idiot decided to park in the middle of the road."

My hand holding my phone began to shake slightly and my palms were so sweaty, I worried I might drop it. I decided if I did, I'd just leave it and run.

"Does your mum know you went to the shop?" Adam's words were sharp and clipped, as though he was trying to keep a lid on his anxiety.

"No. She wanted me to stay at home. She said she'd get what I need on the way back from work, but I was bored."

Adam let out a sigh. "Well you should have let her. Why didn't you call me if you were bored?"

"Because you were going out with Ellis and I didn't want to spoil that for you."

He didn't answer, but it didn't matter; he was on the other end of the line and he was coming to me.

Without realising it, I started to sing, but it was out loud and not in my head as I usually did.

You are my sunshine, my only sunshine
You make me happy when skies are grey
You'll never know dear; how much I love you
Please don't take my sunshine away...

· · ·

"You've got a sweet little singing voice," Adam said with chuckle.

"Oh God, it's awful, isn't it?"

"No, it's not. You're pretty good. Have I heard you sing that song before?" he asked.

My mouth went dry at the thought of telling Adam I sang it in my head when I was scared. What if he thought I was mad?

"Sarah, are you still there?" He sounded worried.

"Sorry, yes... I um, well I sing it when I'm... well when I'm scared. My dad taught it to me when I was little."

I heard Adam's soft laugh and I instantly bristled.

"What's funny? it helps me and if you don't understand that—"

"Hey, of course I understand. It's just, well you always remind me of sunshine."

"I do," I gasped. "Sunshine?"

"Yeah."

Whatever I had felt about Adam tripled in size and filled my chest with something that made my head spin. It wasn't a declaration of love, or undying loyalty it was a simple compliment which had filled me with more hope than I'd experienced in over a year. He'd shown me that I did hold some light in my life. I wasn't all misery and darkness, there was sunshine in there too.

"Adam-"

"I can see you."

I looked up to see him flash his headlights, even though it was daylight and I could quite clearly see his car coming towards me. He sped up and screeched to a halt at the pavement right next to me and my hand holding my phone dropped to my side as I extinguished a huge sigh of relief. Just seeing him made me feel safe and protected. Emotion pushed at my breastbone causing tears to pool at my lashes.

As Adam rushed around the car to me, I dropped the plastic bag to the floor and flung myself at him.

"Oh, God I was so scared."

"Hey, it's fine. I'm here." He pulled me in tight, wrapping one arm around my back, while his other cradled my head against his chest. "Don't cry, I'm here. I'm not going to let you go or let anyone hurt you."

I wept against his thick trucker jacket, wetting the soft corded fabric with a wet mixture of relief and fear. Adam kissed my hair and then brought both hands to cup my face and tilt it back so I could see him.

"Babe there was no one following you, not that I could see anyway."

My eyes widened as I took a half-step back. "I swear, I heard their footsteps, Adam. Honestly."

He looked up and down the road, but there was no one about, except for a woman coming towards us walking a German Shepherd dog.

"Well whoever it was must have disappeared as soon as they heard you talking to me."

He could have been right, but I was sure I'd heard shoes on the pavement only a few moments before Adam turned up; but he would have seen them as he approached me.

I nodded and sniffed. "They must have."

Adam stooped down and picked up my carrier bag before putting his arm around my shoulder and guiding me to the car.

"Come on let's get you home. I'll stay with you until your mum gets home."

"You don't have to. You can go back to the snooker hall to Ellis."

He shook his head and laughed. "No, I don't think so. I need to make sure you're okay, so I'm staying with you."

"Are you sure?"

"Yeah I'm sure. What the hell have you got in this bloody bag by the way. It's heavy." Before I could stop him, Adam opened up the carrier bag and peeked inside. "Oh, shit sorry."

He screwed it together and then quickly passed it to me.

"Adam, they're bloody tampons." I laughed through a lingering sniffle. "You've seen pretty much all of my body and you're embarrassed about tampons.'

His face was bright red and he was rubbing the back of his neck roughly. "Sorry, I shouldn't have looked."

I rolled my eyes and opened up the bag again.

"No, I don't want to look at them," he cried, holding out his hand.

"I'm not getting them out. I wanted to give you this." I handed him the football magazine and the relief on his face made me giggle.

"You didn't have to do that. Wow, thank you." His arm went around my neck and pulled me close so he could land a kiss on my forehead, then the tip of my nose, and finally my mouth. As his tongue prised my lips open, I moaned at the pleasure.

"Excuse me."

We pulled apart as the woman with the dog edged passed us, grunting about us taking up space unnecessarily.

"We'd better go." Adam grinned and steered me towards the car. "And I get to choose the film we watch this afternoon."

"It's my house," I protested, my smile firmly in place.

"Yeah well I'm the eldest, so I get first choice."

I tutted and flopped down into my seat. "Okay what is it then, some action film, or something that's going to send me to sleep within five minutes?"

Adam shook his head. "No, I think you'll be pleasantly surprised."

"Oh my God, Adam. You only picked that to get me back for the tampons, didn't you?"

Adam burst out laughing as the credits for the *Fifty Shades of Grey* film went up. "Want to watch the second one."

"No," I cried and hit him with one of my mum's cushions.

"Well come here then."

He grabbed hold of my ankles and pulled me towards him from my end of the sofa, and then took my hand and dragged me on top of him, tucking me under his chin.

"Fuck, I was so scared earlier," he whispered against my hair. "I was so worried I wouldn't find you, and... fuck I don't even want to think about it."

Reaching up to kiss him, that clawing panic which had crept up my throat in the street returned. I was so sure someone had been there.

"Maybe going into that shop unnerved me more than I thought," I said, pulling away.

"Yeah, it could've been that. Just don't go out on your own if you don't need to. Or at least go to the bloody shop ten minutes away from your house."

He sounded anxious and I wondered if that meant he thought his dad was a danger to me. I didn't dare ask as last time we'd spoken about it, he'd hurt me with his words. I knew it was difficult for him, but selfish as it may be, I needed him to be supportive and tell me he believed me.

"You should probably tell Eleanor what happened today," Adam said, running his fingers along my back. "She'll tell you how to deal with it."

"Yeah I will."

And I would. I realised now it had probably been the trauma of actually going into the shop that unnerved me and had me imagining things.

Deciding to think about it later, I snuggled down on Adams chest and pushed my hands up his soft jumper and under his t-shirt. My fingers loved the warmth and softness of his skin and I could happily have stayed like that for the rest of the half-term, although I was sure my mum would have something to say about it.

"Fancy going somewhere tomorrow?" Adam asked, shifting us both so that he was on his side and I was tucked in front of him. "Go shopping or the cinema and bowling? Anything you want."

"Do you think maybe we should do our history project?" I traced my finger down between his brows and along his nose and when I got to his lips, he pouted them into a kiss for my fingertip.

"We can do that on Wednesday. It won't take us long."

"Says, Mr History Swotty Pants."

"Haha." He caught hold of my finger and nipped the end of it playfully. "You should count yourself lucky you're my partner, because we're going to smash it."

"Why do we always do projects in pairs?" I asked, genuinely interested. "We never did at my old school."

Just thinking of that place made my blood chill. I pushed the images and memories to the back of my mind and flashed a smile at Adam.

"Mr Raymond thinks we become more engaged and invested in the subject if we have someone to bounce off. He's always done it, even when we first started year 7."

"Ah, okay."

"Problem is." He kissed me softly. "He has no clue how much you distract me. How much I think about kissing you and touching you instead of writing a letter home from the Bastille before I get beheaded."

Our lips met and Adam's tongue pushed into my mouth, gliding across mine in a silent invitation to join in. I didn't hesitate and followed his every move. I caught his lip in my teeth and nipped on it before soothing it with a soft kiss, and then repeating it, over and over until Adam groaned and thrust his hips forward.

He dropped his hand to my bum and squeezed as he thrust forward and let me feel his hard length beneath his sweatpants. My breath hitched and when his hand went from my bum to snake up my t-shirt, I felt myself get wet.

"You know I can't do anything, don't you?" I whispered against his mouth as his hands travelled across the places they knew so well

"Yeah, I know, but I quite like this. Kissing and dry humping like we're fourteen." He laughed quietly and pinched my nipple over my bra. "What were you like at fourteen anyway?"

I giggled. "A bit of a princess, but with a wild side. I acted all girly and cute at home, a typical daddy's girl, but when I went out to my street dance lessons, I became real 'gangsta'. I think I told them I lived in Hackney and my mum and dad worked as office cleaners."

Adam frowned and then started to laugh. "What the hell did you do that for?"

"Because I didn't think they'd take me seriously as a street dancer if I admitted I lived in the home counties with my mum who was an accountant and my dad who was a copper in the metropolitan police."

"Did you ever tell them?"

"Yep, I had to," I groaned feeling the embarrassment all over again. "My dad came to pick me up one day and he still had his uniform on. I tried to tell them it was over a DUI, but I was fourteen, couldn't drive and had no idea what a DUI was, it was just something I'd heard my dad say. Of course, Dad came in, as he wanted to see the place considering I'd been going there twice a week for three weeks. I tried to stop him, but he insisted and when he got inside, he realised he'd nicked half of them the week before for spray painting down by Tower Bridge."

Adam's laugh came from deep in his belly and he pulled me closer to him.

"Oh my God, you dick."

"I know, luckily they were all really good about it and it was the story that always came out when anyone new joined."

"Do you miss them, your dance crew?"

I sighed and considered his question. I wasn't sure. They'd never found out about what happened with Mr Mills, but by then I'd already alienated them because of the grief I was wading through.

"I stopped being friends with them when Dad was killed. I was so full of unhappiness I barely spoke to any of them and then when—" I stopped and looked up at Adam, whose mouth was parted slightly, waiting for me to say something. He looked fearful, so I shook my head. "I stopped going to class after a while and they didn't really ask why, so we obviously weren't close, so no, I don't miss them. What about you, what were you like at fourteen?"

Adam rolled his eyes. "Like I am now, or rather like I was when you first came to Maddison Edge, but with less muscle, less pubic hair and a slightly smaller dick and bollocks."

I couldn't help but laugh, but the furrow of his brow and the deep timbre of his voice told me it was something he regretted.

The air weighed heavy with emotional and sexual tension. "Want a drink?" I asked to break it, pushing up from the sofa.

"Yeah, another coke would be good please, babe."

I smiled and stopped short of hugging myself. I knew a lot of girls hated soppy pet names, especially generic ones, but I loved it when he called me babe. It made my insides squidge.

I was almost at the door, when Adam's phone rang out. It wasn't his usual ring tone but a 90's dance track I recognised; my mum and dad used to play it a lot. He practically snatched the phone from his pocket and with a horrified expression looked at the screen.

"What's wrong? Who is it?"

Adam slowly lifted his head and stared at me his eyes wild with unease.

"Adam?" I asked taking a step back towards him. "Who is it?"

He swallowed hard and then licked his lips.

11

ADAM

"It's my dad." My gaze moved up from my phone to Sarah, knowing that the look on her face would likely cripple me. The words had come out of my mouth before I'd had time to think about them.

"I-I don't know what to do," I said, looking back at the phone just as it stopped ringing.

"Why is he ringing you?"

I had no clue; we hadn't spoken since the night he'd turned up at my house and I'd told him not to come back.

"How does he have your number?" Sarah's voice was tiny as she sank down onto the nearest armchair. "Have you been meeting with him?"

I shook my head. "No."

"So how, Adam?"

Letting my head drop back I closed my eyes. "I saw him outside my house. The night I fought with Davies at TJ's."

"That's why you didn't text me that night, and that's why you were off with me the next day and-." She gasped. "That's why you asked me why I'd helped him with the art room, isn't it? He put those thoughts in your head, didn't he?"

She sounded broken and devastated. I hated myself for doing that to her.

"Babe, I'm so fucking sorry. I'd been wanting to see him for thirteen years and it was so hard to turn him away. I knew I should, and that he deserved for me to punch his fucking lights out, but I just couldn't."

I rushed towards her and dropped to my knees in front of her. "We spoke outside my house and like an idiot I gave him my number. I wish I hadn't, but I was hurting and—"

"Adam, don't." Her warm, soft hand cupped my cheek. "I get it, I really do. If my dad had been out of my life for that long, I'd have been desperate to see him too."

"You would?"

"Of course, I would, and I understand why you want to. That doesn't mean I like it, or I want you to carry on seeing him. I can't tell you what to do, Adam, but I swear to you he isn't a good man. He isn't the man you want him to be."

Lifting my hand to cover Sarah's I leaned forward and kissed her, relishing the soft press of her plump lips against mine. Her sweet floral scent filled the air and something inside me shifted. The feelings I had for her, they felt so much bigger than they had before. They were wrapping themselves tightly around me and binding themselves to my soul.

"I'm sorry, Sarah. I know how hard it is for you. We swore this wouldn't affect us, so I won't see him again."

She drew in a shallow breath, her eyes brimming with tears. "But he's your dad and—"

My phone rang again causing us both to inhale sharply. I glanced at it, but this time it was my mum.

"Shit, what the fuck does she want?"

"Answer her," Sarah's keen gaze swept across my face. "I'll get us that drink."

I watched her go from the room and then swiped the screen of my phone. "Yeah."

"Adam, please don't answer the phone like that," Mum complained. "A hello would be nice."

I silently told her to fuck off and then plastered on a smile. "Hello, Mother, how can I help you?"

"Adam I'm really not in the mood." She sighed heavily and I heard a door close. "Your dad has called me; he needs you to call him. It's urgent."

My stomach plummeted and I blinked as my head whirled. "Why did he call you?"

"Because apparently you didn't answer your phone," she whisper-hissed.

"How the hell does he even have your number?" I peered around the door from the lounge and pushed it closed before moving over to the window.

Looking through to the quiet street outside, I watched as four boys of about eleven or twelve walked along, pushing each other and shouting. Each one looked like they owned the fucking world and knew everything there was to know about life. I just hoped none of them were hiding any secrets that would one day turn them from happy go-lucky kids into mean and hard teenagers.

"It must have been through the solicitor who did the divorce."

She sounded less than convincing, but I wasn't in the mood for arguing with her. It only proved what I'd been thinking, that she knew where my dad had been all along.

"Please just call him, Adam. I don't appreciate him calling me."

"And you're okay with that are you, me calling him? Because for the last thirteen years you've done nothing but go on and on about how we're better off without him."

My exhale and inhale were long and deep as I waited for her to answer.

"If it means he stops calling me, and Roger finding out, then yes, I'm okay with it."

And there it was, the kind and generous Elouise Crawford, thinking of everyone else as usual – fucking not.

"I'll call him now."

I ended the call with her and looked down at the phone hesitantly. I knew me calling him would upset Sarah, but I couldn't not; if he'd called Mum to get a hold of me then he obviously needed to speak to me. Maybe something was wrong.

"Hey, babe," I called as I walked from the lounge into the hall. "I need to go."

Sarah came out of the kitchen with two glasses of coke. "Why, what's wrong?"

"Mum needs me to go and pick Lori up from her friend's house. She's not feeling well, or the friend isn't, something like that. I wasn't listening because I was too pissed off that she asked me to go."

Sarah's face brightened. "Oh okay, I can come if you like. We could take Lori to the park or something, if she's not the one who's unwell, obviously." She giggled and held the glass out to me. "Drink this first and then we can get going."

"I can't, I need to go now." I ground out a smile, feeling uneasy.

"Listen, why don't you stay here, and I'll come back tonight, and we can go to the cinema or something?"

Sarah's smile dropped. "Oh, okay. You sure you don't want me to come?"

Leaning into her space I gave her a quick kiss on the cheek and gave her bum a squeeze. "Honestly, I have some maths homework to do anyway. I can get that done and then it means I've got the rest of the week to spend with you to go out, and," I gave her neck a quick nip, "maybe do our history project."

Sarah squirmed and giggled against my lips. I hated that I was lying to her, but I couldn't see any other way. I got that she hated the thought of me seeing or speaking to my dad, but he was *my dad* and the whole situation was fucking ripping me apart.

"Okay." She sighed and turned to take the glasses of coke back into the kitchen.

"I'll see you about seven?"

Sarah leaned against the doorway, lifting one socked foot to rest on the opposite calf. When we'd got back, she'd changed into tight, black leggings and a grey cropped sweat top, showing a sliver of creamy skin. I would have given anything to reach up and pull down her messy bun and run my fingers through her hair while I kissed an orgasm out of her

I leaned into her space and with my hand at the back of her head pulled her in for a kiss.

"I'll miss you, but I'll see you later."

Sarah sighed as I pulled away and I almost, almost, stayed, but had a feeling in my gut that if I didn't call him that my dad would call again.

Snagging my jacket from the bannister on the way out, I jumped into my car and sped off, only to pull up around the corner. I took my phone from my pocket and scrolled through to my dad's number and pressed it.

"Adam." His voice sounded hoarse like he'd just woken up.

"Why are you calling me?"

I heard him blow out a breath before finally speaking.

"I've been beaten up son, and I need your help."

The place that Dad had rented was an apartment in the centre of town. Within the old fire station, it was pretty nice for a man who didn't appear to have a job. At least I didn't think he did, but then there were lots of things I didn't know about him. I hadn't seen him for years and the conversation we'd had since he'd been back had been short and had ended with me crying like a fucking five-year-old.

"Can you pull the pillow up a little?" he asked with a wince.

I pushed his shoulders forward and adjusted the pillow behind him and then stood back and watched him. I'd barely said a word since I'd got to A&E. Silently, I'd been by his side as he'd been examined, given painkillers and then told he could go home. Even when he'd slowly walked to my car, clutching at his side, and holding an ice pack to his swollen cheek bone, I'd remained mute.

When we'd got back to his apartment, he'd told me he needed to sleep.

"I didn't know who else to call. I had no other way of getting home."

"There are taxis." My throat was scratchy as I forced out my first words in almost three hours

He shifted in the bed and hissed. Automatically I made a step towards him, but then pulled up short, caught between helping him and hating him.

"Didn't have any cash on me," he grunted.

I didn't bother to mention that most taxis took cards, it was pointless now that he was home.

"Do you know who it was?" I asked, pushing my hands into my jacket pockets.

He shot me a sideways glance and let out a laboured breath. "I have my suspicions."

"Like?"

"Ask your girlfriend's mum what she's been spending her money on recently."

I tilted my head back, not sure if I'd heard him properly. His eyes narrowed on me, as if daring me to argue.

"Sarah's mum? I don't think I understand."

"Let's just say the guy whispered a little message in my ear when I was doubled up on the floor. 'This is for Sarah', he said. So, unless you got someone to kick the shit out of me on her behalf, there can only be one other person and I'm guessing that bitch of a mother of hers paid someone to do it."

I barked out a laugh. "This is Maddison Edge. Not bloody New York. People don't pay other people to beat someone up."

"Adam, we live on the outskirts of Manchester. Are you not aware of some of the shit that goes down in the city? It wouldn't take much for her to get someone willing to do it for a couple of hundred quid. All she's got to do is go into a dodgy looking pub, mention what she wants and within minutes there'd be two or three guys queuing up to take her money."

"Mrs Danes wouldn't do that, you're wrong."

"She'd do anything for that lying daughter of hers."

I pulled my hands from my pockets and pointed accusingly at him. "Don't you dare speak about Sarah like that."

Dad pinched the bridge of his nose. "Adam, you don't know her like I do. I'm telling you, this was all her mother's doing, I know it."

"Nope, I'm not having it. You're lying that your attacker said that. Mrs Danes is just a lady trying to get over the death of her husband and what you did to her daughter."

His nostrils flared with anger and he reached behind him to adjust his pillow again. "She's lying about that. I told you what happened. We. Were. In. A. Relationship."

There was so much I wanted to say to him. So many accusations I wanted to throw at him, but the words just wouldn't come. They stuck in my throat and dissolved into streams of dread that he was telling the truth, and fear that he was lying.

There were so many things I needed to know, but the truth about him and Sarah wasn't one of them. It was too raw, and I was too much of a coward.

"What happened with you and Mum? Why did she throw you out?"

He curled his lip into a smirk. "Nothing was good enough for your mum. She was needy and difficult and hated that I worked long hours. Of course, I worked long hours because she wanted everything we couldn't afford. I even started doing extra jobs on the side, spray painting cars at the garage after work hours."

"But you left and never came back. I know Mum didn't want you to see me, but you were my dad, you had rights."

"I wanted to see you, you have no idea, but when I left your mum, she told my boss I'd been stealing materials from him to do my own jobs. It was her way at getting back at me for asking for a divorce."

"She says *she* kicked *you* out," I argued. "You didn't leave her."

He looked up at me, his brows raised. "I left her, believe me. She told my boss so he sacked me without any references. I had to go down south for work. When I got there, I couldn't find anything. It was really hard. I ended up drinking a lot."

"What, and the drink made you lose your memory? It caused you to totally forget that you had a five-year-old son who fucking needed you."

My throat burned with the emotion that I was fighting back. I did not want to cry in front of him. I wouldn't, not again.

"I was in a bad way, Adam. I could barely look after myself let alone find time to come and see you. I didn't have the money for a start." The way he looked at me, with his eyes searching my face, I couldn't see any remorse. He didn't think he'd done anything wrong at all.

"You had no clue what I was going through. You left me with her and didn't give a shit what was happening to me. And you changed your fucking name. Why would you do that if you ever wanted me to find you?"

"I was going under Adam, and when I eventually sorted myself out, I needed a new start, so I changed my name and went back to university to get my teaching degree. I didn't think you'd even remember me by then."

"Mum knew where you were," I blasted. "She said she didn't, but she did, I know she did."

Dad's mouth dropped open in surprise. "How do you know?"

"Because I know Mum and I know she's hiding something, so I know she knew where you were. Yet all the time she made me live with man after man and pretend that they were all my dad for the short time they were in our lives."

I wanted to scream at him that she'd let one of them beat me, and had pretended she had no idea, but telling him that would be admitting the shame.

"I'm sorry about that." Dad sighed as he threw the now floppy ice pack down onto his bed. "I am, but I'm here now. You're my son, my flesh and blood. Your genes are my genes. I want to be here for you."

He said the words, but he sounded detached as though he was repeating instructions to some manual on how to raise your child.

"Did you come for me, or Sarah?" I asked, dropping my gaze to the blue and green patterned rug on the varnished floorboards.

"You, of course."

The pause was only a second, but it was enough that I felt it in my chest.

"Don't call me again. You need any help? Call someone else, not me."

As I turned for the door, he grunted something under his breath, and I heard the bed creak.

"Adam don't be fooled by her and that damn little girl act. She'll draw you in just like she did to me. And while you're at it, maybe ask her mother what she knows about how I got beaten up."

I stopped and looked over my shoulder.

"I think whoever kicked the shit out of you did something to your head as well. I don't have a clue who did that to you, but it had nothing to do with Sarah or her mum."

I didn't wait for him to reply but strode off down the short hallway to the front door and yanked it shut with a bang. A woman pushing a bike into through the main doorway, flashed me a smile and I scowled my response. When I heard her tut, I paused about to give her a mouthful of abuse, but my phone started ringing in my pocket. I pulled it out and glanced at the screen; Sarah.

My heart thudded as something pricked at my memory.

"Fuck." The time on my phone showed it was almost half past seven and I was late for picking Sarah up. I hadn't realised how long I'd had to wait in A&E for my dad to be discharged.

I knew if I answered it, I'd have to explain everything about being with the man who she hated, the man who she saw had ruined her life, so like a fucking coward, I dropped her call and turned off my phone. I hated myself for doing it, but I had no idea how else to deal with her. As I got into my car and set off in the direction of home, it crossed my mind to keep on driving until I was far away from all the shit going on in my life, but I knew I couldn't. I couldn't leave her behind. Sarah was one of the only fucking reasons I put one foot in front of the other every day. Without her I was sure I'd fall back into the black and never resurface. Dad's words echoed back at me.

"You're my son, my flesh and blood. Your genes are my genes, so I want to be here for you."

Those words petrified me, because if that were the case, I was sure to send Sarah back into the black, and I couldn't be responsible for that.

12

SARAH

All I'd had from Adam to explain why he failed to pick me up for the cinema, was a bloody text message sent at two in the morning, saying he'd fallen asleep while doing his maths homework. I didn't believe him. Something was going on and I was sure it was to do with the call he'd had from his dad.

It also seemed a bit of a coincidence that his mum had called straight after, and then he'd disappeared.

I wasn't going to sit around and worry about it though.

I'd come too far to stew about a boy.

Even if that boy was Adam Hudson and I couldn't get him out of my head.

I'd called Alannah to see if she fancied going to the shopping centre, which she did, and she even suggested we get Amber to go with us, which was why we were currently waiting for her as she tried on a dress.

"And the only explanation he was gave was that he fell asleep?"

Alannah rolled her eyes as she picked up a shoe with a lethal weapon for a heel.

"Yeah." My stomach churned as I thought about the text and the fact that Adam had then ignored my call after I'd read it when I'd woken up this morning. "Do you think something is wrong at home?"

Alannah put the shoe back and linked her arm with mine. "I hate to say this Sarah, but it could just be Adam being... well, Adam. I know you think he's changed, but maybe he hasn't."

The churning in my stomach changed to a definite swell of nausea at the thoughts running around in my head.

What if he'd decided I was too much trouble?

What if he was with Mackenna?

What if we were over and he didn't have the guts to tell me?

"I need to see him," I said quickly, turning to the shop entrance.

Alannah pulled me back. "No, you don't. You need to wait for a while and see what happens. I might have got it all wrong, and he may well have fallen asleep."

The look of sympathy she had one her face contradicted her words. As far as Alannah was concerned, Adam was back to his old ways.

"You want to say I told you so, don't you?"

"God no. I wouldn't want anyone to feel like that. I know how he can be, and I know how shit he can make you feel. I don't want that for you."

The reminder that my boyfriend had been intimate with the girl who was now probably my best friend, filled my mouth with a bitter taste. I was angry that Alannah had even thought to mention it.

I pulled away from her and stormed over to a rack of sale items and started to look through them. It wasn't long before Alannah joined me.

"I'm sorry, I shouldn't have said anything." She looked contrite, so I flashed her a quick smile.

"I hate that he did that to you, Alannah, you and Amber, but he's not like that with me."

Alannah raised her brows.

"Okay he wasn't like that, but he might be telling the truth."

"Yeah, he might, but there's something that's stopping you from believing that. Some intuition that's making you think the worst."

At that moment, Amber appeared with the dress hanging from a hanger, in her hand. "I'm going to get it," she said, looking less than enthusiastic.

"Why didn't you come out and show us?" Alannah asked.

Amber shrugged. "Just didn't. Come on I need to pay."

As she walked off Alannah shook her head. "See, she makes a career out of being miserable."

Following them both to the cash register, I couldn't help but laugh, but any lightness I might have felt was weighed down with the nagging worry about Adam.

There was only Adam's car on the Crawford's driveway when Alannah dropped me off. Even though she'd tried to persuade me not to go, I knew we needed to talk though. I was glad it didn't look as though anyone else was home , this needed to be alone.

I lifted a shaky hand and closing it into a fist, rapped hard on the door. Within a minute I spotted Adam through the glass. He hesitated for a second but then continued down the hall and opened the door.

"Hey," he said, looking over my shoulder and then down at the floor before finally fixing his gaze onto me.

"Can I come in?"

I looked him directly in the eye, my face impassive despite the fact that part of me wanted to cry. It was there in his eyes; the look which said I wouldn't be leaving his house feeling happy.

Adam stepped aside to let me in and then led me into the lounge. There was music playing and I instantly recognised it as '*Ex*' by James TW. I just hoped it wasn't some sort of a sign.

"What's going on, Adam?" I rounded on him immediately. "No lies, because I know something is. We were fine all afternoon, then you got those calls and you've damn well ghosted me for the last twenty-four hours. Don't lie and say you haven't because I know you have."

He curled his lip and shrugged, displaying hints of the old Adam, the one that I didn't want to be with; the one I didn't deserve.

"Don't shrug at me like that, like I'm not even worthy of words."

"Told you, I fell asleep." He walked past me and threw himself down onto the sofa and sprawled against the cushions. "Been busy this morning, that's all."

He couldn't even look at me; his eyes were everywhere except where they should have been. It was proof that my intuition had been right. There was something wrong and he didn't have the guts to tell me. I didn't have the energy to waste beating around the bush with him about it. My gut told me he was avoiding me, and I wasn't going to tiptoe around the subject.

"I actually thought you cared about me," I said, furling my hands into fists at my side. "I honestly thought we had something. You came to me yesterday when I needed you. You took care of me, you've told me we are perfect, that we fit together. So what the fuck happened between leaving my house and seven o'clock when you were supposed to pick me up?"

I clamped my bottom lip between my teeth, desperately trying to stop the quiver in my chin. To cry in front of him would be the worst thing I could do, because that would mean admitting to myself how deep my feelings for him were. There was no way I could get through what he was going to say, if I didn't close myself off from what he was doing to my heart.

"Well?" I urged when he didn't respond. "And I want the truth."

His shoulders slumped in resignation. "I think I realised that with all the schoolwork I had and having to help out with Lori, that we probably see too much of each other. I'd been with you all day, and just wanted to get my head around things. I think you want something more serious than I'm prepared to give."

He scratched at his chest and then looked over to the window, looking at the empty street outside.

"Liar! If anyone has pushed this into serious territory, then it's been you. You're the one who came to me late at night, you're the one who kicked off if I didn't sit with you at lunchtime. You begged me to believe you about Mackenna, you even came home to make sure I did. Why would you do that if you didn't care?" I took a deep breath. "You're the one with the fucking experience, Adam. You knew that I was scared that I'd get hurt, yet you still..."

I trailed off as I heard his breath hitch and he threw his hands to the top of his head. His face crumpled as he looked at me.

"And that's why I can't fucking be with you, Sarah," he cried. He got up from the sofa and moved to stand in front of me. "I knew you were scared, and I was selfish thinking I could change and be what you wanted, just because I wanted you."

"Who says you can't," I replied, wrapping my arms around my waist. "You're doing a good job of it so far."

"Because the truth will kill me, it'll kill us, and I can't be two people. I can't be the son of a rapist and I can't be the son who is desperate for his dad's attention. Don't you see, I'm pulled in two directions and whichever I choose is going to be bad for you."

I drew in a ragged breath and shook my head. "Being his son doesn't make you like him, Adam. You're *nothing* like him."

"But I am. You know I fucking am. You told me once that he was manipulative and clever and told lies while he domineered people, well isn't that me. Don't I do those things? I did those things to your friends, so don't tell me I'm nothing like him, Sarah."

"But you're not," I cried. "You've saved me, more than once, he would never do that."

My heart beat harder, forcing the fear around my body, making it difficult to breathe because the air in my lungs wouldn't budge. It continued to build, almost suffocating me as I begged Adam with my eyes to listen to me.

His hand reached out to me, but when I moved mine forward, he snatched his back and it felt like he'd reached in and snapped the blood supply to my heart.

"You can't even touch me now?"

Adam shook his head and swallowed hard. "No. Because, if I touch you, I know I'll give in and I'll kiss you. I'll beg you to forgive me and we'll go back to how we were."

"What's wrong with that?"

I closed my eyes on the tears pricking at my eyelashes and

listened to the sound of Selena Gomez singing '*Lose You to Love Me*', and silently prayed that Adam would change his mind.

"What's wrong with that," he continued, "is that one day I will hurt you. I'm not good enough for you, Sarah. I'm Glen Hudson's son. I'm his flesh and blood, I have his genes. He's a manipulator, a liar and he abandons those he's supposed to love. I can't build something with you knowing that one day I'm going to be just like him."

"You have two lots of genes, Adam."

He gave an empty laugh and raised his eyes to the ceiling. "Yeah and the others aren't much better. She's lazy, self-centred and she's also a liar. She's known where he was all this time and lied to me about it, she let a grown man beat me, Sarah. She can fucking dress it up all she likes, but she knew and she let it happen. I was nine years of age, what mother doesn't see that?"

"I don't—"

"I'll tell you. The sort of mother who only cares about herself and what she needs. The sort of mother who suddenly stops checking on her son, because she knows if she helps him have a bath or to get dressed, she'll see the bruises that will mean she's going to be on her own again. So, she might not have seen the black, blue and yellow that covered my back and chest, but she knew it was there. I will not put you through a relationship with me when I have the DNA of two people who are monsters in their own rights."

Tears streamed down both our faces. He was gripping at his hair and his chest heaved at the pain he'd unleashed, as though he'd run a marathon. The determination on his face and in his stance was palpable as his gaze stayed pinned to me.

"This is how it has to be, Sarah. If we stay together, we'll both always be wondering."

I drew in a breath, knowing he wasn't going to change his mind but having to show him how I felt and what could have been.

With one stride I was in front of him, my hands threaded into his hair, my lips on his. Adam opened up immediately and when my tongue pushed inside his mouth, he reacted in the same way he always did, by taking my breath away with his intensity.

I nipped at his bottom lip and scored my nails against his scalp, causing him to groan and his dick to swell. My hips moved forward on instinct and Adam's hands moved, one to the small of my back and one to the centre of my shoulder blades. They pushed me closer while our kiss became more insistent.

Our tongues swept against each other and our teeth clashed as we grew more eager. Hands were suddenly grabbing at clothes and our breathing was heavy and loud. I knew we could be naked, and Adam would be thrusting inside of me within seconds, but afterwards nothing would change. He would still feel the guilt and despair, he would still feel inadequate, and then it would be even harder to accept his actions.

As Adam groaned against my mouth, I pulled away breathing hard, turned on by the animalistic way we'd kissed.

"You're right, Adam," I said breathlessly. "You will always be wondering, but now it will be about the goodness you could have had in your life, not the hurt that might never have come."

As I left the house and walked down the driveway, the dam which had been holding back my tears, broke. I sobbed hard, with my shoulders heaving and a pain in my chest that I knew would take an age to go away.

It was when I reached the pavement that a smooth hand tucked into mine, and when I looked up, I saw my friend walking beside me.

"Come on," Alannah said, squeezing my hand. "Let's get you home."

"He thinks he's not good enough," I whispered through my sobs, as my free hand clutched at my stomach.

"Well," Alannah replied with a sigh. "If he says he isn't, then he isn't."

She was right. If Adam really was good enough, he'd have fought to make sure he never let me down, but it was over now, and we would never know.

13

ADAM

Mackenna grinned as she put her tray down on our table. It was the sort of smile that said, *I knew I'd be back.* I had no idea why I'd even asked her, other than to let everyone know that Sarah and I weren't together anymore.

We'd been back at school for two day and I'd seen Sarah twice. History had been the fucking worst, because we were project partners and sat next to each other – or so I thought. I shouldn't have been surprised when I got there that Mr Raymond announced I was now partnered up with Edward Stokes. I thought I'd at least be able to watch Sarah from my position at the back of the class, but apparently, I'd been moved to sit at Edward's desk in front of Sarah and Shannon's.

No words had been spoken between us and when I'd given her a smile at the end of the lesson, I'd received nothing in return. Sarah had blanked me and then walked out. Hence why Mackenna was now sitting opposite me and pushing salad around her plate and telling me she couldn't eat any more than the forkful she'd already had.

"Are you going to Charlie Douglas' eighteenth?" Mackenna asked, shoving her tray of barely touched food away.

"Nah. Seth Davies is going, and I don't think me kicking the shit out of him would go down too well."

Mackenna giggled. "No, I'm not sure if I'm going either."

"I thought she was your best friend, or one of them?"

I gave Ellis a nod as he sat down. He looked at Mackenna and raised his eyebrows.

"What do we owe the pleasure?"

"Adam asked me to sit here." She preened and then turned to me. "She can be a bitch sometimes, and I think her parents will be there, so who wants to go to a party with a load of oldies there?"

"Where's Tyler and Kirk?" I asked Ellis without acknowledging Mackenna's comment.

"On their way. Kirk got talking to Mr Barnes about his IT coursework and Tyler, no idea."

I was still keeping some distance from the lads, apart from Ellis, but that had been more about wanting to be a better person for Sarah. Now that was no longer necessary. Then as if my brain had conjured her up, she walked into the dining room with Alannah and Amber. She looked so fucking beautiful it made my chest ache. Her hair was in one long plait, hanging over her shoulder and there was no baggy jumper to hide her curves, but a white t-shirt with a red heart on the front with red cropped jeans and a pair of white Vans.

"Mackenna, come and sit here," I barked and pulled the stool out next to me.

Like the good little girl that she was, Mackenna rushed around to my side of the table and sat down, dragging her seat closer to mine.

"We could go to Charlie's party together," she said running her fingers through my hair. "I'll protect you from Seth Daniels."

Her giggle and touch grated on me and was I just about to pull away when I noticed Sarah watching us. She'd stopped dead still in the middle of the dining room with her hand rubbing at her wrist. Alannah was tugging on her arm, trying to pull her on, but Sarah wasn't moving. She looked distraught. All I wanted to do was rush to her and tell her I was a fucking idiot.

I was a fucking idiot.

"Yeah maybe we could do that." I turned to face Mackenna and leaned into her.

She did exactly as I expected and kissed me. Her tongue pushed at the seam of my lips, but I couldn't do it. I couldn't let her kiss me like that. The taste of her mouth on mine was bitter and sour, her arms wrapped around my neck, strangulating and controlling.

I pulled back and half turned away to speak to Ellis.

"What time is the minibus leaving for Rochford Academy?"

We had an away game and I was finally back in the team after sitting out the previous game.

"Four. We've got practice too, don't forget, so we get off last lesson."

My gaze wandered over to where Sarah had been standing to see she'd now moved to a table where she and Alannah had their heads down and were talking. It looked like Sarah might be crying, but her head was down, and Alannah was leaning in closely, obscuring my view.

"Are we going to have some fun with her?" Ellis asked, nodding in Sarah's direction.

"No. *Just fucking leave her alone.*" I hissed, gripping the edge of the table.

Ellis' eyes widened, and he held his hands up in surrender. "Okay, I get the message."

As he went back to his lunch, and Mackenna went back to hanging onto my arm and glaring at every other girl in the dining room, we fell into an uncomfortable silence. It was one of those where you literally want to crawl up your own arse to hide away from it. In fact, it was so awkward that I silently begged for Mackenna to say something in her annoying, nasally whine. After a few minutes, I sighed with relief when Tyler approached the table. That was short-lived though when he grimaced and leaned in to whisper in my ear, "Think you should know Seth Davies is mouthing off about your step-dad."

I shook Mackenna away from me and stood up. "What's he saying?"

"He told me that he heard he knocked you about."

I turned to look over to where Sarah was sitting. At that very moment, her head lifted, and her gaze collided with mine.

"Where did he hear that?" I asked Tyler, not taking my eyes off Sarah.

"Didn't say. Just he'd heard. Not the only thing he said though."

My head swivelled back to Tyler and my stomach began to churn. "What else?"

"The same thing he said that night in TJ's, that Sarah has shagged your dad."

Mackenna gasped beside me. "Ugh gross. What a skank."

"Shut the fuck up." I bent down and leaned into her space. "And while you're at it, fuck off and don't come near me again."

Her mouth dropped open and she shrank back from me. "But I thought... what about Charlie's party?"

"We're not going."

I noticed a few people's heads pop up from their lunches at the sound of my voice, and when I looked down at Mackenna, with her too tight top and short skirt, dressed like it was fucking July instead of February, I felt my anger rise.

"I don't know what you thought might happen with us, Mackenna," I snarled, loud enough for most of the dining room to hear. "But it's not. You're good for one thing and I'm even bored of that. Now, do as I say and fuck off."

Mackenna's eyes filled with tears, and I was shocked. Mackenna never showed emotion of any kind, except hatred.

She glanced at Ellis and then back to me. "You'll be back," she protested as she tilted her chin up and pushed her shoulders back. "I'm the one you always come back to." She then turned towards Sarah and pointed in her direction. "That freak is not who you should be with."

Everyone stopped what they were doing and turned to face our table. Their eyes followed the direction of where Mackenna was pointing and one by one they all stared at Sarah. I could see her cheeks reddened with embarrassment and I wished I could turn back the last fifteen minutes. She didn't deserve the shit that people like me and Mackenna handed out.

"You say one more fucking word," I ground out through gritted teeth, leaning right into Mackenna's air space, "and I'll ruin you. You know I can."

She swallowed and I could see it in her eyes that she was considering opening her mouth again but thought better of it. Instead she scraped her stool back, picked up her bag and teetered away in her whore shoes, everyone's stare on her as she exited the dining room.

"Where is he?" I asked Tyler as I grabbed my phone from the table.

"Outside, next to the gate into the lower school yard. Kirk is with him."

"Adam, don't do anything fucking stupid." Ellis sighed and stood up. "You hit that dick again and you'll be banned for the whole season, not just the next game."

"Ellis is right. You can't afford to get into any more trouble, you could even end up expelled."

I knew they were right. If I was expelled, I'd have no chance of ever going to university this year, next year nor any other year.

"What the fuck do I do then?" I gripped my hair with tense fingers as I watched Sarah and Alannah leaving the dining room. "He can't get away with it, and why the fuck does he even think he can? He knows I can fucking bury him."

Tyler shrugged. "I don't know, but he's acting all cocky, like nothing can touch him. He's always been fucking scared of you Ad. I don't know why he thinks he can get away with this."

Ellis slapped a hand on my shoulder. "Come on, but let us deal with it, okay?"

I looked at Tyler who nodded his agreement of the plan. "Okay, let's go."

We ran from the dining room, pushing past other kids, sending one lad and his tray of food flying. I didn't care though, I needed to shut Seth Davies up before Sarah found out.

As we rounded the corner into the corridor, Ellis pulled up. "You two go, I'll just make sure Mackenna knows to keep her mouth shut."

"No, I'll—"

"No," Ellis butted in. "You've just made her feel like a cheap slag. I don't think she's going to listen to you."

"Okay," I sighed. "Come on Ty, let's go."

When we found Davies, he was leaning against a wall with his mate Jackson cowering beside him. Davies to his credit was facing up to Kirk, even though Kirk was much bigger and had his fisted hand drawn back.

"Kirk, what are you doing?" I asked, pulling on his shoulder.

Kirk kept his eyes firmly on Davies, who I realised as I got closer was gripping his shaking hands at his side.

"Warning this fucker about shouting his mouth off about stupid crap."

"I'm only repeating what I heard." Davies' eyes darted to me.

"Who did you hear it from?" I asked, taking a step closer to him.

He shrugged. "I don't know."

"Fuck off," Tyler scoffed. "You must know. You've spouted this shit once before. Tell us who told you, otherwise we will have to let Kirk loose on you."

"Seth just tell them." Jackson hung his hands off the back of his neck and anxiously turned to me. "It was some lad when we were in TJ's. The night before you kicked the shit out of him in there. He said if Seth spread it around, he'd make sure you didn't hurt him for it, and that he'd pay him a hundred quid."

"Jackson, you fucking grass."

"No, I'm not, Seth," he cried. "You're not dropping anyone in it. You don't have a clue who the fuck he was." Jackson looked between each of us. "He came into the toilet while we were having a piss. Told us that Sarah had shagged your dad and that your stepdad used to beat you. Then he said, he'd protect Seth."

"And you didn't question why some strange lad was telling you this?" Tyler asked. "Or ask how the fuck he thought he was going to stop us from kicking the shit out of you? And did he give you the money?"

Seth's eyes dropped to look at the floor and he shook his head.

"Christ Davies," Tyler scoffed. "You really are a prick."

I was glad Tyler was the one talking to Davies. I didn't want to speak and give away how scared I was. I could barely breathe from the anxiety mixing with my blood supply. If someone out there knew about what happened with my dad and Sarah, then maybe they knew that she'd tried to kill herself too. If that got out it could send her down a black hole and the thought that she might once again feel it was her only option, crippled me with fear. The crap about me and Eric, well of course I didn't want that coming out, but I'd cope. It was a burden I'd carried around for nine years so could let the shame of it slide from my shoulders; Sarah was different though. She was gentle and sensitive, and having to face people knowing her deepest secret could ruin any progress she'd made.

I closed my eyes on the thought of Sarah going downhill and the guilt hit me in the stomach again. Me ending us could have done exactly the same. What if me telling her it was over had sent her spiralling down? Panic started to mix with the fear, and I felt an urge to find her and to make sure she was okay. I couldn't though because Davies started to talk at me.

"After you punched me, the afternoon we watched the girl's new cheer routine, I wanted to get you back," he ground out. "So, when he told me, I didn't care who the hell he was, or why he was telling me. I just had information on you that I knew I could share."

"And you didn't think about Sarah while you were spreading your fucking gossip?" I asked, just about keeping hold of my temper.

Davies groaned as Ellis appeared beside me, breathing heavily.

"Sorted," he said quietly. "What's happening? What's he saying?"

"Some lad told him and Jackson a load of shit about Adam and Sarah, and I'm just about to punch his fucking lights out for it." Kirk gave us a smirk as he waved his fist around. "Even though his new friend promised to take care of his stupid arse."

"What lad?" Ellis asked.

"We don't know. He came in and just told us."

Jackson looked like he might just piss himself at that moment. His face had paled to grey and his hands were shaking at his side.

"What did he look like?" I asked

Jackson turned to me and stared at me with his brows almost in his hairline. "I was taking a piss; I didn't look at him. I'm not fucking gay."

"No one said you were, you dick." Ellis rolled his eyes. "And looking at him or his prick doesn't make you gay, you ignorant knobhead."

"He was quite short and had ginger hair, that's all I can remember."

Jackson swung his gaze to Davies as if shocked that he'd looked.

"Have you ever seen him around here before?" I rubbed a hand over my face, wondering how I was going to find some dickhead who looked like every other lad our age.

"No. He had a Manc' accent."

"Like every other fucker that lives around here." Tyler sighed. "Any chance he was wearing anything recognisable."

"I didn't look that fucking close."

"Can I just punch him now?" Kirk asked, looking bored.

I thought about it. He deserved it. It wouldn't resolve anything, though. It might make things worse; Davies could spread more gossip to a point I wouldn't be able to contain it.

"You better start telling people you got it wrong," I said, taking a step closer to Davies and Jackson. "And I fucking swear, I hear you've repeated any of it ever again, you won't know when or where, but you can be sure I'll fucking batter you, despite what your piss mate told you."

They both nodded and when Kirk dropped his fist, slid from against the wall and ran off, pushing past the handful of people in the yard who were having a crafty smoke.

"You think he'll keep his mouth shut?" Tyler asked, shoving his hands into the pockets of his hoodie.

"Yeah, I reckon. My bet is he knows whoever the lad was and that he won't be able to protect him. I just wish I knew who he was."

"You actually believed that?" Kirk asked me. "Some mystery lad sidles up to him while he's having a piss and acts like some secret agent. Sorry but it sounds crap to me."

"I think he was about ready to shit himself, so probably would've said anything, but yeah I do."

Ellis cleared his throat and ushered us closer to a more secluded area of the yard.

"Is any of it true?" he asked.

I looked at the three of them in turn and wondered how the hell I could get out of telling them. We'd been friends for a long time, they all knew if it was bullshit, I'd have laughed it off.

"Yeah," I replied taking in a deep breath. "Remember the guy Eric, who my mum lived with for a while?"

They all nodded or grunted yes.

"He used to kick the shit out of me. My back and stomach, so no one ever saw it."

"What about your mum?" Ellis asked, rubbing the top of his head distractedly.

I let out a huff of laughter. "Yeah, she said she didn't, but she did. I think she turned a blind eye because Eric brought money into the house and provided her with security. Well security and fucking new shoes when she wanted them."

"Fuck me." Kirk looked like he'd been hit with a truck. His cheeks had paled and he bent over and dropped his hands to knees. I almost put a hand on his arm to keep him upright but didn't.

"Why didn't you tell us?" Tyler asked quietly. "You were just a little kid. You know my mum and dad would have done something."

I shrugged. "I didn't though mate. I thought me and Lori would get taken away, he made me believe that. I couldn't take the risk."

"But you lived with him for years, until he fucked off. Did he hit you the whole time?" Kirk asked, pulling himself upright.

"Pretty much."

"Shit, Ad. I wish you'd said." Tyler shook his head, and I could see he was trying to process it all.

"And what about Sarah?" Ellis asked, his voice tentative. "What about what he said about her and your dad?"

"Yeah, and who did he mean, Roger?"

I turned to Kirk and shook my head. "No."

"So, what?" Ellis asked.

I could lie and tell them it wasn't true, but the look of sympathy in each of their eyes told me they already knew what Davies had said had been true.

"If you repeat this," I said, venom tasting bitter on my tongue, "I swear I'll fucking kill you."

"We won't," Tyler said for them all.

I inhaled and then exhaled slowly before placing my hands on my head, feeling sick to my stomach.

"My dad, my real dad, was her teacher at her last school and…" I paused not sure I could say the words about the man I'd been desperate to have in my life. "He raped her. My dad raped Sarah."

14

SARAH

"I'm not saying I told you so."

"But you are," I replied to Amber who watched me with a raised brow.

She shrugged. "The fact that he's back to getting his cock sucked by Mackenna White should be enough, without me adding to your woes by acting all superior."

Alannah choked back a cough, almost spitting out the water she was drinking from a bottle.

"You okay?" I asked, slapping her back, unable to keep the smile from my lips.

"Yep," she croaked out. "Went down the wrong way."

"Anyway," Amber continued. "The main thing is you've had a lucky escape."

She thought she was right, and if questioned would never have any other opinion, but I couldn't agree. I missed Adam. I desperately wanted to talk to him. My stomach churned constantly, to the point that it ached.

"I think Sarah knows, Amber. It's hardly necessary to keep drilling it home."

I threw her an appreciative smile, grateful that I had at least one friend who understood me.

"Anyway," I said, pulling at some skin around my thumbnail. "We all heard how he spoke to Mackenna yesterday. I doubt she's still hanging around him."

"Sorry to burst your bubble, Sarah," Amber sighed. "But I saw her hanging off his arm only this morning walking into school. They were all over each other."

Bile rose in my throat and tears threatened to spill at the thought of Adam with Mackenna. My body felt bereft of a soul as jagged shards of jealousy stabbed at my insides. He'd promised me so much, but I knew I was to blame for believing the words he'd left unspoken. I should have known everything he said was a lie.

Trying not to think about Adam, we continued walking towards the car park in silence. Amber was scrolling through her phone, but I sensed that Alannah was watching me. I wasn't going to break though; I'd been through too much to let a stupid boy take me down. It would be a close thing though, because my heart was all in with him; the stupid bloody organ.

"Oh my God," Alannah gasped. "What the hell has she done?"

My head lifted and my gaze landed on Mackenna, who was leaning against Adam's car and talking to her friend, Charlie Douglas.

"You're joking." Amber laughed as she shook her head. "Has she done that for *him*?"

Mackenna flicked her long, now blonde hair over her shoulder and laughed at something that Charlie said.

I was dumbstruck. Her hair was the exact same colour as *mine*, she'd even had layers cut into it, like *mine*. From the back, her head could well have been *mine*.

"Does she think that will make him want more from her than her cum swallowing ability?" Alannah asked. "Because I'm pretty sure it won't."

"It's exactly like yours." Amber nudged me. "Are you pissed off?"

I turned my gaze to her and shrugged. "I don't know how I feel." *Apart from weirded out.*

"Shit look at what she's got on her feet too," Alannah gasped.

Gone were Mackenna's usual tower block heels. On her feet instead were a pair of navy coloured Converse. I looked down at my feet, today I was wearing my floral Vans, but usually I wore any one of my four pairs of Converse.

"They don't really go with the hooker outfit," Amber stated. "I mean who the hell wears a silver sequin skirt and pink crop top to school, in February?"

"Mackenna evidently," Alannah replied caustically.

"Oh, and here's her beau now."

The breath left my lungs in a rush as I watched Adam saunter over with Ellis. Mackenna had her back to him, and when Adam spotted her, he stalled, the hand swirling his car key around falling to his side as he stared open mouthed. When Mackenna turned to face Adam, I held my breath and waited, like I was watching an important scene in a film; the one that gave us the biggest clue on how it would end.

It was evident that Adam hadn't seen Mackenna's hair before, but other than surprise it was difficult to know how he felt about it. He had to have seen how alike mine it was, and surely, he had to have wondered why she'd done it, but he didn't stay to find out. He stormed up to his car, ignoring Mackenna and Charlie, got in and screeched out of the car park.

"I think that means he doesn't like her new colour," Amber said.

Mackenna swung around to face us. "What the hell are you looking at?"

I shifted uncomfortably because as much as I didn't like Mackenna, I didn't want to stand and watch her awkwardness. I knew how it felt to be ignored by Adam Hudson and in some ways, it was worse than when he hated you.

"Come on let's go," I said taking Alannah's arm and guiding her away."

"Why?" Amber scoffed. "She's a fucking bitch, it's quite funny to see her getting shit for a change."

That was it, I'd had enough. I pulled to a stop and let out an exasperated breath. "Amber will you just give it a rest, please. I know you dislike her and Adam, but I'm sick of hearing about them. First, you're telling me all about them coming into school together and now you're bitching about her hair. I don't care, *I don't want to know*."

That was a total lie because I did care, of course I cared, I just didn't want to hear about how my ex-boyfriend had moved on so quickly.

"Yeah, about that," Alannah said. "You said you'd seen Mackenna hanging on Adam's arm when they came into school this morning."

"Yeah." Amber pouted and lifted her bag higher on her shoulder.

"Well you never mentioned her hair, or today's choice of shoe for that matter."

My head snapped towards Amber who slumped her shoulders and focused on the ground. "Wasn't taking much notice."

"Enough to see they were all over each other." Alannah shrugged. "Oh well no wonder Adam didn't notice she'd gone from dark brown to blonde since yesterday, if he was all over her this morning."

She flashed Amber a small smile and then grabbed my hand and pulled me towards her car.

"She's such a little bitch at times," Alannah grumbled as we pulled out of the car park. "Why tell you lies about Adam and Mackenna? What does she think it will achieve?"

I shrugged, my eyes firmly on the passing scenery outside.

"Why do you think he stormed off like that?" I asked, moving in my seat to face Alannah.

Her face was one of concentration as she manoeuvred around a cyclist. "No idea. Maybe he doesn't think it suits her." She glanced at me and flashed a smile before putting her eyes back on the road. "I know you probably want his reaction to mean something for you and him, but I'm not sure it does. You've also got to consider the situation with his sperm donor. Do you really want to be around Adam while he's in his life?"

My stomach somersaulted at the thought of Mr Mills and Alannah was right, I could never imagine any scenario where I'd feel comfortable even talking about him to Adam.

"N-no you're right, I don't. And I know we're over, but I just wondered, that's all."

As we pulled to a stop at a zebra crossing, Alannah let out a sigh. "I know what he's like, Sarah, and if he's dumped you, I don't think there's any going back. You don't need him, and you certainly don't want to be around that bastard who helped to produce him. So, why would you want him back?"

Why would I want him back? Because I was catching feelings for him, despite who his dad was, that was why.

"We had fun and he was nice to me," I replied, glancing at the young girl and her mum crossing in front of us. "Believe it or not."

"I admit, he was different with you than anyone else." Alannah put her foot back on the accelerator and continued towards my house. "It takes a lot to change someone from what Adam was like though."

"Yeah I suppose."

Alannah was right it did, but I knew Adam was almost there and I was hurt that I hadn't been enough for him to want to change completely.

When we finally pulled up outside my house, after a little detour, for Alannah to call and get her dad a birthday card—apparently she was thawing to him after his brief affair—I was concentrating on a text I'd had from Mum to say she was running late so would call and get something for dinner.

"Looks like you've got a visitor." Alannah nudged my arm.

My breath caught in my throat, as I looked up to see Adam, looking agitated as he raked his hands through his dark blond hair.

"What's he doing here?"

"Maybe I was wrong," Alannah replied. "Maybe Mackenna's hair has made him realise he'll never get anyone as good as you."

Blowing out a breath, I shook my head and put my hand on the door handle. "I doubt it. Like you said, he's evidently not changed that much."

Alannah gave my forearm a squeeze. "Don't make it easy for him, if that's what he wants."

With a small smile I nodded my head and got out of the car, hoping that my heartrate slowed down in the few steps it took to reach him. I didn't want him to know that I was hopeful nor how much he affected me just by leaning against the wall to my house.

"Hey," I said, reaching into the side pocket of my backpack for my keys. "What are you doing here?"

Adam shifted his feet and looked over my shoulder to where Alannah was slowly moving away from the curb, her eyes firmly on us both.

"She should watch the road, not us," he ground out.

"Yeah well, she's a bit protective of me." I pushed my key in the lock and turned to Adam. "Do you want to come in?"

I inhaled as quietly as I could, trying to steady the adrenalin rushing around my body and the feeling of hope that had lifted my heart.

"No... yeah... fuck I don't know."

Pushing the door open, I took another breath to calm myself. Should I just shut the door on him? He evidently had no clue why he'd come to see me, which meant it definitely wasn't to get back together. Alannah was right though; did I want to be with him while his dad was around?

"Listen, Adam." I sighed wearily. "If you've come here to tell me that you're with Mackenna again, then don't worry about it. It was pretty obvious when she was sucking your face in the dining room at lunchtime yesterday. Seeing you do that kind of reminded me why we probably shouldn't have got together in the first place."

Adam's breath hitched and his gaze became wide-eyed and a little desolate.

"Don't fucking say that," he ground out, with a slow shake of his head. "We were fucking good together."

"Yeah, Adam, for all of five minutes."

Sucking back the tears that were threatening to fall, I swallowed back the words I really wanted to say and replaced them with those that would protect me.

"We were never going to work anyway. It would have ended up being too painful. All I ask is that we try and stay friends and you don't rub my nose in it when you're with other girls."

While Adam stared at me silently, my hand went to my wrist and rubbed slow circles around the bumpy skin. My fingertips soothed and cooled both the skin and my pain. This wasn't what I wanted, or what I'd expected when I saw him waiting for me.

"I just don't know what to do, Sarah."

Bright blue eyes considered me carefully, so beautiful and clear that they made me want to groan through the wrenching pain they created in my heart.

"I'm trying to do the right thing, but it's fucking gutting me. Not being with you is so hard. Not being able to touch you every day. It's not like anything I've ever felt before; it physically hurts, Sarah."

Dropping my bag to the floor, my body sagged. The emotion I'd been trying to hold back sprung forward as Adam closed his eyes and took a long, deep breath.

"I just don't know what to do." He reached out his hand and lightly ran his fingers down my arm. "I miss you so fucking much, but..."

"But what Adam?" Swallowing, I looked him directly in the eye. "Tell me."

He trapped his bottom lip between his teeth and exhaled slowly, as soft eyes studied me. Finally, he shook his head and closed off his beautiful pools of blue.

"But I don't want to believe my dad could do that to you."

A coldness swept across my body, creeping into my bones and

seeping through to the blood pumping through my veins as his words sank in.

"You don't want to believe, or you don't believe?" I asked, my voice quiet and hesitant.

His silence that lasted for far too long, told me everything.

"I think you should go," I said clearing my throat. "I don't even think we can be friends."

"Sarah, no," he cried, reaching for me. "No please I can't be without you in any—"

"No," I spat back, straightening my spine. "I can't, Adam. If you don't believe me, I can't."

"Sarah—"

"Please just go." Tears trailed down my cheeks, my sorrow at losing him, losing his trust and belief, punched into my stomach.

Adam drew in a shaky breath and took a step back, his eyes constantly on me. He looked full of despair and pain, but he wasn't my problem to fix any longer; and I wasn't his.

"I'm so sorry." His chest heaved and he raised a shaky hand to cup my chin, I smacked it away adding more pain to his eyes.

When I pulled back, I heard him inhale sharply before walking backwards down the driveway, back to his car. He never once took his eyes from me until he was in his car and driving away.

Some sort of dam was holding back my sobs, my cries of sorrow and my desire to shout for him to come back. It was a barrier that I knew would fall down eventually and when it did, I knew it was going to be agonising.

As I watched Adam's car disappear around the corner, I pulled back from the doorway and was about to close it on the darkening sky when something, or someone caught my eye across the road. There was someone sitting in a car watching me, I was sure of it. I couldn't see them properly as they were hidden in a baseball cap with a scarf around their mouth, but their stare was definitely in my direction. They didn't even turn away to hide the fact that they'd been caught. With clammy hands I slipped my phone from my pocket and glanced at it. I wondered whether to call Adam and ask him to come back. My mum would be on her way home soon, but he was only a couple of minutes away. Without thinking anymore of it, I pressed the screen, but as I scrolled through to his number, the car with the stranger started up and sped away.

I stepped out of the door and watched as it raced up the street, realising I should have got the registration number but didn't. As it screeched around the corner, I felt the unease continue to creep up my spine, wondering, but thinking I knew, who it was who was watching me.

15

ADAM

When I drove away from Sarah, my chest felt like it was in a vice. I was being crushed from the inside and every inch of my skin felt hot and raw, like I needed to rip it off.

My dirty skin that defined who I was, that held DNA which tainted me.

When I got to the crossroads to turn for home, I turned the wheel at the last minute and did a wide turn in the opposite direction. I knew I shouldn't, that it was the wrong thing to do, but I had to speak to my dad. The weirdest sensation had come over me that I needed to talk to him, to someone who knew Sarah.

I couldn't explain it, but my stomach churned with a mixture of excitement and fear. Thirteen years of missing him didn't just go away, despite the evil things he might have done. It should. I should have been disgusted by him, but for as much as the sight of him made me want to scream and punch him, it also soothed my soul. Seeing him I felt safe after all the years of anger and pain.

Words and thoughts jumbled and span in my head, I swerved

into the car park of the gym, needing some time to think. I needed to process how I was feeling and, if I was being honest, come up with a reason to justify those feelings. Groaning I rested my head against the steering wheel.

"Fuck, fuck, fuck."

I banged my head with each curse, the desire to punch something overwhelming—maybe I was growing up though, because I knew it wouldn't help. The only thing that would was the nagging voice telling me that talking to my dad would.

Sighing I lifted my head and started the ignition, before speeding off to his apartment.

When I got there, I tentatively knocked on the door after having taken about five minutes to pluck up the courage. I heard footsteps on the other side and eventually the lock clicked and there was my dad standing in front of me. His cheek was still bruised but no longer swollen, and there was a yellowish tinge around his eye. He looked like he was about to go out as he had on a jacket and trainers.

"Sorry, is it a bad time?"

"No." He didn't look surprised to see me and there was a definite smirk at his lips.

Instantly I wished I'd not listened to that fucking stupid voice in my head and not gone to visit him.

"You don't seem surprised to see me."

He shrugged. "You're my son, I knew you'd be curious. Plus, no matter what you think you know about me, you've missed me. Like I've missed you."

I let my head drop backwards and exhaled, blowing away all my misgivings and worry, if only for a short time.

"Can I come in?" I finally asked, lowering my gaze back to him.

He didn't answer but stood to one side and patted my back as I walked through to what I remembered was the lounge. There were some shopping bags on the sofa, all from the shopping centre – the sight of which made me to think of Sarah finding my little sister. My heart clenched and my stomach rolled as the image of her once more invaded my thoughts.

"You been shopping?" The question was completely fucking pointless, of course he had.

"Yeah," Dad replied and picked up the bags, almost dropping a Foot Locker one. "I needed a few things. Oh, and I got you something."

"Me?"

He nodded and passed me a bag that I recognised was from the Manchester United shop. My heart sank – I had never supported United. I'd always been a City fan.

"It should fit."

I pulled out the top to see it had Hudson on the back and a number 3. I held it up in front of me and could see at a glance it was too big. That fact and that it had the wrong number and was the wrong fucking colour only drove home how little he actually knew about me.

"Oh shit," Dad groaned out loud. "It's too big isn't it?"

I was quite muscular for my age, but I was toned and only just eighteen, and was obviously not large like the size of the shirt.

"Yeah I think so. Thanks though, maybe I'll grow into it."

And maybe I'll use it to clean my car I thought as I smiled at him, even though it hurt my cheeks to do it.

Dad shook his head and held his hand out. "No, give it to me and I'll sort it out. I'll get you a smaller one."

"Honestly, it's fine." I had no idea why I was arguing with him, there was no way I would put a red shirt on my back.

Before I had a chance to think any more about it, the shirt and the bag were ripped from my hands.

"Honestly, Adam, I'll sort it."

He shoved the shirt back into the carrier and threw it and all the others behind the armchair.

"You want a drink?" he asked, turning to me.

I hesitated, not knowing what to answer. I didn't even know if I wanted to be there.

He must have recognised my hesitation because he flopped down onto an armchair. "I'll put the kettle on in a minute. Tell me how you've been."

"Pretty shit," I replied.

Dad nodded slowly but remained silent as I watched him, trying to pick out something in his features that mirrored mine, but apart from the colour of our hair, I was all my mum.

As I watched him carefully, sitting relaxed in his smart dark blue jeans and pale green jumper, I realised we didn't even have the same mannerisms. Where Dad's fingers were steepled under his chin, mine were entwined, my thumbs flicking against each other. His legs were casually crossed at the ankles, while mine bobbed up and down nervously. I'd bet everything I owned that he was a fucking United fan too.

As the moments of silence got longer and longer, the more the pressure inside of me grew and the more I needed to talk about Sarah, which in itself was totally fucked up.

I wanted to talk about my ex-girlfriend to my dad, the man who'd stolen so much from her.

"Something has upset you. What is it?" Dad finally asked, his question surprising me, seeing as it was fucking obvious.

"Well, we're not exactly in an ideal situation, are we?"

"I suppose not," he mused, rubbing at the stubble on his chin. "Is she giving you trouble about me being here? What's she said?"

I hesitated to reply, guilt momentarily supplanting the need I had to talk to him about Sarah.

"She hasn't said much," I half lied. "I ended it."

"Why?"

My eyes widened as I reared back in the armchair. "Why do you think?"

"You're jealous that I've been in a relationship with her?" he said. He rubbed a hand down his neatly trimmed stubble as his eyes narrowed thoughtfully.

"A *relationship*?" I pushed the word through the dryness clogging my throat.

"Yes, Adam," he said, causing me to swallow hard. "Because that's what it was."

He gave me a no-nonsense stare. A glare which if he'd been my dad for the last thirteen years may well have scared me.

"Is that why you ended it with her? I know she's been spouting these hideous lies about me, but it must be hard for you knowing I was the one she cared about first."

The need to vomit would be imminent if he didn't shut the fuck up. My stomach swirled around like an empty tumble dryer and a sickly feeling travelled upwards towards my throat.

"This was a bad idea," I muttered.

"I'm sorry, Adam. I shouldn't have said anything, ignore me and let's change the subject. Tell me about school."

I should have got up and walked out, but I didn't. Instead, I tried to forget why nausea was rolling around my guts and stayed to talk. The next two hours were difficult for me, listening while he talked and drank a bottle of some poncey Italian lager. During that time I learned about the fact that he loved drawing with charcoals. He told me all about his life in Kent, carefully omitting anything about Sarah. And, just like I'd suspected, he told me he was a United fan. He shared a lot, until he finally looked at his watch.

"Listen, I'm sorry, Adam, I have somewhere I have to be."

"Oh right. Sorry I didn't mean to stay so long."

"It's fine, it's just something I can't get out of."

"Do you need a lift?" I offered.

Dad shook his head. "I can walk. It's not far. I should really think about getting a car soon."

"Okay, if you're sure I'll go." Standing, I felt a little relieved he didn't want a lift, because while listening to him had been great, I realised I was ready to be away from his company. I was starting to feel claustrophobic after all of those years apart.

"It was good to catch up." He looked up and smiled before getting to his feet. "Come back any time."

He moved to the door, so I followed behind, but hesitated when I reached him. I wasn't sure what to do, hug him, shake his hand or do one of those shitty chin dips that men who had no conversation did? Dad took the decision from me by slapping a hand against my back and manoeuvring me into the hallway where he reached around me to open the door.

"Call me soon," he said as I walked over the threshold. "We can arrange to do something.'

"Yeah, okay."

Part of me was ecstatic that he wanted to spend time with me, but another part felt like shit that in some way I was betraying Sarah.

Dad waved me off, but when I turned around at the top of the stairs, he'd already gone inside and closed the door.

For a while I sat in my car the engine ticking over and thought about what he'd suggested. I realised I did actually want to see him again; we just needed to take things slowly. With my anxiety slightly abated and the five-year-old in me feeling excited, I drove away thinking, as always about Sarah. She was constantly in my head and tonight was no exception. Just because I wasn't with her any longer didn't mean I didn't care. I still wanted her to be happy and safe, so as I did most nights, I headed back in the direction of her house, just to check on her, because I never settled until I knew she was safe inside.

16

SARAH

To say I hated being in the sickly warm hall, talking to a bunch of strangers was an understatement. There had to be some way I could escape and leave the group therapy session behind.

"Are you hating this too?" a voice whispered in my ear.

I turned quickly and almost smashed my nose against the face next to mine.

"Oh God, sorry."

"No problem." The dark-haired boy laughed quietly. "I shouldn't have been so close. "I'm Jack by the way."

He held his hand out, so I took it and gave it a quick shake.

"Sarah."

"Who made you come; parents, teachers, your therapist?"

I smiled. "My mum and Eleanor; she *is* my therapist." I nodded towards Eleanor who was listening intently to a girl with an auburn coloured pixie haircut, as she spoke about the death of her twin brother in a drowning accident. It was tragic and heart breaking, and

I didn't want to listen to any more stories of despair. I had my own to deal with.

He pointed to the itinerary. "We're scheduled a break in five minutes. I'm sure we could sneak off early," Jack whispered, tearing my gaze away from the girl crying on Eleanor's shoulder.

I thought about it for a second and then nodded. "Okay, let's go."

We quietly got up from our seats and tiptoed away, and as the door to the hall clicked shut behind us, we both heaved a sigh of relief.

"As much as I feel bad for everyone," Jack said. "Listening to their problems is really depressing don't you think? I'm trying to deal with my own stuff."

I nodded and smiled, quickly taking in his appearance. Dark hair fell into brown, mischief filled eyes.

"My mum and Eleanor told me it'd be good for me, to share what happened but I'm dreading my turn. And as for the thought of role playing." I shuddered and glanced at Jack to see understanding on his face.

"God no." He grimaced and paused to look over his shoulder. "Do you fancy a coffee or something?"

When I didn't answer, he laughed nervously.

"Shit, I'm not normally that pretentious. I expect you're used to lads asking to take you to the pub, or for pizza or something."

I shook my head and gave him what I hoped was a gentle smile. "There's nothing wrong with coffee."

When he didn't reply, but stared at me, I looked down at my feet, unsure what else to say.

"There's a Costa around the corner," he rushed out a little breathlessly. "How about we go there? Maybe we could forget the time." He nudged me, and I couldn't help but smile.

I should probably have been more cautious or felt more nervous about spending time with a boy I barely knew, but he had a kind face and nothing about Jack worried or scared me. After all we'd be in a busy coffee shop with plenty of other people around.

"Okay," I said. "Sounds good to me."

Only ten minutes later we were sitting down at a table and I was blowing on the hot black coffee in a huge mug. "I'll be hyper by the time I've drunk all of this caffeine," I said raising my eyebrows. "I thought you were going to get me a regular."

Jack shrugged and grinned around the cream on top of his hot chocolate. "It only seems big because your hands are so tiny."

Instantly my mind went to dirtier things as I remembered me saying the same to Adam one night when I had his dick in my hand. We'd been joking around and he'd been boasting how well-endowed he was and that had been my retort. I sighed as I remembered the tickling session that he'd landed on me as payback. Happy times when I felt as though my life was beginning again.

"You look really sad, you know that," Jack said and kicked at my foot with his under the table. "Want to talk about it? I won't make you role play, if that helps."

I just about managed a smile as I pushed my mug to one side, waiting for it to cool down. "My dad was killed in an armed robbery. He was a policeman."

Jack's hand instinctively reached for mine and gave it a quick squeeze before he snatched it back and wrapped it around his mug.

"Shit, I'm sorry. I know we've all come to talk about grief, but to lose your dad and in such an awful way. Fuck."

"There isn't really any nice way to lose someone is there." I shrugged and leaned forward with my arms crossed in front of me on the table. "What about you. Why are you here at Eleanor's session?"

"I lost my Grandma about six months ago, and my mum and dad seem to think I'm not accepting it. We were really close and well, she's the first person I've ever lost, so it's been pretty hard going."

"Why don't your parents think you're accepting it?" I asked.

"Probably because I've been bunking off school and generally being a pain in their arses ever since," Jack replied with a shrug. "I've always been the good kid you see; it was always my older brother Nathan that gave them trouble. Nothing serious, you know the stuff, drinking and smoking, staying out late. Now they're worried I'm going off the rails, just as Nathan has pulled himself together and got a decent job."

I studied his face and watched as the pulse in his temple sped up.

"*Are* you struggling to accept it?" I asked.

Jack tilted his head to one side and grinned. "Are you therapying me?"

"God no," I gasped. "I just know how hard it can be to believe that the person you love is never coming back."

He ran his finger through the cream around the edge of his mug and then licked it away before looking up at me.

"I used to stay with her every summer for three weeks. Me and Nathan, but he stopped going when he was about fifteen, so I've been going on my own for the last six years. Even when my mates wanted to go away on holiday last year, I made sure I went to Gran's as well. She was always there for me. You know everyone falls out with their parents from time to time, so she was always the one who helped me to see things from their point of view, or even my point of view a lot of the time. She was brilliant." He looked wistfully out of the window. "I suppose me bunking off is a big fuck off to the world for taking her away from me. She'd go mad though and more than likely give me a kick up the arse for doing it."

"Well we all do things we probably shouldn't when we're grieving." I shuddered as I thought about how I'd trusted Mr Mills and even though I'd blamed my mum for working all the time, even I could now see that I'd pushed her away too.

"Anyway," Jack said brightly. "Tell me about yourself. Are you in sixth form as well?"

"Yeah." I nodded and risked a sip of my coffee. "Maddison High. I only started there a short time ago. We moved from Kent."

"Ooh." He grimaced. "Being the newbie is never easy, especially in the final year. I thought that wasn't a local accent; far too posh for around here."

I rolled my eyes. "Hardly."

"Well you don't sound Manc, that's for sure," he said with a laugh. "How's it going for you? Have you made any new friends?"

My throat went dry as I thought of Adam and the emptiness came back, creeping up on me once again when I thought I might get through a few hours without thinking about him.

"A couple of girls, they're really nice."

"Boys?" Jack eyed me over the rim of his mug, his tone edged with something more than inquisitiveness.

I cleared my throat and shook my head. "Nope, no boys."

"Good to know," he replied wiping his mouth with the back of his hand. "Very good to know."

Jack and I stayed and had another drink, until it actually *was* too late to go back to the group session. I knew my mum would be disappointed when I told her, but she'd also said it was my decision. Her and Eleanor had made it very clear though that they thought I should attend, but at least I'd given it a try and knew it definitely wasn't for me.

"I'll text you about going for a drink," Jack said, tapping the screen of his phone. "And I won't take no for an answer."

I'd told him that I wasn't interested in anything other than friends, but I had the feeling he had the confidence of most eighteen-year-old boys and was convinced he'd eventually persuade me otherwise.

"I'll be happy to go for a drink with you, Jack, so long as you remember that's all it is."

He gave me a grin and then leaned in for a hug. I wasn't expecting it and stiffened a little as his arm went around my shoulders. It wasn't that he scared me, but his touch was unfamiliar; it wasn't Adam.

"Right, I'd better go, my dad will be outside the centre in five minutes."

"I hope you don't get in too much trouble for not staying in the session," I called as he started to jog away.

Still moving he turned to face me and held up a hand. "It'll be fine. I tried it and that's the main thing. Thanks for the chat and I'll speak to you soon."

He then turned and ran off in the direction of the centre. With a sigh I glanced at the time on my phone, glad to see it was only ten minutes until the bus that went closest to my house came into the bus station. I'd persuaded Mum that I'd be fine getting the bus home. She'd been desperate to have her hair done for weeks and this afternoon had been the only appointment she could get, so I'd been insistent. I was definitely nervous, particularly since spotting the car across the road on the day Adam had been to the house. At the same time, I didn't want to live my life in fear any longer. Mum had called the police, but their response had been limited, except maybe drive past the house from time to time. I guessed they had better things to do as far as they were concerned.

The fear of bumping into Mr Mills while I was alone was definitely at the forefront of my mind. I knew how manipulative he was and if he found me when I was alone, who knew what he might do. I was still convinced I was being followed the day I'd gone to the shop and had needed to call Adam, but he'd been just as convinced there had been no one around.

Maybe I was imagining things and my paranoia was merely spiking since Adam's dad had come into town.

Adam's dad – I couldn't believe I had to use both words together to describe the man who'd raped me. It really didn't seem real and if I hadn't seen it first-hand how desperate Adam had been to see his dad, to find him, after thirteen years apart, I might have thought it all to be one big set up – Adam making me fall for him, knowing his dad would soon be back to haunt me.

Sighing heavily as thoughts of Adam invaded my head, yet again, I glanced up and down the road before darting across it, reaching the other side just as a man on a scooter whizzed past.

"You really should be careful, Sarah."

The voice sent a stream of iced fear through my veins. I'd conjured up my greatest nightmare.

"Mr Mills."

The words tumbled from my mouth on a heavy tremoring

breath. He smiled at me, making my body rigid, the words of my song rang out in my head as my hand went to my wrist.

You are my sunshine

My only sunshine

"I think we know each other well enough for you to call me Joshua, don't you?"

A quiet whimper gurgled at the back of my throat as Mr Mills smiled at me and took a step closer. We were in the town square with shops bordering it as people shouldered past us going about their normal day to day activities. I wanted to grab one of them and tell them I was scared. I wanted to yell that the man standing beside me was a danger, but I was mute and paralysed.

"Or what about Josh?" he asked. "Yeah, I like that. Call me Josh."

When he lifted a hand, I shrank back, and another pained sound emitted from me.

"I'm not going to hurt you. I've never hurt you."

His ridiculous words were like a shock to my system, electro-cuting me into moving. I took a step back and shook my head.

"You raped me," I hissed. "You made me believe I was safe with you and then you forced yourself on me."

Mr Mills glanced around before leaning the top half of his body closer to mine. "Depends how you look at it. You came into my art room in your short little skirt and tight top and then laughed and joked with me. You wanted me, Sarah, don't pretend you didn't."

I shook my head vigorously, taking a step back. "No. No I didn't. I just needed someone to talk to and I certainly wasn't dressed inappro-priately. You were my teacher. You were supposed to take care of me."

"And I did."

I felt the vomit rise in my throat as his words embedded themselves into my brain.

And I did.

Turning quickly, I retched and vomited all over the pale grey stone of the town square. The two large mugs of coffee I'd had with Jack came back up, the acid taste burning my throat as I clutched at my stomach. Tears seeped from the corners of my eyes as I heaved twice before breathing heavily through a sob.

"Are you okay, love."

I looked to my side to see an elderly lady dressed in a navy-blue coat, staring at me with sympathy. I nodded my head with a hand still resting over the top of my jacket and oversized jumper.

"Yes, thank you. I think it's something I ate."

"You need me to call someone for you?" She held up an old-style flip phone.

"Honestly I'm fine, thank you."

"Okay, love as long as you're sure." She gave me a reassuring smile and moved away.

I remembered then why I'd been sick, and I wanted to call her back, ask her to help me, but when I looked up there was no sign of Mr Mills. I looked around the square, my eyes searching through the crowds, but I couldn't see him. I hadn't even registered what he'd been wearing, he could have been standing in a dark corner watching me now for all I knew.

With a shaking hand I reached inside my pocket and pulled out my phone. There was only one person I wanted to be with. I needed Adam to hold me and tell me that I was safe. The feel of his arms wrapped around me were the only things I could envisage comforting me.

Tapping the number on my phone I held my breath until after three rings it was answered.

"Hey, Sarah."

"Alannah," I said on a sob. "I really need you; can you come and get me please?"

17

ADAM

"You ready for this?" Ellis asked, kicking the ball to my feet. "Because you look like shit to be honest."

I rolled my eyes at him and kicked the ball back with force.

Admittedly thinking about what to do about my dad and Sarah had been keeping me awake at night, but I knew whichever route I chose it was going to hurt someone – fuck, it was going to hurt Sarah. I had a feeling that if I chose not to have contact with my dad, he might actually get over it pretty quickly, yet I still felt the need to see him. My want to see him was overpowering my need to be with Sarah and I had trouble understanding it.

"You're not still pining for Sarah, are you?" Ellis asked.

"I've got a *load* of fucking shit going on in my life, Ellis. I'm hardly going to look like I've just been offered a first team place at City, am I?"

"I suppose not, but I thought at least you'd be happy your dad is back in your life. Have you seen much of him?"

"We've spoken on the phone a couple of times and he said he's going to come today."

"You don't actually sound like you want him to." Ellis raised an eyebrow. "I thought you'd be fucking loving having him at a match."

"Yeah well, I kind of felt bad asking Roger not to."

He kicked the ball back to me, which I trapped with my foot and then immediately sent back to him.

"Really? You getting on better with him then?"

I shrugged. "He's not a bad bloke. At least he was okay about not coming, unlike my mum who did her usual dramatics. Apparently, I'm a horrible boy for picking the man who abandoned me over the man who takes care of me."

"Never mind the fact he abandoned you, what about the stuff he was supposed to have done to Sarah? How do you feel about that?"

Ellis stooped to pick up the ball and tucked it under his arm, watching me carefully. He knew me better than anyone, so always seemed to know what was bothering me. His friendship had meant a lot over the years, particularly during my time with Eric. He hadn't know what the fucking bastard was doing to me, but he'd been a relief from the nightmare. He'd made me laugh when no one else could, his mum and dad had often invited me for tea or to sleep over a fair amount. I had a lot to thank him for. Him questioning me about my dad and Sarah though wasn't what I needed from him. If I talked about it, it would make it real, then I'd have to face up to the fact I was the son of a rapist. Currently I was more than happy to bury my head in the sand and think he was found not guilty, so that must be true.

I knew that wasn't fair to Sarah, but my eighteen-year-old brain didn't know how else to cope.

"I don't want to talk about it," I growled, looking around to check no one else was listening. "And don't mention it again. Sarah would go mad if she knew I'd told you."

"It's not like you're going out with her anymore," he replied, frowning. "Why do you give a fuck what she thinks? I'm surprised you've not told everyone in school. You normally would."

I shuddered inwardly at his words, because he was right, that *was* something I'd normally do. Sarah was different though. Sarah was the one person, apart from my sister, who I never wanted to hurt, which was fucking stupid considering that was exactly what I'd done.

"Doesn't mean I don't care about her," I snapped back. "Let's go, Mr Jameson is calling us all over."

Ellis looked over my shoulder, to where Mr Jameson had his arm in the air beckoning the team over, probably ready to start our pre-match drills.

"Just one thing," Ellis said as he drew level with me. "You've made a decision, so live with it. Okay?"

I turned my gaze to his and exhaled. "Okay. Now let's go and beat that shit other school."

We'd been playing for ten minutes when I finally spotted my dad in amongst the crowd of people stood around the halfway line. He was standing at the back, wearing a black baseball cap and black coat against the February wind. I could tell it was him by the way he stood, with his shoulders and back ramrod straight even with his hands stuffed into his neatly pressed dark jeans. As I ran into some space and called for the ball, I heard him shout my name, so quickly glanced over and gave him a wave. He waved back and then started to saunter down towards the goal line. The ball went out of play and I turned to watch where he was going, feeling some pride that he knew the goal was where I was headed. In almost slow motion I noticed Sarah a few feet away, in the direction he was walking.

My heart, thudding against my chest, dropped to my stomach when I realised that she was standing alone, right on the touchline where there was a gap in the spectators. As if sensing I was watching her, Sarah's head turned towards me and she offered me a small smile. I hadn't even considered she would turn up to watch, she hadn't before. Feeling a fucking host of butterflies in my stomach I smiled back.

She looked beautiful with her hair in a high ponytail, loose strands whispered around her face, but the minute the cheer girls started to chant while waiting for one of Ashworth High School's trainers to come on to a player who'd gone down, she glanced in their direction and spotted my dad. Instantly her smile dropped, and I could see from my spot on the pitch that her face had gone white as she lifted a shaky hand to her mouth. She really was petrified of him.

"Sarah," I called and jogged towards the sideline where she was standing.

Dad was still walking towards her, and when I looked over to him, to ask him to go back, I noticed that his eyes were firmly on her. My head spun back to Sarah, but when I looked, she wasn't there and all I saw through the crowd of people was the back of her head and the high ponytail swinging as she pushed through them and away from the pitch.

As the whistle went to restart the game, I heard Mr Jameson yelling at me to drop into space in midfield. My pulse was racing as the adrenalin rushed around my body waking up all my senses.

I wanted to go to Sarah.

I needed to get my head into the game.

I had to stop my dad.

"Hudson get in that space now," Mr Jameson shouted.

Running backwards I looked over my shoulder and heaved a sigh of relief to see Dad had stopped in the gap where Sarah had been and had his eyes firmly on the pitch. He clapped his hands together and leaned forward.

"Come on, Adam, show them how damn good you are."

Flashing him a smile, I turned back to face the play just in time to see Tyler shimmy past one of Ashworth's defenders and fizz the ball straight to my feet.

Despite playing well, we lost the game two nil and I had to admit it fucking stung. Ashworth were two places below us in the league and had been missing their first-choice striker, so we really should have beaten them. We peppered their goal with chance after chance, but their Keeper had a worldy of a game and saved everything.

Shaking the opposition's hands, I looked to where my dad had been standing, expecting to see him there, but it was an empty space. Quickly scanning the thinning crowd there was no sign of him, I couldn't even see his disappearing back. The dread I'd felt when I thought he'd been making his way over to Sarah spiked again.

He hadn't said he'd wait for me, and neither had we agreed we'd meet up after the match, but the fact that he wasn't on the sideline waiting for me had me shit scared. What if he'd gone after Sarah? I had no fucking clue how long he'd been gone. Once Sarah disappeared and I was sure Dad was staying, I'd got my concentration back on the game and had spotted him a couple of times early on, and then once at the beginning of the second half, but that was all. For all I knew he could have left and gone over to her house. Or what if she'd decided to go back into school and do some extra study... he might have followed her in there.

"Ad," Tyler yelled. "Mr Jameson wants us to go straight to gym."

He rolled his eyes because we all knew what that meant – the fucking bleep test. Mr Jameson always did it when we got beat. He reckoned anyone that passed it obviously hadn't worked hard enough on the pitch, so they then had to run around the school field four times. You couldn't even fail it on purpose either, the sneaky bastard just knew if you were faking and then you had to do six laps.

"Okay, I'll be there is a minute."

Tyler strolled off, puffing hard with his hands on his hips. He'd definitely been one player who'd tried hard to get us the win—he wouldn't be running around the pitch later. As I watched him go thoughts raced around my head on what I should do. I couldn't go and find Dad because all my stuff was in the changing room and Mr Jameson would probably catch me sneaking in. The best I could do would be to get the bleep test done and hold just enough back that I didn't look like I'd been slacking in the game.

As I ran from the pitch, Alannah came into view. She was walking along, chatting to Jessie Morgan, a girl in the cheer squad who had a crush on Tyler. Hoping that Alannah didn't tell me to piss off, I rushed over to her.

"Hey Alannah, can you do me a favour?" I asked.

"Oh, and hello to you too." She slapped her hands to her hips, and Jessie sniggered.

"Sorry, but I haven't got much time. Can you call Sarah for me and check she's okay?"

Alannah's face blanched as she glanced at Jessie and then back to me. "Why?"

I gave her wide eyes which hopefully said, *don't ask questions.* Thankfully, she understood, because she pulled her phone from the outside pocket of her bag and tapped at the screen.

Waiting for Sarah to answer, I held my breath, only letting it go when Alannah spoke.

"Hi, where are you? I thought we might go to TJ's... oh, okay... yep, will do... see you tomorrow."

With the call evidently over, Alannah looked up at me and licked her lips.

"She went home, she didn't feel well."

"Is she home now?" I asked, rubbing my hand across the back of my neck.

"She says she is. She said she's in her room watching a film."

I nodded at her hoping that Sarah wasn't lying. "Okay thanks."

"Should I go around there?" she asked.

I considered it for a second. "Yeah, it might be an idea."

Alannah nodded and jogged away leaving Jessie looking confused and me hoping that Sarah was telling the truth and she really was okay. One other fact was startling clear to me. I didn't trust my dad, and that made me feel sicker than the dreaded beep test ever would.

18

SARAH

Throwing my phone onto my bed, I wondered whether I should call Alannah back and agree to meet her at TJ's, Mum had nipped to the supermarket on the way home from work though, and I didn't want to have to ask Alannah to come and get me then have to drive back into town to go to TJ's. I knew she would, but it didn't seem fair, plus I wasn't in the mood.

Seeing Mr Mills had really shaken me, especially it being back in a school environment. Adam must have asked him to go, which pissed me off. Surely, he must have known how much it would upset me to see his dad there. Maybe he didn't know though, it was obvious he didn't believe me.

Frustration, fear and anger all buzzed around my head in equal measures. I slid off my bed, deciding that I'd start dinner for mum. I knew she hated supermarket shopping and making dinner would be the last thing she'd want to do when she walked through the door. Walking into the kitchen I flicked on the light, because although we were in the second week of February it still got dark quite early in the evening. With a sigh, I went to the fridge and pulled out a packet of minced beef and whatever else I needed to make chilli.

I took it all over to the counter next to the sink and set about preparing everything, when the calendar hanging from a hook on the wall caught my eye, making me groan. It was Valentine's day in three days and the card and stupid bloody teddy bear I'd bought for Adam would be staying put at the bottom of my wardrobe. I'd been in two minds whether to buy them in the first place. I'd been an idiot though and listened to the stupid pathetic girl inside of me; the one who thought he'd love the teddy bear dressed in a City kit with a number seven on its back.

"Oh, piss off," I griped at the picture of a woman tossing a pancake over the top of the days of February.

After putting the beef into a large pan and starting to fry it in oil, I ran the cold tap and began to wash the excess dirt from the mush-rooms. I'd almost finished when movement in the garden caught my eye. It wasn't quite pitch-black outside, but too dark to see properly. I knew for definite there must have been something there because the security light came on.

My heart started to pound as I moved to the back of the kitchen and turned off the light and peered out from what I felt was a safe spot, away from the window. There was nothing out there that I could see, the garden was only small and just lawn with a shed tucked in one corner; there really wasn't even anywhere anyone could hide. I was seriously paranoid and was beginning to believe that Adam was right, and no one had been following me that day.

Tentatively, I went back to the window and pulled down the blind that we barely ever closed. We had no need, our garden backed onto another garden and we had a seven-foot wall all the way around it, although that hadn't stopped Adam scaling our garden gate. Trying not to think about whether anyone else could get over the six feet high gate, I still felt safer by closing off my view of the darkness outside.

After eventually calming down, I finished making the chilli and had it on a low heat when the doorbell rang. The shrill sound made me jump and almost drop the lid of the pan. Taking a deep breath, I peeked into the hall from around the door. Our door only had two thin panels of frosted glass in it, so I couldn't make out who was there. I decided to ignore it and hope whoever it was just went away. It was probably the Amazon man delivering something Mum had ordered online, but he'd leave it by the front door if he had to.

The bell went again but at the same time my phone buzzed on the kitchen table. I snatched it up and pressed at the screen, not wanting whoever was outside to hear it. When I read the text, I gave a massive sigh of relief.

Alannah: I'm outside, can you answer the door?

I didn't bother replying but ran to the door and flung it open.

"Oh my God," I said breathlessly. "I had no idea who it was."

Alannah frowned and stepped forward peering at my face. "Are you okay? What's going on, Adam asked me to call you?"

"You'd better come in."

She shook her head. "I can't I have to get home; Dad is taking me and Mum out for dinner. The TJ's thing was a ruse because Jessie Morgan was standing next to me."

"Adam asked you to come over?" I licked my dry lips as I waited for Alannah to answer.

"Yeah. He seemed really worried about you. What happened?"

"His dad was at the match earlier. He was coming towards me, so I just left. Adam saw it all."

"Shit," Alannah groaned. "No wonder he wanted me to call you. His dad didn't speak to you, did he?" Concern flashed across her face as she took hold of my hand.

When I shook my head, she visibly relaxed.

"If Adam was so worried, he shouldn't have invited him to come along," I muttered.

"I can't believe it. He's a total dick. I told you he was and now he's just proved it." Alannah's mouth thinned into a grimace as she folded her arms over her chest. "God, Sarah, you are so much better off without him."

I didn't argue with her, not because I necessarily agreed, but because I didn't have the energy.

"You should speak to the police," Alannah added. "Tell them he's harassing you."

"He didn't even speak to me, Alannah." I'd already told her that I'd seen him in town and what the police had said. She'd been amazed that they weren't willing to slap him in cuffs and arrest him straight away.

"If he comes near you again then call them straight away."

"I will. Now you go or you'll be late for dinner with your mum and dad."

She leaned in and gave me a quick hug. "Okay, I'll see you tomorrow at school. Now go inside and lock the door."

Smiling I gave her a salute and did as she said.

I hadn't even got back to the kitchen when the bell went again, and assuming it must be Alannah I pulled it open, only to be faced with Mr Mills.

"No," I gasped. "No, you can't be here."

"I'm only here to deliver a message," he said lifting his chin haughtily. "I just came to say I forgive you for lying. I forgi—"

"I didn't lie," I broke in. "You know I didn't lie."

"Like I said, I forgive you for lying, but I also need you to know that you ruined my fucking life." His tone was quiet and calm which made it all the more menacing as he leaned closer to me. "So, it's only fair I ruin yours. First thing I did was take Adam away from you, then it'll be your friends and maybe last of all that dance class you love giving so much."

"I'll call the police," I sobbed. "My mum will call the police."

"Oh God, I almost forgot about your mum. Maybe I'll take her away from you too."

I shook my head as I reached for my wrist. "No, you can't. I'm going to call the police right now."

"Try it, Sarah," he snarled. "And see what I'll do. I've got someone who will say I was at the park, sitting on a bench reading a book." He pulled a dog-eared paperback from his pocket and held it up to me. "And plenty of people saw me at Adam's match, so don't waste any more police time than you already have."

Another sob ripped from my lungs as Mr Mills sneered at me. He had someone to lie for him? There was someone who was willing to go along with his sick game?

"Actually, you tell the police," he said as he turned to leave. "Because when you're proved to be wrong, they'll just think your mental health is suffering again. That'll make it so much easier for me to ruin your life."

Tears and snot ran down my face as I silently watched him

calmly walk away, pulling his baseball cap further down on his head. His stride was long and confident, and I knew that my nightmare had started up once again.

19

ADAM

Since the match I'd tried to call Sarah and check she was okay, but each time my call had been dropped, which was a pretty good statement of how she currently felt about me. My dad on the other hand had called me a few times in the two days since then and had explained he'd had a call about a job during the second half, so had rushed off to meet the guy in the park as he was working close by. The job was in a garage, spraying cars again, but the owner had taken someone else on. It all sounded dodgy to me, who met someone in a park to talk about a fucking job?

In fact, the more I considered everything, the more I realised everything about my dad seemed dodgy. He had no job yet had bags of new clothes. He had a nice apartment and time on his hands, but still didn't make any real effort to see me. I was beginning to think I'd picked the wrong person to support.

With a sigh of frustration, I pushed my textbook away and leaned back in my chair to stare at the battered photograph of him which was lying on my desk. Leaning forward I snatched at it.

"Why the hell did you come back?" I hissed.

Staring down at the picture I recalled all the times I'd wished he *would* come back and rescue me. Now that he was here, all I wanted was for him to disappear and for me to get my life back. I wanted to be a teenager who enjoyed sex with his girlfriend whenever possible. I didn't want to be a teenager who worried for hours every night about whether I'd done the right thing by taking his side.

Sliding open my drawer, I threw the picture inside and noticed Sarah's notebook that I'd taken from TJ's. I thought about opening it, but now that I knew what all the notes, words and poems were about it felt wrong. The death of her dad was something she was still struggling with and those words were what had helped her get through. I decided I'd take it back to her, but first I needed to get her to speak to me. I had to get us back to being friends at least. I groaned and dropped my forehead to the desk. What the fuck was I thinking; get us back to being friends... and then give her the stolen notebook back? What a shit idea that was? All that would do would drive us further apart.

"Shit," I cursed and banged my head on the desk.

"Are you okay?" I turned to see Roger peering around the door. "I was calling you, but you obviously didn't hear."

"Just having a mild breakdown," I grunted, sitting up and twizzling around in my chair to face him.

"Can I come in?" he asked, hovering by the door.

I thought about it momentarily and then nodded. Things had been thawing between us the last few weeks, mainly because I'd stopped acting like a dick around him. Part of it was also because I'd begun to see that out of all the parents I'd had over the years, Roger was one of the better ones, my mum included. After all, Lori fucking adored him, and kids were usually right about things like that.

"You want to talk about it? Or I can get your mum because I assume it's about your dad and Sarah?"

"I'm worried about her," I replied without even questioning it. "She's not spoken to me in days."

"You finished your relationship with her. Isn't that sort of normal for teenage girls to do that to the boy who dumps them? What do you kids call it, ghosting?"

I let out a humourless laugh. "Most girls probably, but not Sarah. She's really different to most girls. We *were* speaking, but she saw Dad at the match the other day and since then she's kind of avoided me."

Roger pointed towards the bed, and when I nodded, he pushed a pair of jeans and a jumper away to make room for himself to sit down.

"I think you have to realise that was probably not your best idea."

When I opened my mouth to speak, he held up a hand.

"I get why you wanted your dad to go to the match, Adam, but maybe you should have told Sarah first. It would have been better than her being side-swiped by seeing him."

He had a point it would have been much more respectful to her.

"Shit, you're right." I dropped my head back and stared up at the ceiling. "I'm such a dickhead."

"No Adam, you're just a boy who hasn't always had the best influences in his life. If you've never been shown how to respect people, then how would you know."

"Yeah, well some of Mum's choices of partner have been less than stellar to say the least."

Roger raised his brows at me. I knew he must agree, but as always, he was loyal to a fault to my mum.

"Oh, come on, Roger, you know she's a crap judge of character." He scratched the tip of his nose and cleared his throat. "Okay, maybe you're the exception."

"Woah," he said on a laugh. "Are you actually admitting that you like me a little bit, Adam?"

I shrugged, not wanting to admit anything about him that in two days, or even two hours, might well change. I was still a dickhead at heart, it was only Sarah that had changed me and without her I had no reason to be decent.

"Have you tried to talk to her?" Roger asked, evidently realising he wasn't going to get a response on whether I liked him or not.

"No."

"Well it might be a good place to start. Tell her how you feel, how torn you are over wanting to be with her, but also wanting to have your dad around."

"I tried, but she can't get past it." I chewed on my lip. "Do you think I'm wrong for wanting him to be around?"

"That's not for me to say, Adam." He leaned forward, resting his forearms on his thighs. "I do think it must be hard for Sarah. The man... well he allegedly raped her."

"Do you think he did it?" I asked.

"Again, it doesn't matter what I think. All I'll say is she doesn't seem to me like a girl who would lie about something so serious. She's sweet and polite and Lori adores her. If, and it's a big if, she's got it all wrong, then she honestly doesn't believe it. Which makes me think that if they were in some sort of a relationship your dad still took advantage of a vulnerable young girl, and he did something she wasn't comfortable with, despite their status."

He was fucking right. Everything he said was right, and what made me feel like shit was that it wasn't any great genius theory. It was something I should have realised as her boyfriend, the one person who was supposed to support her. I should have known all of that, because even though we hadn't been together long, we had something special. In the grand scheme of things, if we'd been any other teenagers, if she'd been any other girl, we'd probably have lasted as long as the majority of other teenage romances. The problem was she wasn't just any other girl, she was someone who I didn't think I would ever be able to live without.

Thinking of her made my heart feel as though it was being squeezed inside my aching chest. When she wasn't around my eyes constantly searched for her, and when I found her my stomach turned sending a thousand fucking butterflies to take flight. She was the girl who I could see my future with. She was the girl who had cracked open the darkness around my heart and helped the light to break through. She was the girl I was in love with.

"Have you thought about how you'd feel if it was Lori in this situation," Roger said, his words dragging me into reality and causing my heart to miss a beat. "If a man who she'd said had raped her came back. How would you react?"

"I'd fucking kill him, whether he'd got off or not," I spat back. "There's no way I'd let him be around her." My stomach rolled at the thought and what my response meant.

"What if he said he hadn't done it, but Lori was adamant he had, who would you believe?"

I dropped my head and let out a moan.

"I've messed things up so badly, Roger."

"You didn't just want to believe your dad, Adam. If I know you, there's more to it, and if I know you it's because those damn demons in your head are pecking away at you."

He watched me with the grace of a man who had all his shit

199

together. A man who I should have respected more the last two years for facts other than he'd been my stepdad.

"But what if I'm like him? What if his DNA is so strong that I end up being the same sort of man? I've been a shit to practically everyone since I was nine years old. What sort of kid behaves like that?"

I drew in a shuddering breath and felt the pain of regret squeezing my lungs tight. The people I'd hurt with my arrogance and hatred weren't deserving of it, there was only one person who was, and who knew where he was or what he was doing with his life.

Roger leaned forward and placed a large hand on my knee, his gold wedding ring shining under the bright light of my desk lamp.

"Adam, you are not your dad. You're nothing like him, if you were, Lori wouldn't adore you and you wouldn't be tossing and turning every night worrying about all of this." He smiled when my mouth dropped open. "I check on you every night. You're restless and you talk in your sleep, when you actually get to sleep. A parent knows when their child isn't coping, but I've bided my time and waited until I knew you'd accept my help and advice."

My throat got scratchy. Not even my mum had ever said anything to make me think she cared about me. She said the words I love you, but never I care, or I'm worried about you. Roger was the only person who ever had.

I wanted to say I was sorry to him, to apologise for being the stepchild from hell, but the words were too big. I couldn't get them past my tongue, so I said nothing. I didn't even smile at him. Roger did though. He smiled as he stood up and came forward to place a hand on my shoulder.

"Adam, I think of you as my son as much as I think of Lori as my daughter. Please don't ever think you can't come to me, or that I won't listen, because I will. I'll always be there for you. Remember this though, you have to stop punishing yourself for the sins of your parents. Be the better person you want to be, but do it for yourself, not just for the girl you're falling in love with."

He gave my shoulder a squeeze and then moved towards the door.

"Dinner is ready when you are, come and eat with us and then get a good night's sleep. Tomorrow is the weekend, so it might be a good idea to think about things and then once you're sure speak to Sarah."

"Do you think I should wait until we're back at school on Monday?"

"I think you should wait until you know exactly what you believe is the truth. Then when you know that, consider what you want, because I don't think Sarah is the sort of girl who gives more than one chance. You don't want to squander that chance, do you?"

I shook my head as I gripped the arms of my chair and swallowed back the tears that were threatening to fall. Tears that I barely ever shed.

"Good," Roger said. "Now hurry up because if I have to listen to Lori break into a rendition of a Frozen medley once more, I might just leave home."

He laughed good-naturedly and went to join the family, humming 'Let it Go' as he walked down the stairs.

20

SARAH

"Are you nervous?" Alannah screeched down the line.

"No," I ground out. "Because it's not a date."

I rolled my eyes even though she couldn't see me. I knew I shouldn't have told her that Jack had asked me for a drink. At first, I'd said no; I didn't want to leave the house if I could help it. Going to school the last couple of days since Mr Mills had visited had been hard enough, especially as I hadn't even told Mum what had happened. It was stupid, I was aware of that. The consequences of me keeping secrets from her once before had almost been catastrophic, but this time I had a plan. At least I thought I did. I was going to try and get more evidence against the bastard who was terrorising me and then I'd go to the police. If I told my mum now, she'd insist we went to them immediately and he was right, I'd look like a liar and an idiot. Worse still, they might think I was a danger to myself again.

A stupid plan probably, but I had no idea how else to deal with it, other than bury my head in the sand and hope he got bored and went away.

Hearing him talk about Adam had been hard, it made my heart clench with longing for him. Which was another reason why I'd said no to Jack, I didn't want him to get the wrong idea. I would never think of him as more than anything than a friend, not while I still had feelings for Adam.

Despite my argument, Jack had been insistent and so I'd finally agreed to go out with him – just as friends. I hoped he really did understand that. He was pretty self-assured though - Adam would probably call him a cocky twat - and I was worried that he'd keep pursuing something more between us.

"It could be a date though," Alannah said pulling me back from my thoughts. "If it goes well."

"Alannah, it's not happening. I don't want to date anyone."

She sighed wearily. "Okay, but just keep an open mind. He may be the perfect person for you."

"But I'm *not* interested." I looked through the window and saw a red Corsa pull up and my heart started to beat wildly. "I've got to go, he's here."

"Oh my God," Alannah screeched, almost bursting my ear drum. "Text me regularly."

"Okay, bye."

I didn't bother waiting for her response but snatched up my phone and keys and rushed down the hall shouting a goodbye to Mum who was in her room.

"Wait," she called and appeared at the door. "You call me if you need anything, okay?"

I resisted the urge to run into her arms and beg her to keep me in them forever. If I didn't go Mr Mills would win, and I wasn't going to allow him to rule my life ever again.

"I won't be too late," I replied, my hand on the door handle.

"It's fine, just be safe."

Her eyes were troubled and wary, and I knew how hard it was for her. Me going out with Adam had been one thing, a boy she'd never met filled her with dread. "Are you sure I can't come and meet him, just speak to him?"

"No, Mum. I don't want him to know about what happened to me. I want to try and be normal." And I did, but it was like hiking up Everest. Every step was hard, and it was difficult to breathe, but I had to do it.

"Okay."

"I'll text you regularly."

Mum shook her head. "No, you're right you need to try and be normal. I'll text you every couple of hours and you just reply with a kiss if everything is okay."

I smiled, glad that she would be checking on me, but relieved I didn't have to explain to Jack why I was texting my mum every few minutes.

"See you later." I took a deep breath to calm my nerves and pulled the handle down to open the door. "Lock up after me."

"I will." She gave me an indulgent look and followed me to the door. "Have fun and I love you."

When I stepped out of the house, Jack was already out of his car and grinning at me. I had to admit he looked good in his ankle length trousers and smart shirt tucked in, with black leather loafers on his feet. He was dressed like lot of boys, with his hair cut into a fade and side parting, but I couldn't help but compare him to Adam. They had similar dress sense, but Jack wasn't as tall as Adam's six feet one and he certainly didn't have the same athletic body; not from what I could see anyway. I was positive I wouldn't be seeing him without clothes but was pretty sure he wouldn't have the ripped abs and defined v that Adam had.

"Hi," he said. "You look nice."

I looked down at the yellow ditzy print dress I was wearing with my black Dr Marten boots and black leather biker jacket. It had all meant to be friend casual, so I hadn't expected him to compliment me.

"Thank you, so do you."

He smiled. "So, I thought maybe we could go to The Brass Monkey. They don't really check for ID in there, as long as we don't get fall about drunk. I'll leave my car there and we can get a taxi home." He blushed and glanced at the ground before looking back up to me. "My mum gave me the money for it, she said it was only proper I pay as it was our first da-night out."

My heart plummeted at his almost slip up and I wondered if I should have agreed to go out with him.

"Jack, you know this isn't a date. We can only be friends." I scratched my brow wondering how on earth I could get out of this without hurting his feelings.

"Yeah I know," he replied, sounding resigned. "I did tell her that, but she's ever the optimist."

I took a breath to consider everything and when he playfully pouted, I couldn't help but smile.

"Okay, let's go."

***

Jack snorted as my face crumpled with disgust. We'd been in the bar for an hour or so, drinking, laughing and even dancing. I had to admit I was enjoying myself. I was feeling a lot drunker than I should have on a couple of vodka and cokes and the brandy that I'd bet Jack I could down in one.

"That's disgusting," I groaned as the amber liquid burned my throat as it went down.

"You're a wimp. Oh my God, your face."

Jack dropped his head back and laughed as I continued to gag.

"It's not funny. It's vile. I feel like I've swallowed the contents of the cigarette bucket from the beer garden." I stuck out my tongue and grimaced, which quickly morphed into a grin. "Oh God I love this song."

As 'Could be You' by Michael Calfan and Danny Dearden came on, I tried to sway to the beat, but only managed to stagger into the high table we were standing at.

"I think you need some water," Jack said, putting a stabilising hand on my elbow. "You're pretty far gone, Sarah."

He frowned and looked around, before grabbing a stool and dragging it to the table.

"Sit here and I'll go and get you some water."

"I need to pee first," I replied, giggling at how slurred my words were.

He chewed on his bottom lip. "Do you want me to come with you?"

"No," I cried, waving him off. "I'm not that bad. I'll be fine."

"Okay, I'll wait until you come back before I get you some water, I don't want us to lose this table."

The bar was filling up with all the pre-drinkers finally making it into town, because as Jack had said, it was a bar where your ID was rarely requested.

"I'll be back asap."

I flashed him a smile and giggled, pushing my way through the growing crowd towards the toilets. Even though I was stumbling a little and my head was started to spin, I felt good. I felt free and had pushed all the crap in my life to one side just to be a teenager.

Pushing through some double doors to the back hallway, I felt a hand on my shoulder. If I hadn't known who it was, I might have frozen and screamed, but I knew instinctively it was Adam. When I swung around to face him, it was obvious that he was as drunk as I was, if not more. His eyes were red-rimmed, and he was swaying and licking his lips as he looked at me.

"Who the hell is that?" he demanded. "Why the fuck are you with him?"

Letting out a long breath, I closed my eyes, but quickly opened them when I felt the floor tilt beneath me.

"Adam, please don't."

"Don't what?" he asked with a slur. "Spoil your date."

"It's not a date. He's a friend." I pointed at him but stumbled again before continuing. "We're just out as friends and anyway it's none of your business."

"Yes, it fucking is and why are you so drunk? Has he been spiking your drinks?"

"No," I cried and put a hand to my stomach. "I'm just a light-weight. Actually, I haven't eaten all day so that might be it."

Adam's eyes went dark as he leaned into my personal space.

"Why the hell not?"

I shrugged not wanting to say because I'm living on my nerves that your rapist dad is going to hurt me again. I should have said it, I should have told someone, but Adam was not that person.

"Anyway, like I said its none of your business."

Turning to walk away I wasn't surprised when his hand landed on my arm.

"It is my business." He gently pulled me back around to face him. "You're my business."

When he took a step closer, my pulse sped up. His familiar smell and touch were a heady mix with the alcohol running through both our veins. The concoction zapped my senses and startled my heart into action. It thudded hard and fast causing my chest to heave and Adam's eyes were firmly on it; his gaze turned on and excited.

"Is that all I am to you, Adam," I croaked out. "A pair of tits."

His eyes snapped back to mine. "No and don't be so fucking ridiculous. You know you're not. You know you're so much more; you're everything."

Without any chance to reconsider, or to prepare myself for the onslaught of feelings, his lips, soft and warm, crashed against mine.

My fingertips instantly tangled with his hair, while his hands went to my bum and pulled me closer. There was no space between us as his hard on rubbed against me but not in the place I wanted it the most. Anticipating my need, Adam lifted me up so that my legs were tight around his waist and he was able to stumble down the hall, his lips and tongue still demanding of me, he took us to a dark recess behind a pillar.

"Adam," I groaned feeling my clit pulsing and throbbing inside my dampened knickers.

"You *are* my business," he said against my mouth. "You're my business and my *everything*, remember that."

Desperate for him, I reached between us and started to undo his trousers.

"Are you sure?" he panted; his eyes locked on mine.

"Yes, positive," I replied and pulled his zip down.

Adam pulled out his rock hard dick, I pulled my knickers to one side and as 'Sweat' by David Guetta and Snoop Dogg pumped out in the bar behind us, Adam pushed inside of me.

"Fuck," he said against my mouth. "I've missed you so much."

He pulled back and thrust back into me so hard it pushed me up the wall. His lips sucked on my nipple, over the top of my dress, so hard that my mouth opened on a loud gasp. My fingers gripped his hair tighter and I yanked his head back and sucked on his neck until I got the tangy taste of blood in my mouth.

"Harder," I panted.

As the music got louder, Adam's pumps became harsher and faster keeping in time with the beat vibrating all around us. His hips punched in and out, and with each thrust I felt myself get closer to screaming out from the pleasure. The build was quick and intense and when Adam pulled the top of my dress to one side and yanked down my bra to take my nipple into his mouth again, I felt the waves of my orgasm start from my core and swell through my body like ripples in a pond. My clit throbbed in time with Adam's thrusts and the beat of the music until nothing else existed around us. I didn't care if people were watching or could hear my cries of his name; all I cared about was the hedonism of the moment and how it was making me come long and hard.

As I clenched my legs around Adam's waist, I felt his body go rigid and with one last, firm pump he groaned out against my skin.

"Oh, my fucking God," he cried, his fingers digging into my bum, clutching at it as if it was his lifeline.

The waves continued washing over me, making my skin tingle as I dropped my head to Adam's shoulder and breathed heavily. Soft lips kissed my neck and up to my jaw as the music changed and Launa's 'Thinkin'' started. As soon as the tune began to infiltrate my brain, I felt the heaviness of regret pushing down on me. I shouldn't have done that. He wasn't my boyfriend anymore, there was too much that needed to be resolved between us and having him again would only make it harder for me to move on.

Adam nibbled on my earlobe, and when I stiffened in his arms, he immediately pulled his head back to look at me. "Sarah?" His eyes were questioning, and his arms loosened around me and allowed my feet to drop to the floor.

"We shouldn't have," I whispered. my breath trembling. "We're not even together."

Adam's face hardened. "Are you with him?" he demanded. "Is he your new fucking boyfriend?"

"No, I told you, we're just friends. As if I'd do that with you if he was."

"So why are you pulling away from me? Don't do that." His voice was desolate, almost pleading.

"Because this is wrong. We're not together, and I can't be with you if he's around. If he's in your life. But I would never tell you that he shouldn't be. I don't think he should, but I won't be the person to make you choose."

"But you fucking are," he yelled and pulled away from me, tucking himself back into his trousers and fastening them up. "You won't be with me because he's here, so if that isn't making me choose then what the fuck is?"

I watched him carefully, as I readjusted my knickers and smoothed down my dress, not daring to reply. I had to stay silent and make it easier for both of us to go our separate ways. I needed to keep my thoughts to myself to avoid saying something I might regret. Finally, Adam looked up at me, his eyes narrowed and watchful.

"Just go back to him but remember I'm the one who he'll smell on you when he goes down on you later. It'll be my cum that's dried around your pussy and legs when he decides he wants to fuck you. It'll be me you'll be thinking of when he pushes inside of you."

I couldn't stop my hand as it reached up and slapped his face, the noise echoing around us in the dark corner we were ensconced in.

"You're a bastard," I hissed. "I have no idea why I..."

With a gasp I stopped myself from saying anything else, because I'd been about to say something that I knew I'd regret. Something that Adam would never let go.

"Oh, just go," he snarled turning away from me. "Go back to your little boyfriend."

With my stomach turning over, and Adam's cum on the inside of my thighs, I did just that. I stumbled to the ladies' bathroom and drunkenly cried because the boy I loved had no idea. He didn't know that all I wanted to do was go after him and ask him to forgive me and beg him to protect me from the man he called Dad.

21

ADAM

When I walked back into the bar, the first sight to meet me was fucking Mackenna. She was talking to Kirk, who looked bored as shit that she was there. When I registered what she was wearing, I sucked in a breath. She could have been Sarah, with a cheap imitation of Dr Marten boots, a pair of baggy jeans and a crop top that just about covered her tits. The top was all Mackenna though, because there was no way Sarah would wear anything like that.

Thoughts of her, and what we'd just done, made my lungs expand painfully. If I closed my eyes I knew I'd be able to summon up that feeling of being inside her. It was like nothing I'd ever experienced before. Nothing reached the high that Sarah gave me when her pussy tightened around my dick and she gripped my hair to the point of pain.

"Adam," Mackenna called as she spotted me and dragged me from some amazing thoughts. "Kirk said you'd gone."

"I thought you had," Kirk muttered looking at her sideways. "You've been ages."

"Yeah well I needed a long piss. What do you want, Mackenna?" I pushed past her, elbowing my way into a space by the shelf where my bottle of beer still stood.

"I came over to see you. Charlie, Libby and Caitlin are over there. I thought maybe you'd all like to sit with us."

Ignoring her I turned to Kirk. "Where's Tyler and Ellis?"

He nodded towards the bar. As I looked over, I saw the pretty boy that Sarah was with. He was scrolling through his phone, sending quick glances to the back of the bar where the toilets were. I sniggered to myself, wondering whether I should just go over there and tell him I'd just shagged his girlfriend against the wall, and it had been one of the best fucks of my life.

"What's so funny?" Kirk asked.

"Nothing." I turned back to Mackenna. "Listen, I told you I don't want you around me, so I'm asking you nicely, please just fuck off."

Her face dropped for a split second but was soon eased back into the sickly-sweet smile that *she* thought was sexy.

"Don't be like that."

I let out a frustrated breath. "Mackenna, just because you've started to dress like her and," I flicked at the long tresses of her hair, "you've dyed your hair the same colour, it doesn't mean I'll forget about her and attach myself to you instead. You are not and never will be anything like her, so once again, I repeat, fuck off."

Mackenna's nostrils flared as she curled her hands into fists at her side. I was pretty sure she was about to plant one on me, but something over my shoulder caught her eye. Her concentration moved away from me and her back straightened.

I didn't need to look to know it was Sarah. Mackenna's reaction told me, but I could sense she was there anyway. Any time she

214

entered a room, I could practically taste her. We were linked more than I would have ever thought possible.

Not moving my gaze, I waited until Sarah appeared in my eyeline and watched as she swayed towards the little dick waiting for her. When she got to the table, he pulled out a stool for her and then leaned in to say something close to her ear. The music wasn't so loud that he needed to, so in my eyes he'd been promoted from dick to cunt.

"You see that?" Kirk asked.

"Yeah."

I kept my eyes on them and inhaled sharply when Sarah almost fell off the stool. She quickly righted herself but the lad, who was walking a close line to getting a pasting, grabbed her hand and held on tight. He said something else and when Sarah nodded, he moved away to the bar.

"Adam," Mackenna whined. "She's obviously moved on."

"Mackenna," Kirk growled. "Do yourself a favour and go back to your friends, because I won't be responsible for what he does to you at school on Monday if you don't."

I had no idea what she or Kirk did because my gaze was still on Sarah, whose head was now lolling like her neck was boneless. When she put out her hand to rest it on the table and missed, I knew I'd seen enough. She hadn't seemed that drunk when I'd had her against the wall, but then the adrenalin had taken over, and now that buzz had died down that of the alcohol was taking over – I knew because I felt the same way.

Marching towards her, I heard Kirk mutter an 'oh fuck' close behind me but ignored his worries and continued to Sarah.

"You need to go home," I breathed against her ear, placing one hand under her armpit and the other over the top of her hand.

She shook her head. "No. You can't tell me what to do."

She sounded like a petulant kid, just like Lori when she was told to do something she didn't want to do.

"Sarah, I'm telling you, as a friend, you've had enough."

"We're not even friends anymore." Her voice broke and I was sure I saw tears pooling against her lashes. She quickly turned away and sniffed loudly.

"I'm going to call a taxi and I'm going to take you home."

As I reached for my phone, her little boyfriend appeared with a pint of water.

"Too fucking little too late." I scowled at him and pointedly looked at the glass.

"What's going on? Sarah, do you know these two?" He placed the water in front of her and then moved to her side, stooping down to look into her eyes which were lowered to the floor. "I need you to drink some water."

"No," she slurred. "I need Alannah to come. I need to go home."

"If you go home like that your mum will bollock you," I said moving in on her other side. "Drink the water that *he* should have given you earlier and I'll call a taxi. You can come back to my house for a while."

Her head shot up and her eyes went wide. "No, I'm not coming to *your* house."

"What the fuck did you give her?" I demanded, now feeling totally sober.

"She's had four drinks, that's all, but what the fuck does it have to do with you?"

Kirk stepped forward and placed a hand on the lad's shoulder. "Listen mate, I wouldn't if I was you. Adam is her boyfriend and he's likely to fucking punch you if you carry on."

"Boyfriend?" he asked at the same time that Sarah slurred, 'No he isn't'.

"Temporary ex-boyfriend," I replied hitting a number on my phone. "But all you need to know is that she's leaving."

Lifting the phone to my ear, I watched him carefully as he whispered something to Sarah who shrugged and then dropped her head to the table.

"What's going on?" Tyler came up beside me and handed me one of two bottles of beer.

Ellis did the same to Kirk and grinned. "Shit, she's really fucked."

"Yeah thanks to that dickhead," I ground out through gritted teeth as I stared at Sarah's *'friend'*.

"I told you, she's had four drinks that's all." He tried to push towards me, but Kirk's big hand on his chest stopped him.

"And if you'd been any sort of a *friend*," I hissed, emphasising the word friend. "You'd have discovered she's barely eaten today and isn't capable of holding two drinks never mind four."

He puffed out a breath and turned to Sarah. "Why didn't you say? I would never have suggested the brandy if I'd known."

"You gave her fucking brandy?" My temper was near boiling point but luckily for him the phone was finally answered. "Where are you... can you get to The Brass Monkey as soon as you can...? Yeah, she does... thanks."

"Who was that?" Ellis asked before taking a sip of his beer.

"Alannah," I replied, my eyes firmly on the dick with his arm around Sarah's slumped shoulders. "She's coming to get Sarah."

"I can take her," the dick said, eyeing me over the top of her head. "I'll organise a taxi."

"And take her where, because I promise you if you think I'm

fucking mad, wait until her mum finds out you let her get this pissed."

His face paled as he slowly pulled his arm away from Sarah – fucking chicken piece of shit.

"You can go," Tyler said. "If you want to."

To give him his due, the lad shook his head. "No, I'll wait until her friend gets here."

The silence that followed was pretty uncomfortable as we all drank in silence while he kept asking Sarah if she was okay, only to get one-word answers. I kept my eyes on her and intermittently made her drink from the pint of water. The fact that she wouldn't look at me felt like a blade to my guts, but that was something I'd deal with when she was sober. Finally, Alannah appeared, wearing what could possibly have been her pyjamas, her damp hair in a ponytail and her glasses perched on the end of her nose as she surveyed the bar looking for us. When she spotted us and then Sarah, her glare swung to the lad who I still had no name for.

"What the hell happened?" Alannah demanded.

"She only had—"

"She's not eaten anything all day and had *four* drinks," I explained as I encouraged Sarah to take another sip of water. "Can she stay at yours, if her mum sees her like this, she'll go ballistic."

"Of course, but what do I say to her mum?"

I leaned closer to Sarah and stroked a hand down her hair. "Sarah, babe, give me your phone."

"Not your babe," she muttered, but reached into the pocket of her leather jacket took out her phone and handed it to me.

Like the prick I was, I couldn't help but smirk at the dick head, even laughing when I typed out her passcode to get into the phone and his mouth gaped open.

"He was her boyfriend," Kirk said with a shrug.

Noticing a string of messages already sent between Mrs Danes and Sarah, I quickly typed out a text, feeling pretty amused with myself as I did.

Sarah: Hi Mum, date was a disaster, so Alannah came to pick me up. We've gone back to hers to do our nails and watch...

I paused wondering what film they'd watch and then grinned.

...and watch Fifty Shades. I'm going to stay over, will be home in the morning.

After a few seconds a text came back which also made me smile, but for different reasons. It made me smile for Sarah.

Mum:Okay sweetheart. Enjoy your night and sorry it was bad, but I thought you said it wasn't a date!! Oh and 50 Shades...really? Lol. Love you loads and glad you have a good friend like Alannah. Sleep tight xx

As I slipped the phone back into Sarah's pocket, I realised I was also glad that she had a friend like Alannah, which made me feel even more of a shit for the things I'd done to her. Clearing my throat, I looked up at her and smiled.

"Thanks for this, Alannah."

"No problem, but I can't believe she only had four drinks," she sighed as she took Sarah's hand in hers and rubbed it gently. "Sarah, you okay to come back to mine?"

Sarah lifted her head and nodded. "Please. My mum will kill me."

I sighed in relief, glad that I done the right thing and happy that she was lucid enough to know exactly what had happened and that she was going to Alannah's. It was selfish of me, but I wanted her to remember how I'd felt inside of her in that dark corner of the hallway. To remember how fucking good we'd been together and the high we'd given each other that I was sure no damn drug would equal.

"Tyler can you help me," Alannah said. "My car is right outside."

I stepped forward but Ellis put a hand on my arm. "Just leave it for now."

Sighing, I knew he was right. Not that it made it any easier to watch Tyler with his arm around Sarah and helping her out of the bar. It made my skin crawl and set my teeth on edge, so to ease the discomfort, I snatched up my bottle and took a long swig.

The dick who'd been with Sarah started to follow them out, but I quickly reached for him and grabbed his arm.

"You're not going anywhere dick head. We're going to have a little chat."

When my bedroom door swung open, banging against the wall, I almost let out a string of expletives, but caught myself when I heard my little sister's sweet voice.

"Adam get up quick," she cried as she came alongside my bed. "Someone's here to see you."

"Go away, Munchkin," I groaned pulling the duvet over my head. "Tell them I'm too ill to get up."

"You mean you've been drinking dirty beer. Daddy had to throw three bottles in the bin this morning. Mummy told him you'd had a party and just you were there."

I peeked out from under the covers and looked at her with one eye closed to find her frowning.

"She said it was a pity party, whatever that is." Lori curled her lip and shrugged.

"It's what you have when you've been a twat," I grumbled under my breath. "Who's here anyway?"

"Oh Sarah," she said casually before smacking my stomach over the duvet. "So, shake a leg sailor."

The ridiculousness of her statement went way over my head. It was too far gone with the fact that Sarah was visiting me.

I threw back the duvet and jumped out of bed, causing Lori to scream and run out of the room.

"Ugh that's disgusting. You're so rude," she yelled.

It was only then that I looked down and realised that I was naked. I usually slept in boxers at least but was obviously so drunk the night before I'd just abandoned my clothes and fallen into bed.

"Sorry, Munchkin," I shouted after her as I snagged a pair of jeans from the floor and pulled them and a t-shirt on while running from my room.

When I got downstairs, I headed for the voices in the kitchen where Lori was showing Sarah a toy catalogue. My sister was chatting away about her upcoming ninth birthday, while Roger leaned against a cupboard watching her indulgently

"Hey," I said running a hand through my hair. "How're you feeling?"

Sarah looked up and me and swallowed. "Okay, a bit of a headache." She placed a hand against her stomach, and I guessed she'd probably puked at some point.

"You as well, hey." Roger said with a grin. "Adam, was worse for wear when he got home and then proceeded to down another three bottles of beer." He raised his brows at me. "I don't suppose you remember me waking you up in the chair at three this morning?"

A vague recollection flitted through my mind. "Sorry."

"Ah that's what being young is all about." He smiled and moved over to Lori and placed a hand on top of her blonde head. "Okay you, let's go and pick Mummy up and leave Sarah and Adam in peace."

"Where is Mum?" I asked, glancing at Sarah to see her rubbing her temple.

"The nail bar," Lori grumbled. "She's having Flamingo Pink nails and wouldn't let me go with her."

Roger rolled his eyes and chuckled. "You're too young, we told you that. Say goodbye to Sarah."

"Bye, Sarah," Lori said with a pout before stomping out of the room.

"Bye, Lori, see you next week at Street Dance."

She gave Roger a sweet smile, even though she looked a little green in the face. "Bye, Mr Crawford."

"Bye love, nice to see you again."

We watched each other in silence until the front door clicked shut and as soon as it had I moved to sit next to her at the table.

"You sure you feel okay?" I asked leaning forward with my elbows on my knees.

"Pretty much. I think the water you made me drink helped. That and the other three pints Alannah practically poured into me." She looked down at the catalogue which Lori had left on the table and traced her finger around a picture of a scooter. "I need to thank you for calling her and texting my mum too."

I shook my head. "No problem. I just wanted you to be safe."

We fell silent and the air crackled with intensity as Sarah avoided my gaze. I didn't take my eyes off her. Eventually, when I could stand it no longer, I cleared my throat, ready to speak. "Do you think we need to talk about what else happened last night?"

Her fingers knotted together and without looking up she shrugged. "I don't know, do we?"

"Yes, we do. We had sex, and you can't just ignore it."

"I'm not," Sarah replied, shaking her head and finally looking up at me, her eyes full of trepidation. "But it doesn't change anything."

I clenched my teeth. She had to know it changed everything. I knew I'd agreed with Roger I'd wait until I was sure what I wanted, but after being inside her last night there was no doubt in my fucking mind.

"So, you and that lad, you're just friends, right?" I asked, thinking that veering her away from a discussion about the sex she evidently wished we hadn't had, might keep her in my house for a while longer.

She raised a brow. "Yes, Adam, *Jack* and I are friends. That's all."

"He didn't think that," I scoffed.

"Well, that's not my problem. I made it clear that was all it was." She sounded irritated as she huffed and pushed her chair back. "And as far as you and I are concerned, what happened shouldn't have. I just wanted to apologise. I was drunk, as you know, and I should have just walked away."

Well that was a way to hurt my male ego.

"You didn't have sex with me just because you were drunk, Sarah. We both know that, so don't try and kid yourself."

"You don't know what I was thinking," she said, her gaze snapping to mine.

"No, but I know when someone wants sex for reasons other than being drunk, and you most definitely wanted me in spite of being pissed." I felt my dick twitch as I thought about how willing and wet she had been. "I'm sorry it happened, but only because you deserve more respect that a shag against a wall in a bar, so I apologise."

She started to push her hand up her sleeve, so I leaned forward and pulled it to me instead. "Don't," I whispered.

Dragging her hand from mine, Sarah closed her eyes and licked her lips before taking a deep breath and then looking at me.

"I need to go, I just wanted to say thank you. Oh, and thank you for not punching Jack."

My spine stiffened me. "How do you know I didn't?"

"I spoke to him this morning." She cleared her throat and entwined her fingers together. "He said that you ended up walking home with him."

I reared back in my chair trying to ignore the fact that she'd spoken to him. "I did?"

"Yes, you did," she said with a hint of a smile. "Apparently, you told him he was your new best mate."

"Well he isn't. He's a twat."

"Adam!"

"He is," I protested. "He let you get drunk."

"It was my fault, I hadn't eaten." She chewed on her bottom lip, looking uneasy. "I need to go."

"You could stay. I could make you..." I looked at the orange LED clock on the cooker and saw it was almost two. "Shit, I could make you a late lunch."

She shook her head and pushed back her chair. "I have to go I promised my mum I'd watch a film with her this afternoon, and I need to pick her up, she's gone to a yoga class followed by a woman's meeting that I dropped her off at earlier. Clarice just started them this week." Suddenly a beautiful smile flashed across her face. One that brightened not only her eyes but my world too. "Oh, and talking of films, Fifty Shades, really?"

I shrugged and gave her my cocky, I'm-so-fucking-funny, smile, one that I knew she loved. When she took a deep breath and sucked her bottom lip into her mouth, I knew it was the best one to bring out.

"I didn't know what else you and Alannah might watch."

"Hmm, I'm sure. You could have actually asked Alannah or mentioned any one of a thousand romantic comedies." She shook her head, but there was a little grin on her face which told me I wasn't really in trouble.

"I can drive you, if you like," I offered.

"I have my mum's car, but thank you." As she stood up, her mobile buzzed with a text. "That's probably my mum reminding me to call and get chocolate."

As Sarah pulled her phone from her pocket, I watched her carefully. My eyes grazing over her deep pink lips, the milky skin of her neck and the sexy curve of her perfect tits. She was so bloody beautiful, and I'd fucked everything up for a man I'd seen a handful of times.

"Oh my God," she gasped. "That's awful."

"What is?" I pushed up from my chair ready to comfort her, she looked so upset.

Sarah looked up at me with wide eyes. "Jack just went to pick up his car and someone has scratched the paintwork."

I wasn't surprised as he'd hardly left it on the safest car park overnight. "It's dodgy around there. He was a bit stupid to leave it."

"You don't understand," she said quietly, tears brimming at her lashes.

"Sarah, what the fuck is wrong?" I rushed to her side and threw an arm around her. "What's wrong, babe?"

She passed her phone to me which was showing a photograph that Jack had evidently sent. I looked down at it.

"What the fuck?"

With my heart hammering and anger simmering almost to the point of exploding, I looked at a photograph of a red Corsa with the words "Whore Shagger" etched into its side.

"Fucking Mackenna," I yelled. "I'll fucking kill her."

22

SARAH

Seeing the words etched into Jack's car had made me feel sick to my stomach. How could someone could be so nasty. One thing I was sure of was that I agreed with Adam in that it was probably Mackenna's work. Despite Adam wanting to sort it, I'd passed on Mackenna's name to Jack and explained she hated me because of Adam.

The whole thing made me sick and I wasn't sure I actually wanted to help my mum eat both the family size bars of chocolate, chocolate coloured peanuts and a huge bag of popcorn, I'd bought. I did wonder if I'd overdone it. My hangover was lingering though, and junk food was the only thing that would do.

Approaching Mum's car, I thought again about the sex Adam and I'd had against the wall in the bar. It wasn't the sort of thing I'd ever imagine myself doing, not until I'd met Adam. He drove me bloody crazy with need for him in every way. My cheeks heated up as I recalled how amazing it had felt having him between my legs and how he'd sent me free falling over the edge of bliss.

Blowing out to cool my face, I reached the car and pointed the key at it to hear the bleep of the lock. When I sat inside, I put the key in the ignition and smiled sadly when Gracie Abrams' 'Stay' sounded out through the speakers. I'd been playing it on repeat for the last few days, revelling in the pain it created in my chest because it reminded me so much of Adam and me. It also reminded me that Adam's dad was the creeping hand of fear that stopped me from taking what I wanted and us from being normal teenagers.

Pulling my seat belt across my chest, I noticed a bright, flashing orange light on the dashboard with the message 'Tyre Pressure Low' next to it was the number 6.

"Shit."

I knew what that meant. Dad had made sure I knew how to know how much air was needed in a tyre. This meant I was aware that a pressure of six meant it was pretty much flat.

Unbuckling my belt and getting out I walked around the car to see that the front passenger side tyre was indeed as flat as a pancake. The problem was Dad may well have taught me all about tyre pressure, but never once had he shown me how to change a tyre. I looked around to see if there was anyone around who might be able to help, but apart from a frazzled mum and her two small children there was no one.

Sighing heavily, I pulled my phone from the back pocket of my jeans and called Mum.

"Hi, love, you on your way?"

"Not really, Mum." I looked down at the tyre and kicked it. "I've got a flat tyre."

"Flat. What totally flat?"

"Yep. What shall I do?"

"Do you think you could change it? There's a spare underneath the boot." She didn't sound optimistic and she was right. It was a Ford Kuga, so quite a big car, too big for me to jack up on my own.

"I don't think I can. Shall I call roadside assistance?"

Mum thought for a moment. "I think I have to be with the car. Bloody hell, I meant to put your name on it too. Do you think you could call Adam?" she asked tentatively.

"Mum," I sighed. "No not really."

I couldn't say, *no because he shagged me against a wall and I just told him it was a mistake*, but thankfully she didn't push me on it.

"No, I suppose not. Okay love, you go home and then I'll call them in the morning and arrange to meet them there. It'll be fine there overnight. There's no point us missing our film night. I could be sat there for hours waiting for them."

I was a little surprised that she was happy for me to leave the car but loved that she didn't want to miss out on us having some time together. Her new car would have been important to her at one time, but now she really was trying to put me first.

"Okay, but how will you get home from yoga?"

"There's a lady called Tricia who lives on our estate, she offered but I said you were coming for me. We're just about to start the meeting, so I'm sure she won't mind."

"That's good." I smiled glad that Mum seemed to be making friends. She hadn't really mixed with anyone since we'd lost Dad, so when Clarice had told me about the yoga and women's meetings she was starting, I knew I had to persuade her to go. "Well I'll have the chocolate and popcorn ready for when you get back."

"Ooh good," she said happily. "I'm going to make stir fry for dinner, and I have wine in the fridge too."

My stomach turned over at the thought of alcohol but didn't mention that fact as we said our goodbyes.

The shop was only a ten-minute walk from home but only stocked non branded stuff. While I wasn't a snob generally, if it wasn't Cadbury chocolate or real diet coke, it wasn't worth buying. Today though I couldn't face talking to Rita or Murray, so cheap chocolate would have to do

Taking a deep breath and giving my surroundings a quick scan, I set off thinking that if I hadn't decided to go and see Adam, I wouldn't have needed to borrow Mum's car and get her a flat tyre. Also, if I hadn't decided to go and see Adam, I wouldn't be feeling hot and bothered and remembering him inside of me and his lips on my skin.

Trying to push the thoughts of lust away, I zipped up my jacket against the wind, which was blowing directly at me, and put my head down as I marched on swinging my carrier bag at my side. With our bungalow in sight, I came to a place where the footpath narrowed as it skirted a path which led down to a kid's park, I was about to cross over the road when a man dressed in a thin black bomber jacket, and jeans with a black baseball cap on his head stepped out in front of me. I jumped backwards and my heart thumped in my throat, beating uncontrollably.

"Well, we meet again," he said as he gave me a smile which barely moved his lips.

The nightmares I always had about him were nothing compared to how he looked in that moment. He looked determined and vengeful as his black heart and soul spoke to me through unforgiving and narrowed eyes. In those nightmares, I would open my mouth to scream and there would be nothing but silence. I would try and run from him, but my legs would be stuck in place as he moved towards me.

This wasn't a dream though, this was real life and I wasn't going to let him hurt me again, so with every ounce of strength and power I had I lifted my feet and ran.

23

ADAM

"Why the fuck are you so het up about her?" Ellis asked as he lounged on my bed and flicked through the pages of the football magazine that Sarah had bought for me.

About five minutes after Sarah left, Ellis turned up to play FIFA, but when I'd told him I wasn't in the mood because of what Mackenna had done to Jack's car, and that it had upset Sarah, he'd just shrugged and made himself comfy with my magazine.

"She's got a pussy," he said. "But so do plenty of other girls. It's nothing special."

I snatched the magazine from him and standing above him, got into his face. "You fucking speak about her like that again and best friend or not, I'll fucking annihilate you."

Ellis reared back, but his usual grin wasn't there. He looked disdainful with his lip curled as though he could smell shit. I had a feeling he'd been on the weed, before he came over, because his eyes were red rimmed and lazy.

"For fuck's sake, Adam, stop getting so arsey."

"You know what I think about her. This is the last thing she needs after everything that's happened to her. Mackenna is a cunt for doing it."

Ellis looked up at me and frowned.

"You've fucking lost it, Adam. All over a girl who fucked your dad."

And that was his step too far.

The red mist dropped like a lump of concrete from a great height and without even thinking about it, my fist landed on his face.

"You fucking twat," he cried, wincing as he scrambled up the bed away from me. "I'll end you."

"Go on then," I yelled, spittle spraying all over him. "Try it. I dare you."

Ellis snarled and rolled off the bed to stand face to face with me. His breath was heavy as he forcefully pushed my forehead with his.

"You're a prick, Adam. No wonder your dad fucked off and left you."

"Tell me something I don't know." I pushed Ellis hard against his chest. He stumbled back a step, but he quickly righted himself and got right back in my face. "Say what you like about him, but not Sarah."

"You think she's so amazing, yet not one fucking girl in her last school had a good word to say about her."

"*What?*"

Ellis gave me a sickly smile. "Oh yeah I talked to them all, but not one of them liked her; your precious *Sarah*."

My stomach bottomed out and my lungs cinched. "What the fuck did you do, Ellis?"

"I went looking for her secret, just like you asked us to. This is all on you Adam," he scoffed. "Your dad being here, it's all because *you* wanted to break her, well it looks like you got your wish Mr Fucking Big Shot."

My hands clenched into fists, ready to punch him again, but not until he told me everything. Not until he spilled about the vile shit-storm he'd instigated. As I breathed heavily and stared at the lad who'd been my best friend for years, I could see the venom practically seeping from him. His sneer and the entitled tilt of his chin told me everything I should have seen before.

"You brought him here, didn't you? You brought him here to hurt her. He didn't come for me, did he?"

Ellis grinned. "He didn't even know you were here. Fuck I didn't even know he was your dad; it was a pure, magical coincidence."

I shook my head and stretched out my fingers, they were desperate to claw at him. "Why, after all the things I've done for you?"

"What the fuck have you done for me?" he laughed out. "Except let me be in your *gang*." He smirked and turned away from me and as he did, I was conscious of hearing yelling from downstairs – fuck could the day get any worse.

"I covered for you," I cried, spinning him around by his elbow my attention back on him. "When you set fire to the school dining room, I was the one who got you out of there. I was the one who went back for the lighter with your dad's company name on it. I was the one who got Kirk to hack into the school CCTV and wipe it. I," I said poking his chest, "was the one who persuaded Mr Jameson to let you back on the team."

One day last year, Ellis had come to footy practice having downed a bottle of vodka and almost broke another lad's leg with a ridiculous tackle when he came running out of goal. When Mr Jameson ordered him into the changing rooms, Ellis gave him a mouthful of abuse earning him a total ban from the team. The next morning, even before the caretaker had arrived, Ellis broke into school and set fire to a load of books from the library in the dining hall. Tyler thankfully had an idea he was up to something and persuaded us to find him. Kirk did his magic and pinged his phone or some crap like that and we got there just in time before the fire spread to the actual kitchen where there were all sorts of flammable stuff. In the end it was mainly smoke damage but all bad enough that a total refurbishment was needed.

"Oh, the great number seven pulled some strings for me, well like I fucking care."

I stared at him, not recognising the affable, cocky lad who I'd grown up with. His usual white toothed smile wasn't there, there were no laugh lines around his eyes; just hatred.

"What the hell is wrong with you? What the fuck did you do it for when you knew what she was beginning to mean to me?"

"Because you fucking dropped us like hot turds," Ellis yelled in my face. "We'd done all sorts of crap for you for years, and then she comes along and all of a sudden you decide you want to be Mr Nice Guy, and we're not good enough for you. Well it's too fucking late, Adam because like I said, you started all of this."

"I told you to leave her alone."

"You told *Kirk* to find out her secret, and when he couldn't, I did." He actually looked pleased with himself and patted his chest with his palm.

"Even when you found out what my dad did to her?" I asked, amazed. "You still thought it was okay?"

The pounding in my chest was so hard and fast I thought I might be having a heart attack. I couldn't comprehend what he was saying to me. I'd always thought him and me were tighter than anyone.

"Are Kirk and Tyler in on it?" I asked full of dread.

"Are they fuck, do you really think I'd bring that pair of dick heads in on anything. No, this was all me with the help of Mackenna."

"Mackenna?"

Ellis smirked. "Why else do you think she's been hanging around like a bad smell trying to split you up. That's why she told Sarah you'd left your hoodie."

"Fuck the blue hoodie." Ellis and I both owned the same hoodie, which was why Lori had written my name in mine with her loopy childish handwriting. I'd come home in Ellis' once, with his phone in the pocket and Lori had found it really funny for some weird reason.

"I have to admit it was her idea to dress like Sarah. I was as surprised as you at that one," he added.

Staring at him, I tried to take it all in, unable to believe what they'd done just to come between me and Sarah. This wasn't the Ellis I knew. This Ellis was a fucking bastard.

"You brought a rapist back into her life," I cried as I gripped at my hair. "Didn't you think what that would do to her?"

"He fucking denied it and everyone else said she was lying," he cried, holding his arms out to his sides.

I took a step towards him with my fist clenched, when my bedroom door flung open. I swung around to see Roger in my doorway, with my mum hanging on to his arm.

"Roger no," she cried.

Roger shook her off and looked angrier than I'd ever seen him.

"Ellis, I think you should go," he said more calmly than I'd expect with the rage he was evidently feeling. "We need to talk to Adam."

"No problem at all," Ellis muttered and went past me, barging his shoulder into mine.

"We haven't finished, Ellis," I warned. "I'll be coming for you."

"What's happened?" Roger asked as my ex-best friend stamped from the room.

"He's a fucking prick."

I knew that he and my mum were in my room for something serious because Roger didn't say anything about me swearing in front of my precious mother.

"What's going on?"

"Tell him," Roger demanded of my mum as he strode to the window, both his hands linked at the back of his neck.

"No, it's not important."

Mum turned to leave the room, but Roger must have had some sixth sense, because without even turning around he barked at her, "Don't you dare leave, Elouise, and just bloody tell him."

I looked at my mum who was gnawing at her bottom lip, her eyes darting between me and Roger.

"*Elouise.*"

"Mum, for God's sake what?"

She swallowed and then rubbed a hand across her brow, all delaying tactics, but there was no way Roger was going to let her get away with whatever it was.

"Mum, just tell me."

Whatever it was I needed to know, because I had to get out of there and find my dad and tell him he had to leave Maddison Edge. Sarah was more important to me than him, I knew that without a doubt. The sooner he went meant the sooner I could beg Sarah to take me back.

"Adam, I'm so sorry. I just thought it was for the best, that I was protecting you."

I sighed. "If you're going to tell me you knew where Dad was all this time, then don't bother. I guessed that one a while ago."

"Oh no," Roger scoffed turning back around and raising his arms in the air. "If only it were that insignificant."

Looking between his crimson angry face and Mum's pale worried one, I had no clue how she was about to tilt my world on its axis.

"Tell me."

"I can't, Roger, you do it."

"Will someone just fucking tell me what the hell it that is so important. I need to go and see Glen, or fucking Joshua, whatever his name his."

"No," Roger snapped and dropped a hand to my shoulder. "I don't think you should go."

I shrugged him off. "Well tough, because I am."

"You can't," he replied shaking his head. "That's what we have to tell you." He looked at Mum who was doing her usual weeping and wailing routine she always did when she didn't like a situation. "Well, I suppose I have to tell you. What he did to Sarah, he did it before, when you were little."

24

ADAM

"W-what do you mean." My blood ran cold and my legs felt like jelly as I staggered over to my desk and dropped into the chair. "He didn't fucking touch me did he?"

"God no, son, no." Roger knelt in front of me and pulled my hands between both of his. "Your mum caught him in the house with a fifteen-year-old girl. She used to babysit you from time to time."

I tried to think back to any girl that might have looked after me, but no one came to mind, apart from vague recollections of a girl with blonde hair who had one of those huge sheepdogs like those from the paint advert.

"There was a girl who used to let me go for a walk in the field with her and her dog," I said, as sketchy images flashed through my head.

"Angela," Mum said, venom rich in her voice. "The little bitch's name was Angela."

Roger gave her a disdainful look and then turned back to me. "He did the same to her, raped her while you were playing in your bedroom. Your mum came home and found the girl crying in the corner of their room, while your dad was... shall we say, getting dressed."

Everything in the room went hazy. Roger's face swam in front of my eyes. The curtains at my window looked like they were blowing in a breeze. The floor moved up and down like a rollercoaster and my body felt chilled to the bone despite the fine sheen of sweat covering it.

"I feel sick." I gulped in some air and looked at Mum. "What did you do?"

My hands were shaking even though they were trapped inside Rogers and I could feel his grip tighten as my tears splashed onto his skin.

Mum shook her head and clamped a hand over her mouth. A movement that couldn't have been more symbolic if she'd tried.

"What did she do, Roger?"

"She." He drew in a deep breath. "She didn't do anything. She told the girl is was her word against both of theirs and she'd give your dad any alibi he needed."

"Fuck." My gaze shot to my mum. "Please tell me you didn't."

She nodded as she cried silently.

"You let him go," I whispered and looked at Roger, who seemed to have lost that adoring look in his eye for my mum. It was replaced with a hardness as his steel grey eyes flashed to her and then back to me.

"I threw him out," Mum protested.

"I can't be in the same room as her," I said to Roger, my voice anxious and breathy. "I need to leave; I need to find Sarah."

Roger kept a firm grip of my hand and looked me directly in the eye. "I think you should stay here, and I'll call the police. I know how hot headed you get, and you'll go straight round to his place and then he'll run."

"Sarah," I croaked out. "I need Sarah."

Roger pulled me up with him and dragged me into his arms. My arms wrapped around his waist and I dropped my forehead to his shoulder.

"Please, Roger, let me call Sarah. I need her here. I need to know she's okay."

"Okay, son," he whispered soothingly. "Let's call her and see if her mum will bring her over." He blew out a breath. "I'm so bloody sorry."

"Adam, sweetheart."

When Mum started to sob, I pulled away from Roger and turned on her.

"Shut up, I don't want to hear it. I don't want any excuses from you. You helped him get away with rape and then he raped Sarah. You're as bad as he is."

She gasped loudly and staggered backwards.

"I think you should leave him alone, Elouise," Roger said quietly, his head bowed. "Go and see to Lori."

"But I—"

"No," Roger commanded. "For once in your life just do as I damn well ask."

She whimpered for a few seconds, but neither Roger nor I said anything as she slipped from the room.

"How could she have done that?" I asked, swiping at my eyes with the heels of my hands. "He's a fucking monster and she let him go."

Roger exhaled slowly. "I don't know. There's a lot of things your mum does that amaze me, but this," he paused to scrub a hand down his face. "This is just about the limit."

Something inside of me wilted as I thought of Roger leaving our lives. I hadn't realised how much I'd warmed to him over the last few weeks. How much I had realised that he was the one who had parented me for the last two years or so, despite everything I'd done to push him away.

"You're leaving her," I stated, acceptance in my tone.

Roger tilted his chin up and shook his head. "No," he said determinedly. "As much as I can't stand the sight of her, I love you and Lori. I won't abandon either of you, but your mum...well, I will never forgive her for this."

With his shoulders hunched and his back stooped, he looked destroyed and defeated. My mum had done it again but this time she'd managed to lose a good man. The fact that he said he'd stay for us, for me and Lori, made him my fucking hero. As for Mum, I had no sympathy for her whatsoever.

"Roger, I'm so sorry."

He patted my shoulder.

"There are only two people to blame for this shit, Adam, and you're most definitely not one of them." Rubbing his bald head, he sighed heavily. "We'll try and make things as normal as possible for Lori's sake, but me and your mum are finished. I knew she had Glen's contact details all this time, but to find out she... well, that's unforgiveable."

"But I—"

"Adam, mate your mum let me up."

Kirk came bounding into the room his face was pale and his hair was messed all over the place as though he'd been running his hands through it.

"I don't want to talk about Ellis," I groaned, as I wiped the residue of my tears away.

"I don't know what you're talking about." He stopped dead in front of me and grabbed both my upper arms. "I was listening on the police radio—"

"Kirk, lad, you'll get into trouble for that if they catch you," Roger sighed. "You boys, I don't know."

"No, Mr Crawford, really I need to tell you this." Kirk's chest heaved and he was looking at me as if my dog had just died.

"Nothing else, please," I groaned.

"You need to hear this," he insisted.

"Okay what?"

"They've found a girl's body in the park. She's drowned in the lake."

The way he was looking at me, I just knew.

"No," I said, shaking my head. "You don't fucking know that." I scrambled across the room, pushing Roger out of the way to get my phone from my bed.

"What?" Roger asked. "What's going on?"

As I stabbed at my phone to get to Sarah's number, Kirk's voice lowered to a worried quake.

"She was blonde and." He took a deep breath. "And they said she was around seventeen and had one blue Converse missing.

It was then that the phone dropped from my hand the last thing I remember the thud of it landing on the floor.

25

ADAM

Roger was holding my head up while Kirk wiped a wet flannel over my face when I came around. As soon as my eyes regained focus, embarrassed, I tried to stand up, sending Kirk flying onto his arse.

"Just hold on a minute," Roger said, pushing on my shoulders to keep me down. "You need to be sure you're okay first."

"I'm fine, I need to find out what's happening. I have to know if it's Sarah."

"Okay, okay." Roger patted my shoulder. "Take it steady."

As quickly as he'd let me, I got to my feet and then held my hand out to him to help him up. He breathed in sharply through his nose and momentarily closed his eyes and in that moment, I knew he would always look out for me and my sister, no matter what happened.

"I'm so sorry, mate," Kirk said as stood up. "I wish it hadn't had to be me to tell you, but—."

"No," I said, shaking my head. "It's not her, I know it isn't. I'd feel it in here." I slammed my closed fist against my chest and took a deep breath. "I would fucking know."

Kirk nodded and instinctively knew not to say anything else.

"If I can't get hold of her, can you go home and carry on listening?" I asked him.

He looked at Roger and then back to me. "Well, yeah if you want me to."

"I need to know for certain. Where's my phone?"

Roger passed it to me, his eyes grave and concerned. "Adam if it's the worst news, I think you should be at home."

"I need to find her. It's not her." I tapped on my phone and then lifted it to my ear.

It felt like it had been ringing forever when her voicemail kicked.

"Hi, you've reached Sarah Danes, please leave a message and I'll call you back."

Shit she sounded so bright and alive and I hoped with everything inside of me that she was okay.

"Hey Sarah, please call me as soon as you get this message... I... please, babe, just call me." I pocketed my phone and then snatched up my car keys.

"Adam, I'm not sure—"

"I have to Roger. I have to find her."

He nodded once and then stood to one side. "I can come with you, if you'd like me to."

I thought about it but knew that if for one minute I thought my dad was involved in the fucking nightmare, or that he'd even looked in Sarah's direction, I'd want to pummel him until he begged me to stop. Roger wouldn't allow that.

"I'll be fine. Stay with Mum and Lori and make sure Lori doesn't find out. She loves Sarah."

Fuck she wasn't the only one, that was something I was sure of.

"I'll go back home and see what I can find out." Kirk ran a hand over his head, and I could see apology and pity in his eyes.

"Thanks, mate. I really appreciate it."

"Least I can do."

As I followed him down the stairs, it was strange to realise how wrong I'd got it about him. I'd always thought Ellis was the one I could rely on, but Kirk was the one who had worried about me and yet again was willing to help me.

Once in my car I went to put the key in the ignition, but my hands were shaking too much.

"Come on, pull yourself together," I muttered to myself.

I took a deep breath and finally managed to get the key in and start the car, speeding off towards Sarah's house. I had no idea what I would find there, all I knew was I had to make sure she wasn't the blonde girl who would never draw another breath. If it was her then I wasn't sure how I could continue to draw my own; I loved her that much.

26

SARAH

As my feet pounded the pavement towards our house, I knew that Mr Mills was close behind me. I could almost feel his breath on the back of my neck.

There was a certain sense of inevitability deep inside me that knew he'd catch me, but I would do everything in my power to try and make sure he didn't. The house was in sight, if only I could get there before Mr Mills gained on me. I wanted to shout for help, but no one was around; even for a Sunday it was quiet. No kids were playing in the street, no one was washing their car or walking their dog, it was deserted.

The carrier bag of chocolate wasn't heavy, but it wasn't helping me to run, so I threw it to one side, glancing over my shoulder as I did. Mr Mills was almost within touching distance of me, his arms and legs pumping in unison.

"You can't run from me for long, Sarah."

His breathless voice reached me over the air rushing past my ears as I tried desperately to outrun him. With the house only feet away, I reached into my pocket for my key and had it pointed ready, even though I wasn't sure I'd make it.

Reaching the house, I pushed the key in the lock and before I'd even got it open my hair was grabbed, my head pulled back and then crashed hard against the door.

The pain zigzagged through my head as my body jerked and then slammed forward, with my cheek pressed up against the door.

"Open it." Mr Mills' voice was quiet and menacing as his breath whispered against the bare skin of my neck.

"My mum will be home soon, you can't do this," I managed to gasp out.

Mr Mills laughed. "No, she won't, she's at that meeting for fucking women and don't even try and tell me she's not. I know. I also know you are more stupid than I thought," he sneered. "You really should have run to a neighbour instead of here where no one's home."

I let out a pained whimper, realising he was right. I'd been stupid. Too scared of the man who had snubbed out the light in my life. Too scared to think logically.

"You won't get away with this."

He snatched my fingers from the key and turned it. "Yeah well I've nothing left to lose, thanks to you."

He pushed me into the hall, sending me flying and when my hands and knees hit the floor, he pushed his foot against my back so that I fell flat on my face.

"Since meeting you, my life's been a fucking mess. I lost my job and reputation and yet here you are living your perfect life, with *my* fucking son. *Fucking* my son as well."

I crawled along the floor and managed to drag myself to the kitchen door, holding on to the door frame I pulled myself up. If he was going to hurt me then I was going to face him while he did it, so I turned with my back against the wall.

"Adam will hate you for this," I breathed out in between gulping for air.

"Like I care what he thinks."

Mr Mills lifted his leg behind him and kicked the door closed.

"He's your son. You came back for him."

As I said the words, I knew that they were totally false. In my heart of hearts, I'd always known he came to Maddison Edge for me, not to reconnect with Adam. My chest ached as I thought of Adam, how I loved him and how this man had stopped us from being together. How the monster in front of me had manipulated his son, who was already broken and full of pain, into believing he was back to save him.

"I had no fucking idea he was here," he sneered, taking a determined step closer to me. "When that friend of his contacted me to tell me where you were and asked if I wanted to know so I could mess with you for 'setting me up' I had no idea he knew Adam."

My mouth went dry as his words resonated in my head. "F-friend?"

"Yeah, the black kid. Managed to connect with that friend of yours, Harley, on Facebook. She told him everything about you and what you did to me. Then she spotted me in town one day and organised for us to talk."

He looked me up and down disdainfully, but all I could think was that Ellis had been the one to bring him here. Ellis who was supposed to be Adam's best friend. Not Kirk, or even Seth Davies, but Ellis. Ellis and that bitch Harley. How ironic this was partly down to her after the lie I'd told Alannah that day.

"Bit of a shock is it?" Mr Mills asked, leaning his face closer to mine. "Well I can only thank him. He wanted to split you two up, so he was the one who paid some kid to spread the word about us."

Ellis had paid for my darkest secret to be spread around like salacious gossip.

"There was no us," I whimpered, veering away from him, and banging my head against the wall.

He gave an empty laugh and shook his head. "Angle it whichever way you like, but you know what the truth really is."

Mr Mills lifted a finger and ran it down my cheek, turning the blood in my veins to ice. The feel of his fingertip was all too familiar and created a crack in my soul. The track he'd followed felt as though it was scarred, and I could practically feel the skin blistering and puckering as he continued to stare at me.

"There's no loyalty with any of you fucking kids," he said, his lip curling. "Even that girl who Adam let suck his dick from time to time."

"Mackenna?" I gasped. "W-what did you do to her?"

His dismissive shrug made me realise that whatever it was, it was nothing to him. His actions were inconsequential as far as he was concerned.

"Well I bought her some clothes and shoes, and paid for her to have her hair done, so she was more than happy to give me what I needed. More than happy to give herself whichever way I wanted."

Bile rose in my throat as images of Mackenna with hair like mine and dressed like me washed in front of my eyes. My hands started to shake at my sides, drawing Mr Mills' gaze.

"Worried that she might take your place with Adam?"

"You're sick," I managed to utter, taking huge breaths of air to stem back the need to vomit. "We're seventeen years old, how could you?"

Mr Mills cupped my chin gently, but when I reared my head back, he gripped and squeezed hard; his stare deathly.

"I can because I love you and you love me. No one will ever come between us, not my son, not your mother, not anyone." He laughed, shaking his head. "It was so easy to make Adam believe your mother paid for my beating, so easy to slice a shadow of doubt between you. Think of how he didn't trust you."

His words were dark, menacing and low, sending a cold, fearful pain throughout my body. I could hear the thump, thump, thump of my heart pounding in my ear drums as his fingers loosened their grip and slowly caressed my jaw. His touch made me feel dirty, it made me want to crumble and go back into the dark. All the feelings of self-hatred and shame were back as I remembered what he'd done to me, what he was probably going to do to me again.

You are my sunshine

My only sunshine

You make me-

"Shut the fuck up with the song," Mr Mills said, pinching my chin tighter. "I don't want to hear it."

I opened my mouth to sing again, but a screech of tyres outside the house pulled a gasp from my lips instead. Instantly Mr Mills dragged me in front of him and clapped a hand over my mouth.

"Make a noise and I'll do to you what I did to that cheap imitation of you."

My heart stopped and fear took a firmer hold of me. Did he mean Mackenna? What had he done to her?

The banging and thumping on the door started and for a brief second I felt elation, until he whispered into my ear.

"I mean it."

Bang, bang, bang.

"Sarah, Mrs Danes, are you in there?"

Bang, bang, bang.

"Babe, please if you're there open the door. I need to speak to you, something bad has happened and I need to check you're okay."

Bang, bang, bang.

"Sarah, please."

Adam sounded desperate, his voice breaking.

"Please babe, just answer the fucking door."

Bang, bang, bang.

"Sarah, you have to be in there. I need to know you're okay. Please, babe."

The last two words were dragged from his throat as a sob and tears ran down my cheeks as his despair echoed through the hallway. I had never heard him sound so anxious or broken and it was hurting my heart. I had no idea whether he loved me, but I knew it would shatter him if anything were to happen to me. He would always blame himself for letting his dad back into his life and his soul would never recover.

I would not allow that to happen.

Lifting my leg, I flexed my foot and kicked it back into Mr Mills' leg, landing the heel of my Dr Marten on his shin. It wouldn't have been enough to maim him, but it was enough of a surprise and hard enough that he loosened his grip on me.

"Adam help me!"

My cry was louder and more powerful than I'd ever imagine I'd be capable of. My fear I'd be mute like in my nightmares wasn't reality.

"Sarah, fuck, Sarah."

Adam pounded on the door, a huge barrier between us stopping him getting to me. He thumped and kicked, pounded and punched all the time screaming out my name.

Desperate to get to him, I kicked, elbowed and pinched trying to do my part to make sure Adam could reach me. Mr Mills' arms went firmer around my body, but I was determined. I wasn't going to let him take anything more from me.

I didn't know how, maybe adrenalin increased my strength, but I managed to get free and made a run for the door, but I slipped and screamed as his hand grabbed the back of my jumper. Clawing on the floor, I tried to drag myself away, but he was slowly pulling me back, his low, menacing laugh melting in with the noise of Adam banging against the door.

"No," I screamed. "Adam, help."

Despite me fighting with everything I had, he soon had an arm over my chest and one around my waist, his fingers digging into my flesh.

"You, stupid fucking girl, you've just made things a whole lot worse for him now."

I could feel his breath against my skin and the panic began again.

"Please no. Don't hurt him."

Mr Mills turned around and shoved me into the kitchen sending me crashing against the table. My hip banged against the corner and pain shot through me. "Oww."

"If you hadn't been so stupid, this would all be over by now." He grabbed my ponytail which was almost down and dragged me over to the utility room. "You can stay in here until I've dealt with Adam."

I inhaled sharply knowing that if he hurt Adam, I would be the one who'd never forgive themselves. Not that I had long left to live with my guilt.

I knew without doubt, he was going to kill me. He was going to kill us both.

As he pushed me forwards, I knew I had to do something. Once I was locked in that room, that was it. My eyes quickly darted either side and I knew in that instant that my dad was looking down on me. Right next to the wok on the side, my mum had already put out her chopping knife.

Without a second hesitation I reached for it with my left hand and did a perfect Street Dance step and twist, bringing my arm around and stabbing him right in his side.

"You, fucking little bitch."

Mr Mills screamed as I pulled the knife back and jabbed at him again, this time I hit his hand that was clutching at his side. When I tried to go again, he managed to grab my forearm and grip it tightly, shaking it to try and force me to drop the blade.

I clung on to my weapon, with every ounce of the strength I had left in me and pushed my head forward and then sharply pulled it back to try and headbutt him, but he moved and brought his bloodied hand up to my throat. In the struggle our position shifted, and he finally had me inside the utility, pushed up against the washing machine as he fought for the knife while blood pumped from his side.

"I'm going to make you fucking scream for your life before—"

The hardness of his body was gone and before I had time to turn around, I heard deep, angry grunts alongside the sound of flesh being hit. Turning around, I found Adam straddled over his dad and punching him repeatedly in the face.

"Adam, no," I cried as he rained another closed fist against Mr Mills' cheek. "No more."

Mr Mills was out cold, a dark red patch on his jacket which was spreading and blood smeared on his face from what looked like a broken nose.

I put my hand on Adam's shoulder and he immediately stopped, looking up at me. His eyes were full of anger, but red-rimmed from tears. He breathed out a sigh and scrambled up from on top of his dad, pulling me into his arms.

"Oh my God, I thought I'd lost you. I thought he was going to kill you. Fuck."

He pulled away from me and scoured my face, running his hands up and down my body.

"Are you okay? Did he hurt you?" He pulled me close again and buried his face in my neck. "I thought..."

"I'm okay," I sniffed, giving up on trying to stem my tears. "I'm okay. Nothing that won't heal."

My hip hurt, my knees were sore, and my head ached, but I was alive. I'd fought hard so that the monster on the floor didn't take anything else from me.

"How did you get in?" I asked, snuggling closer, breathing Adam in.

"Your bedroom doors were open."

I gasped. "Oh God, I must have forgotten to lock them this morning."

When I'd returned from Alannah's I'd gone for a lie down to try and ward off my need to vomit, I'd opened the doors to let some fresh air in. When I'd left in a rush to drop Mum off, I'd obviously forgotten to lock them.

"Thank fuck you did."

Adam's lips were soft and gentle on my cheek as I heard him breathe in, taking in my scent. I knew that was what he was doing because it was what I was doing to him.

"How did you get him off me?"

Adam let out a quiet laugh. "Thank fuck your mum left her wok out."

I peeked around his shoulder to see the wok on the floor next to Mr Mills' body.

"God, Adam, I thought he was going to rape me again, and then kill me."

Adam's hold on me got tighter as he kissed my temple. "Me too. I'm so sorry I let him come between us. I knew what he'd done, yet I still took his side."

"It doesn't matter. I understood how torn you were. But how did you know to come to the house?"

He let out a long breath and pulled back to look into my eyes. "Kirk heard something on the police radio and I...I thought it was you."

Everything he'd said about Mackenna drilled against my brain.

"Mackenna," I cried. "He's done something to Mackenna."

Adam's body went rigid before he moved away from me and knelt down by the side of his dad and lifted him by his collar.

"You fucking bastard," he spat at him and then punched the unconscious man once more.

Letting him drop back to the floor, Adam came back to me, pulled me close and we both wept. We cried for everything we'd lost, but most of all, for everything we'd saved.

27

ADAM

As I knocked on Sarah's front door, a shiver ran through me. The last time I'd been trying to get into this house I thought my world was about to end.

The pain I'd felt at hearing her scream my name, begging me to help her, had been nothing like I'd ever felt before. It was like jagged glass piercing my skin, my heart and my lungs. I never wanted to feel it ever again.

Thankfully, I hadn't had to experience the true consequences of what Glen had done that day. Unlike Mackenna's family who were having to come to terms with her death. For them things would never be the same again thanks to Glen Hudson. The man was, and always would be a waste of oxygen and I hated myself for allowing him into my life.

Even though deep down I knew he hadn't come to Maddison Edge for me, I'd still wanted to believe that we could have had some sort of relationship. I should have known that it was all too good to be true, I should have listened to Sarah and kept him out of my life.

Hindsight is one of those things though. It's fucking great after you've been shat on from a great height.

At least he was locked up and waiting for his trial. The police had told us that he was being advised to plead guilty, especially if Mackenna's post-mortem proved her death wasn't an accident, but if I knew him, he'd try and lie his way out of the facts. I just hoped whatever happened he went down for as long as possible and someone shanked the bastard while he was in there.

While my biological dad was someone who I never wanted to set eyes on ever again, Roger had been awesome. Something in his gut had told him there was something badly wrong, so after getting Sarah's address from Kirk, he'd jumped in his car and gone around to her house. As soon as he'd seen my car abandoned at an angle with the engine still running, he called the police. He even stood over Glen with the wok just in case he came to, which he did. Thank God for Roger because by that point Sarah and I were in shock and apart from clinging to each other, there wasn't much else we could have done. Luckily Glen was too groggy and had lost too much blood to be able to fight back, so he accepted his fate and lay there until the police turned up. Roger had also been with me at every single interview and statement I'd had to give to the police, a supporting hand on my arm or shoulder each time.

When the door to the neat bungalow opened, Mrs Danes smiled broadly at me. I sighed with relief. In truth I hadn't known how she would greet me.

"Hi, Adam, come on in," she said as she stood to one side and let me in.

I hovered in the hallway as she closed the door and locked it and I noticed two bolts had been added, offering me a small sense of comfort for them both.

"Sarah's in her room, go on through."

"Thanks, Mrs Danes."

She gave me another smile and then went back to the lounge, leaving me alone. It wasn't the first time I'd seen Sarah in the three days since the attack, but it was the first time we'd been alone. There'd always been parents, friends or police around and I was nervous that she might tell me to get lost. I hoped not because I had a surprise for her, two really but both were connected, and I hoped that she liked them.

I moved to her bedroom door, further down the hallway and gently knocked, waiting for her to call me in.

"Yeah."

I pushed it open and almost dropped to my knees with relief when she instantly jumped off the bed, ran to me and wrapped herself around me.

"Oh God," she whispered as she peppered kisses to my face. "I've missed you so much."

"I only saw you yesterday," I replied with a laugh as I carried her back to her bed and sat down on it, Sarah still clinging to me like a little monkey.

"But my mum and Roger were there and then when I came out from finalising my statement you'd gone."

"Yeah, Lori has been a bit anxious since it all happened, and Mum rang to say she was upset and wouldn't settle until she knew I was okay. Roger thought it best to go home as soon as I'd finished."

Sarah kissed me fully on the mouth and squeezed me tight. "It must have been really scary for her. At least we're okay, not like poor Mackenna."

I nodded and tried not to over think the fact that it might well have been Sarah in the lake and not Mackenna.

"Glen is still saying it was an accident," I sighed. "He's also still saying they were in a relationship and she fell during an argument about you and hit her head."

"So why dump her body in the lake?" Sarah stiffened so I rubbed a hand gently down her back, instantly feeling her body ease out. "Why doesn't he just tell the truth, he killed her."

"The post-mortem is tomorrow, and the police are hoping that will prove otherwise. One of them told Roger that they think he may have suffocated her, as there was no evidence of hitting her head, but we'll soon find out."

"I hope so, if only for her family's sake." Sarah rested her head on my shoulder. "I can't believe he persuaded her to dress like me."

I shuddered. "It's fucking sick. I also can't believe she sneaked out in the middle of the night to see him. Her mum and dad must be devastated that they didn't hear her."

Sarah nodded. "He's a monster no doubt about it. Do you think Ellis realises what he did by bringing him here?"

"I hope so, because even if Glen did kill Mackenna, Ellis is responsible too."

My jaw ticked as I thought about my ex best friend and not one ounce of my thoughts had any sympathy for him. The fact that Tyler and Kirk had dropped him as well would hopefully make him realise he'd done something unforgivable.

"Alannah said Miss Davies has suspended him," Sarah said as she played with the pocket on my flannel shirt.

"Yeah, Tyler told me. Someone told her about his part in it all."

"Who?" Sarah's head shot up and a cute frown furrowed her brow.

I grinned. "It was anonymous but put it this way, it was flashed on every PC in the school along with some CCTV footage of him setting fire to books in the school dining room last year."

"Oh my God," Sarah squeaked. "That was Ellis? Alannah told me about it on my first day."

"Yep that was Ellis. I didn't realise Kirk had saved the footage, but now Miss Davies has seen it he's been suspended while she investigates. It looks like he'll be expelled."

She looked at me warily. "Aren't you worried you'll be implicated?"

"How do you know I was?" I asked, unable to help the smirk.

She rolled her eyes. "Aren't you worried you'll be implicated?"

I laughed that she'd not answered my question but repeated her own to put her point across.

"No, Kirk has definitely deleted any other CCTV and while he's a fucking twat, Ellis isn't a grass."

"But Kirk is and that's fine?" Sarah said with a knowing smile.

I shrugged and then playfully nipped at her neck, glad that I was finally able to feel and smell her again. Our time apart had been fucking shit and I never wanted to experience it again.

"What about you and Kirk by the way?" Sarah asked when I pulled away. "Are you back to normal?"

I blew out a breath as I considered her question. It was difficult because he'd done things that I couldn't forgive him for, but at least he'd owned them, unlike Ellis.

"Him and Tyler are off to Uni soon, so maybe it's time to step back. Time moves on and things change, so perhaps our friendship should too. All the stuff with Kirk made me reassess things and now Ellis, so maybe we shouldn't be friends. Maybe I'm too much of a bad influence on them and for me to change I need to move on from them."

Sarah pulled away from me and pinned her gaze to mine. "You could all change together," she said softly. "They've been really supportive this last couple of days. Tyler even called me to check I was okay and whether you were okay when they weren't around."

As she cupped my cheek, I leaned into her touch and savoured her again as I tried not to think of what alternative day I might have been living in if I hadn't got into the bungalow when I did.

"I'm not going to try for Uni this year," I told her, wanting to change the subject. "I talked to Roger last night and we agreed that it's probably better to have a year out."

Sarah's eyes brightened with excitement. "You are?"

"Yep, so I thought maybe we could work for a couple of months during the summer, save some money and then go travelling."

"Together?"

She looked surprised, which in turn surprised me.

"Of course, together. Who else would I go with?"

"I just... I wasn't sure how... are you serious about me?"

I couldn't help bursting out laughing. The girl who I'd crowned my dad with a wok for and then punched until I broke his nose and fractured his cheek bone, wanted to know if I was serious about her.

"Am I serious about you?" I breathed out. "Well, I thought I was going to die when I heard you screaming for me. If you hadn't stopped me, I would have killed him for you. I can't imagine ever being with anyone else. You're all I think about every minute of every fucking day. So, am I serious about you?" Rubbing my nose against Sarah's, I exhaled slowly, wanting my voice to be steady as I said the next words. "I love you more than I ever thought possible. Although we're only young, I know that I will love you until my last breath. You are my eternal sunshine."

Sarah's hand clasped her shirt over her heart and a small sigh came from her slightly parted lips.

"You do?" she asked, her voice quiet and unsure.

"I do."

She gave me the most beautiful smile and with both her hands cupping my face she gave me the words back.

"I love you too, so much. *You* are all *I* think of every minute of every day. *You* are the only person *I* can imagine being with. *I* will love *you* until *my* last breath. *You* are *my* eternal light."

I had so much I wanted to do and say to Sarah in that moment, but it could wait because we had more time than I could ever imagine and firstly I wanted to give her the surprises. I kissed her lightly on the cheek and then lifted her to sit her on the bed.

With Sarah's back against the headboard, I shifted to kneel in front of her.

"Okay," I said as she looked at me quizzically. "I have two surprises for you."

"Okay." She frowned and looked so fucking cute I almost jumped her.

"First this one." I reached into my jeans' pocket and pulled out a flat, square, black box and handed it to her.

"Adam, you shouldn't have bought me anything."

"I wanted to, call it a late Valentine's gift."

She blushed and rolled her eyes. "I have one for you but have a feeling it's not going to be as good as this."

"Open it and see."

I leaned forward expectantly, hoping that she loved the gift. I was sure she would but couldn't help holding my breath as she flipped up the lid.

"Adam," she breathed out. "It's gorgeous."

Bright eyes looked down at the two-coloured gold necklace in the shape of a sun. The pendant and chain were both delicate but were everything I needed to say about how strong I thought she was.

"It's real gold, the jeweller in town made it for me," I said feeling nervous and hoping she realised it wasn't some cheap piece of jewellery I'd bought without a thought from some website. I'd had to borrow money from Roger for it a couple of weeks back, before everything went tits up between us, but I was so glad I had. The engraving had been a recent addition when I'd picked it up the day before.

"Adam that's so thoughtful. Thank you."

"Look on the back." I swallowed, hoping that I hadn't got everything totally wrong about us.

Sarah turned the pendant over and gave a quiet whimper. When she looked up at me, I knew I'd been right to have the words, 'You are my sunshine, only ever you, love Adam' engraved on the back

"I love you, so much. Thank you."

She launched herself at me, with the box still clutched in her hand she kissed me long and hard, but I pulled away so that I could show her the second surprise.

"Wait, there's something else."

"Hurry up then," Sarah huffed making me laugh.

"Sit back." I steadied her with my hands on her shoulders and then when I thought she was watching carefully I started to unbutton my shirt.

"Woah, you said I had another surprise first." Sarah's eyes went wide and her fingers went to the hem of her t-shirt.

"Hang on," I playfully smacked her hands. "I do. Just wait. Surprise first, orgasms later."

As I undid the first three buttons, Sarah's breathing got faster and as if it had a direct line to it, my dick it started to get harder. I just hoped she liked this surprise too, otherwise the pole in my boxers would be totally wasted.

When I finally had all the buttons undone, I pulled off my shirt and waited. Her cry of excitement was instant. Yet again I'd hit the fucking jackpot with my ability of giving the best surprises.

Sarah reached forward and with her fingertip, traced the pattern of the eternity symbol. Even though my eyes were watching her face, I'd stared at the tattoo in the mirror enough to know that when she stopped tracing and licked her bottom lip, she'd reached my name. I knew she would stop at hers and I was right, but this time she captured her lip with her teeth and sent all sorts of messages to my dick.

"You like it?" I asked.

Sarah's eyes were bright with unshed tears as she looked up at me and smiled.

"I love it. It's absolutely perfect."

Instantly, our lips found each other, and with passion and a fierce, fiery love, we kissed away our worries. The heaviness I'd been carrying for thirteen years had lifted and I finally had someone who loved me for who I was. Someone who could see past the armour of hatred and vitriol and who knew that underneath I was just an ordinary boy who craved the love of an incredible girl.

EPILOGUE

THIRTEEN YEARS LATER

Sarah

There are times in your life when you have to look back on every-thing that went before and be thankful for them, the good and the bad, because they are what got you to that place. Your happy place, your contented place, the place you were meant to be. Today was that time for me. As I watched Adam help our son to kick a football, while our daughter watched on with pouty pink lips, I had never been more grateful for the reasons I'd had to move to Maddison Edge.

They'd been hard and painful, but they'd given him to me. The broken boy with a heart that had been hidden by doubt, insecurity and resentment was gone and in his place was a great man. A man who loved me with all his heart and who adored his children whose names had been added to his eternity tattoo.

Ethan was six now and had been into football for around a year and loved nothing more than doing penalty shoot outs with his dad.

Adam usually let him win, but there were some occasions when he couldn't help the competitive side of his nature. Those usually ended with Ethan vowing to beat him next time – he certainly was his father's son. As for Paige our four-year-old, well she was the image of her aunt Lori and unfortunately had her talent for dance too. My skills must have skipped a generation because that girl was a whirling dervish of uncoordinated mess. She had an awful lot of enthusiasm, but that was where her aptitude for dance ended.

I sighed contentedly as I watched them and when Adam left the kids to play and walked over to me, I ached with need for him. At thirty-one he was even more handsome than the boy I'd met at seventeen. His body was more muscular than that of the lean teenage football player and his features more defined, not to mention the things he could do in the bedroom with the power of that amazing bum behind him.

"Hey gorgeous," he said softly as he pulled me into his arms. "You think we have a future Premier League star on our hands?"

I watched as Ethan kicked the ball into the five-a-side nets and nodded. "Yeah, he's had a great teacher though, so of course."

Adam leaned down and kissed me, his tongue urging my mouth to open, not that it needed much encouragement.

"Never gets old," he sighed when we finally pulled apart.

"Good, because after all this time I need to make sure I keep you interested." I grinned and squeezed his bum.

"Oh, you do, you can be sure of that." His smile was cocky and secretive evidently thinking of the night before when the kids had stayed over with my mum and my stepdad Pete. Let's just say we'd made the most of every surface in our new house. A house that we'd arrived at through some hard, mostly happy but always love filled times.

Before we both went to Uni, we took a gap year, travelling for six months of it after taking two jobs each for the previous five to pay for it. After that we went to London. Adam studied at UCL for a combined honours degree in maths and history, and that was where he stayed to do a post graduate course in education, once he realised that he wanted to be a teacher. I went to Kingston University and gained a BA Honours degree in dance, teaching dance and choreography. Then after we both graduated, we decided to stay in the capital. We rented an apartment in Shoreditch not far from the high school where Adam eventually taught and the community college where I'd held dance classes and had done for the extra year it had taken Adam to complete his PGCE. And, while it wasn't a palace, we loved it and were happy there.

Then, on my twenty-fourth birthday Adam surprised me with the most beautiful and simple proposal. My back was to his chest, with his arms wrapped around me as we watched the fountain display from the pavement outside the Bellagio hotel and, as Tiesto's *Footprints* played, he whispered into my ear how much he loved me and then slipped a stunning pear-shaped diamond ring into my hand. Obviously, I said yes, as long as we could do it while we were in Vegas. My dad wasn't around to give me away and even though I was close to Roger and Pete, my mum's new husband, it didn't seem right to ask anyone else. We married two days later in The Chapel of the Flowers. I wore a white sundress and Adam wore shorts and a white shirt, rolled at the sleeves to show his sexy forearms and it was perfect. My mum cried when we called to tell her, but she understood. All we had ever needed was each other and that would never change.

Then, on Adam's twenty-fifth birthday, I surprised him by announcing I was pregnant. We hadn't been trying but we both agreed it was a gift from my dad and I'd never seen Adam more excited or happy. So, although I never did get to work as a dancer in film or TV I didn't care. What I had was so much more than anything else I might once have wished for.

Now though we were back in Maddison Edge after twelve years, ready for Adam to take up his dual role as History and Maths teacher at Maddison High. When the vacancy came up it hadn't been a difficult decision for him to apply, we were ready to come home; ready to leave the hustle of London behind. The kids were an age where moving didn't really matter to them, Ethan made friends easily and Paige thundered through life without a care, and as for me I could teach dance anywhere and had constantly been in touch with Clarice, who offered me my old Street Dance slots back, so it was all good.

It was also the right thing to come back for Adam because his Mum was ill. It was the second time she'd had breast cancer, but things didn't look too good this time around and while they still didn't have much of a relationship, he wanted to at least try and give her some peace before she died. He had never got past the fact she hadn't reported Joshua, or Glen as he'd been then, or what Eric had done to him right under her nose. I understood his anger, but Elouise was a weak woman and always had been and only really ever cared about herself. She and I weren't close and never would be, but I respected her as the grandmother of my children, which she was great at, but that was as far as it went. Admittedly she'd expressed her regret over the years about her poor parenting, but it really was too little too late as far as Adam was concerned.

As for Glen Hudson, he didn't fare well in prison. He was immediately targeted for the nature of his crimes and spent a great deal of time in solitary confinement, according to his solicitor. We only found out that much detail because Adam got his wish; Glen got shanked during lunch one day, just eighteen months into his sentence. Apparently, he was too mouthy for some people's taste. When he died Adam didn't shed a single tear, in fact when we found out, my gorgeous, broken boy toasted the man who'd done it with a bottle of the beer he'd once seen his dad drink. It was his way of metaphorically spitting on his grave.

As for Adam and Roger, well they had a lot of love and respect for each other. Adam realised over time how much his stepdad loved him and Lori. Roger had been the one who'd kept the family together when Elouise was so apathetic about her role as a mother. He was the father figure Adam could finally look up to. Although Roger and Elouise divorced when Lori reached sixteen, Adam always introduced him as his dad. Roger was the first person Adam went to when he needed advice and before we came back Adam spoke to him every week on the phone.

Lori still lived in Maddison Edge too, she hadn't gone to university but had a job working as an administrator for a construction company and loved it. She split her time between Elouise and Roger, although mostly her mum since she'd been ill. Word was though that she was pretty serious with her boyfriend, Elliot, who happened to be Tyler's younger cousin, so Adam had already had a 'friendly' word. Whatever happened between them though, Lori was beyond excited to have her big brother back in town, especially as he came bringing two little cherubs whom she adored.

As for Tyler, well Adam had reconnected with him and Kirk over the years of school reunions and visits home, but Ellis was never around. We'd heard that he was living in Spain working as a DJ, but no one was actually sure, or actually cared. Kirk ran a successful IT company in Manchester, but still lived in Maddison Edge with his wife Ali and their twin boys Teddy and Theo, while Tyler was the PE teacher and football coach at Maddison High, so he was going to be one of Adam's new colleagues. I'd met his girlfriend a couple of times and she was really sweet, so hopefully we could have a few dinners together and continue to build bridges.

"Are you nervous about tomorrow?" I asked. "All those rowdy boys you've got to keep in line and hormonal girls who'll be flirting with you."

He laughed and dropped a kiss to my forehead. "Nope. I ruled this school remember I'll tell them a few stories that will keep them in line."

"Adam," I cried. "You can't. Mr Monroe will sack you before you've even got started."

"He won't, he's on my wavelength." He winked at me and I knew then he was joking.

Mr Monroe was only four years older than us, so when he'd taken over the job from Miss Daniels at the end of the last school year, he'd decided a few changes were needed. One was getting rid of some of the old, bored and frustrated teaching staff so when Mrs Baker our old maths teacher was pensioned off, Adam decided to apply. Lucky for him Mr Raymond, our history teacher had decided to move back to Surrey, so he'd been the one to recommend Adam for the dual role when he'd put his CV forward. The new head also had zero tolerance on bullying and elitism in the school. He liked that Adam had been honest with him about some of the things he'd done in his past, which was why Adam was also heading up the school council. Kids would be able to air their worries and grievances about what went on in the school and it would be a place for them to have open honesty without fear of any consequences. More importantly there would always be a trained counsellor on hand, should Adam feel any of them needed it.

"What time are you meeting Alannah?" he asked, a shadow passing over his handsome face.

"Half seven," I replied and rubbed at the frown line between his eyes. "We're having an early dinner as her flight home is practically in the middle of the night."

He nodded and then glanced over his shoulder to check on the kids.

"She would like to see you, you know," I said and tugged on his sleeve.

Adam turned back to me and shook his head. "No, I think the past is best left in the past as far as me and Alannah are concerned."

He still felt haunted about the way he'd treated some of the girls, particularly Alannah and Amber as they'd been my friends. He didn't understand how Alannah could move on and still be in contact with us, still send birthday and Christmas cards and still like to meet up with me if we were ever in the same place at the same time. Although, meeting with Alannah was rare as she worked as a designer for a car company in Germany and was rarely in the country. It had to be said, she was a pretty forgiving person and claimed none of us were the same people because life shaped you and life changed you. I was lucky to have her as a friend and happy that she was home visiting her family at the time we moved back.

"Well you'd be welcome," I replied. "And Amber won't be there."

Adam rolled his eyes. Amber definitely hadn't forgiven him, in fact she was generally anti men full stop and had given up her nursing career to travel the world campaigning for women's rights.

"I would definitely not be joining you if she was," he said with a grimace. "I'd be worried for my bollocks."

"She's not that bad," I lied. "She just doesn't like you and I don't blame her."

"Exactly."

He pulled me in for another heart stopping kiss and just when things were getting interesting a little voice caused us to break apart.

"Daddy, I'm hungry." Paige ran across to us with a face of consternation at the fact that it was evidently our fault she hadn't been fed almost an hour.

Adam swung her up into his arms and blew a raspberry against her chubby little belly.

"You only just had lunch and if you keep eating, this thing," he blew her belly again, "will pop."

Paige giggled and wiggled in his arms and not for the first time, I wondered whether she constantly complained of hunger just so Adam would do that and say those exact words to her each time.

As Adam continued to tickle her, I looked over to Ethan who was concentrating on his dribbling skills around some cones placed in the gym. We may have laughed about him being a future Premier League star, but the coach at the football coaching sessions we'd enrolled him into in London, had said he was pretty good for his age. I guessed that's what happened when on the day you were born the first thing your daddy did was buy you a full-size football and place it in your Moses basket.

"Hey, Mummy," he shouted to me with a wave of his hand. "I think I'm getting better, do you?"

My gorgeous, blond haired, kind-hearted boy who, apart from having my colouring, was the mirror image of Adam, filled my heart with joy every time I looked at him. Both my kids did, and I cherished every moment with them. Even at their age I made sure they knew they could tell us absolutely anything, there were to be no secrets in our home and they knew if anyone told them to keep a secret from us then they should check with Aunt Lori or their grandparents if it was the right thing to do. I wanted an open household, but surprise parties and gifts were another thing after all.

"I think you're amazing," I replied, and I truly did. I still marvelled that two messed up kids had produced these two miracles. "You ready to go to the new house now, buddy. Daddy's finished setting up his classroom."

"Okay, just one more dribble."

"Okay, just one more."

I smiled because I knew that as soon as we got to the new house, he'd be out in the large garden at the back, kicking balls into the kid's size goals that Adam had already put up for him.

"You ready, gorgeous?" Adam asked as he walked towards me with Paige in his arms.

I nodded and took one last look around the gym. I took in the climbing ropes hanging from the ceiling and the usual pile of gym mats in the corner. In place of the speaker Alannah had pumped her cheer music through, there was now a top of the range Bluetooth sound system proving that Maddison High was moving forward. Finally, my eyes went back to our son kicking a ball with the name Hudson and the number 7 on his back, just like his daddy.

We were where we started, where we'd hated each other and where we'd fallen in love with each other. It was one of those times where I was thankful for everything and knew somehow my dad was still looking out for me, my husband and my two beautiful babies. Walking away, I touched the pendant at my neck, now my anchor instead of my fading scar, and started to sing quietly. My smile was wide when Paige and Ethan joined in with the song we now sang as a family in times of happiness, and I felt content.

You are my sunshine, my only sunshine

You make me happy when skies are grey

You'll never know dear; how much I love you

Please don't take my sunshine away

The End

ACKNOWLEDGMENTS

Well, Adam and Sarah's story is over and it's time to thank those who helped me. It's another big list, so sit back and relax.

Anna Bloom thank you once again for your editing skills on this one. I know you found parts difficult to read, but you did it and made it a much better book with your words of wisdom.

My two alpha readers, *Lynn Newman* and *Sarah Dale*, I can't thank you enough for your love and encouragement for this book. You immediately understood my boy Adam and the sort of person he wanted to be, and you never once mistrusted the journey I was taking him and Sarah on. One day we are going to publish those messages and all your theories!

To my beta readers, *Cal Sleath, Lesley Robson, Kirsty Adams* and *Claire Cutler* thank you for all your honesty about Love Struck. I couldn't think of a better group of people to trust with telling me the truth. I hope that I listened carefully to what you all had to say and thank you for taking this ride with Adam and Sarah, I really do appreciate it.

Thank you, *Lou Stock* for making me another amazing cover. You never let me down and you never, ever lose your patience with me. As always, it's been a pleasure.

Claire and *Wendy* at *Bare Naked Words*, thank you for your promotion skills even if I did kind of land it on you last minute.

I was also going to thank my *mum*, but I'm not sure I can. She was supposed to help out with some proof reading, but while my other proofreader found over seventy spelling mistakes etc, Mum found *one*, which wasn't even a mistake – according to her my spelling of weird looked weird! Anyway, she didn't do her job because she was too engrossed in the story. To be honest though, it's great to think two seventeen-year olds have given my seventy-three-year-old mother a book hangover.

Last but not least thank you to *all of you* for following Adam and Sarah's love story, because that's exactly what it is. You can call it a bully romance or an enemies to lovers romance, but deep down it's simply a love story. A tale of, in Adam's words, an ordinary boy who craved the love of an incredible girl. I hope I gave them both the story they deserve and that you all fall in love with them as much as I have. If not, you at least gave it a try so thank you.

If you love music, then please listen to the playlist for the two books. There are some incredible tunes on there, and most were chosen by the Queen of Angst *Chloe Walsh*, so you know they're going to be good.

Thanks again and please stay safe and healthy.
Much love, Nikki x

Hate Struck/Love Struck Playlist on Spotify

https://open.spotify.com/playlist/
1BVmvEF0LrvFebyHHEPE5u?si=v4s_ruroSDaT1Yag3rDdcA

NIKKI'S LINKS

If you'd like to know more about me or my books, then all my links are listed below.

Website:
www.nikkiashtonbooks.co.uk

Instagram
www.instagram.com/nikkiashtonauthor

Facebook
www.facebook.com/nikki.ashton.982

Ashton's Amorous Angels Facebook Group
www.facebook.com/groups/1039480929500429

Amazon
viewAuthor.at/NAPage

NIKKI'S BOOK LINKS

Guess Who I Pulled Last Night

mybook.to/NAGuessWhoIPulled

No Bra Required

myBook.to/NANoBra

Get Your Kit Off

mybook.to/GetYourKitOff

Rock Stars Don't Like Big Knickers

myBook.to/NARockStars1

Rock Stars Don't Like Ugly Bras

myBook.to/NARockStars2

Rock Stars Do Like Christmas

myBook.to/NARockStarsXmas

Cheese Tarts and Fluffy Socks
myBook.to/NACheeseTarts

Roman's having sex again
myBook.to/RomansHavingSex

I wanna get laid by Kade
myBook.to/NAVJKade

Box of Hearts (Connor Ranch #1)
myBook.to/BOH

Angels Kisses (Connor Ranch #2)
myBook.to/AngelsKisses

Secret Wishes (Connor Ranch #3)
myBook.to/SecretWishes

Do You Do Extras?
mybook.to/DoYouDoExtras

Pelvic Flaws
mybook.to/PelvicFlaws

Elijah (Cooper Brothers #1)
mybook.to/ElijahCooper

Samuel (Cooper Brothers #2)
mybook.to/SamuelCooper

The Big Ohhh

mybook.to/TheBigOhhh

Hate Struck

mybook.to/HateStruck

Audio Books

preview.tinyurl.com/NikkiAshtonAudio

Printed in Great Britain
by Amazon